"First-rate stuff; lean prose, co[...]
telling. Don't miss it."   —R[...]

"Bill Eidson, author of *The Lit[...]
a story....The tale, reminiscent in a way of the nemesis-
haunted work of Cornell Woolrich, crackles and splashes its
way to a gory and surprising finish."
                          —*The Los Angeles Times Book Review*
                          on *Dangerous Waters*

Praise for *Adrenaline*

"*Adrenaline* looms as *the* big book of the summer, so I suggest
you reserve your copy now."
                          —Dick Sinnott, "The City Scene,"
                          The Post-Gazette (Boston)

"Indulge yourself. *Adrenaline* is a terrific read comfortably
encased in some really good writing."
                          —*The Providence Journal*

"Some thrillers give you a roller-coaster ride. Bill Eidson's
Adrenaline will put you in free-fall. Eidson's novels are
bloody, punchy, hit-you-in-the-gut stories and *Adrenaline* is
the best of the breed."
                          —Frank M. Robinson, author of *Waiting*

"A careening adventure tale that virtually defines taut, no-
nonsense plotting and lean muscular prose."
                          —*Ft. Lauderdale Sun-Sentinel*

"The book lives up to its name; open it at any page and Eidson
will soon have your *Adrenaline* pumping."   —Dean Ing

"There's lots of action, lots of excitement, and a hair-raising
conclusion. Eidson really delivers."   —*Mystery News*

"Eidson is closest in style to Elmore Leonard's novels, filled
with funky dialogue, fascinating secondary characters, lots of
action and suspense, and a fine sense of location....The pace,
action, and suspense never slacken."   —*The Mystery Review*

Other Forge Books by Bill Eidson

The Guardian
Frames per Second

ADRENALINE

BILL EIDSON

TOR®

A TOM DOHERTY ASSOCIATES BOOK
NEW YORK

ADRENALINE

Copyright © 1998 by Bill Eidson

Edited by David G. Hartwell

A Tor Book
Published by Tom Doherty Associates, LLC
175 Fifth Avenue
New York, NY 10010

www.tor.com

Tor® is a registered trademark of Tom Doherty Associates, LLC.

ISBN: 0-812-57773-6
Library of Congress Catalog Card Number: 98-5549

First edition: June 1998
First mass market edition: October 1999

Printed in the United States of America

0 9 8 7 6 5 4 3 2 1

For Donna and Nick

Acknowledgments

I would like to thank Frank Robinson, Richard Parks, David Hartwell, Jim Minz, Karen Lovell, Catherine Sinkys, Bill Eidson, Sr., Rick Berry, Kate Mattes, Nancy Childs, and Sibylle Barrasso for their help with my career and this story.

Chapter 1

They finished the climb and waited on their bikes for the light to change. Ahead of them, the street plunged for five straight city blocks down the kind of hill for which San Francisco was famous. If a walking man tripped, he wouldn't stop rolling until he reached the flat of the next intersection. At the bottom, the street took a hard left turn before heading uphill again.

Royal sniffed.

Traffic was heavy up ahead, and the sun was hot enough to make the air shimmer. Royal could smell the oil that the sun brought up to the pavement surface. Cars crossed at the intersections.

"I don't feel so good," he said.

Beside him, the blond man smiled and breathed deeply. "Me, I feel great. You should be terrific at this. Much better than me."

"You can get hurt too, man."

"Of course I can." The blond man handed him a hundred-dollar bill. "That's the fee. You know how to get the prize."

"Ah, man, look—"

"Shut up, Royal. Talk is not what I'm here for."

Royal stared back at him. The fucker was dressed in black skintight spandex. Red stripes, leather waist pack, helmet, bike shoes, the bit. Couple years past thirty, probably. Blue eyes, smiling WASP face. In any other circumstance, with any other guy with a similar description, Royal would have put him on the ground.

Royal knew this, but something about this guy made him take it.

Royal told himself it was the craving. He had it something bad. Two hundred more bucks if he raced to the bottom of the hill first. Money in his hand, and he needed that, no shit. Fire up the pipe. Plus the guy got him right where it counted—the one thing Royal could do was *ride.*

Royal's legs were pumped hard as rocks, and he knew his machine. He rolled back and forth on the bike and snapped his brakes, feeling their solid clamp on the wheel rims. Even through the jones, he took pleasure in the absolute, oiled perfection of his all-terrain bike. He had picked out the frame and put the rest of it together one part at a time: a Shimano derailleur, Scott handlebars. That was before he had started smoking the crack. Lately, he had been thinking about selling the bike, but he needed it for his messenger job, and there were other things to sell, other things to steal.

And he had a hard time seeing himself without the bike. It was like if it was gone, he was gone.

Gonna to take care of business with it today, he told himself.

Royal licked his lips, but his tongue was dry. Could he count on the bastard to keep his promise? The guy had shown Royal the cash already. Flashed it right after he had pulled up beside Royal, Lucine, and Burlie. The three of them had been drinking some pop, letting the sweat cool. The guy said he had been asking around, and that Royal who rode for Abbanat Messenger was supposed to be fast, was that true?

"*Is* fast," Royal had said, and then the guy made the bet. Then Lucine had told Royal that he wasn't going to race. Bitch said it right in front of Burlie. "This dude's weird and you ain't taking him on, and I mean it, Royal."

He could tell right away she knew she had stepped in it. But there was no way she could take it back. And no way he could let it go, not with the two others right there looking at him. "You on, Homey," he'd said. Lucine had taken off, face set like one of them frigging sphinxes, and Burlie had gone with her, shaking his head and grinning at Royal.

Royal had felt bad about Lucine. She was bossy as hell, but she was all right. But he wanted to race the guy. It wasn't just the money. There was something about him that made Royal *want* to show him how fast he could ride.

Now the guy waved down the hill. Far below, right down at the bottom, Royal saw someone wave back. It was a woman. Royal could see her yellow hair from there, could even tell from that far away she was a looker.

That gave him a bad jolt. "What's this shit? You got some fucking cheerleader, man?"

The guy shrugged. "Hey, your girl could've come. Don't know that the two of them have that much in common. But I'd have made the introductions."

Royal looked at him hard. "The fuck's that supposed to mean?"

The guy ignored the question. "Light's about to change. Remember, not just to the fifth light, but around the bend where the hill starts to climb again. You've got to beat me."

Royal set himself. "Oh, I'm gonna."

"One other thing." The blond took out a pair of wire cutters from his belly pouch, and faster than Royal could've imagined, the guy reached over and cut Royal's front and rear brake cables.

"What the hell?"

The guy calmly snipped his own.

Royal's heart flopped. "You cocksucker!" A quick glance at the traffic below, the sickeningly steep plunge down to the hard left. The short little guardrail. The girl's face turned up toward them. Royal's voice turned high-pitched. "You crazy?"

"Hell, yes." The blond guy was sweating, too. But it was more than from the ride up. He looked excited, happy almost. "The prize just went up. Five hundred."

"We're gonna be hitting sixty by the time we reach that fifth light!"

"So back out."

The light turned green.

Royal hesitated. Behind them, a car horn sounded. The guy watched him, grinning. He clutched at his throat mockingly. "Choking? Tell your chick that. She'll tell you you're still a man." He shoved off down the hill.

"Motherfucker," Royal spat, and then he shoved off too.

Royal clicked the brakes automatically. Nothing. He reached back with his right foot and braced his heel against the frame and let the wheel rub against the bottom of his shoe. The bicycle slowed, but that would only be good for setting up, it would never stop him.

He was already going too fast just to bail out—not without losing lots of skin on that asphalt. Royal had made runs as fast before, but with the full use of his brakes to adjust. He started looking ahead, trying to find his path.

The hill seemed to suck him down. Already the wind rushed past his head, blurring his vision. He snapped down his sunglasses and pedaled hard, catching up to the blond in the first traffic-free block. The intersection came up fast, and he let his arms absorb the impact as the front wheel hit the flat of the cross street. When he reached the other side, he simply pushed the wheel down and tucked. Beside him, the blond lifted the front wheel and flew a couple of feet.

Showy bastard, Royal thought, and kept his head down.

He rode the yellow double line for most of the next block, sweeping past the cars braking for the next light. The blond was right behind him. Royal looked far ahead: Guy coming up the hill in a big old Plymouth looking left, was he going to turn in front of him? The guy didn't have his signal on.

Yeah, thought Royal, his quick eyes picking the broken glass of the turn signal. *This car don't tell.*

Royal kept his front wheel kissing that double line, and when the dickhead in the Plymouth suddenly pulled a hard left in front of the oncoming cars, and then stopped, Royal was ready. He pumped hard in his top gear and raced around the ass end of the big boat just before the next car up the hill blocked the intersection completely. Its horn blared, the tires screeching as the driver was suddenly faced with two bikers.

Royal wondered suddenly if he had gone too far.

The guy behind him didn't scream. Royal put a fast glance over his shoulder and was amazed to find the guy still drafting him, less than a foot behind. *Paint. He must have scraped through on paint.*

Up ahead, a paneled van was crowding the left lane. Royal whipped in behind a Toyota and plunged down the right side of the hill. The blond guy stayed with the double lines. Royal was doing risky shit, but he could still see over the cars on his left. Even though he was approaching forty miles an hour, he kept his hands light on the handlebars and kept an eye on the left-hand mirrors of the parked cars. A face appearing in any one of those could mean an opening door, or worse, a driver about to pull out.

I'm on it, Royal told himself. Doing what I do best.

Even so, when the big white lady stepped out from the curb at the next intersection with her arms full of groceries, Royal used all his considerable arm strength to clamp the useless brake grips to the handlebars. It wasn't until he was upon her that his body broke into the magic that years of riding had taught him.

He slipped around her, bumped into the side of a moving panel truck and kicked off. The truck's horn wailed behind him as he crossed the next intersection.

The blond bastard was ahead of him by at least one bike length, and still pedaling for all he was worth. Pedaling. Didn't that bastard see the next light was already turning yellow?

Course he did, Royal realized, and poured on the power too. Who knew what they would do at the light after that, but running this light was the only way to live this block out, and the one thing Royal had learned in his twenty-two years on the street was that if you were still moving, you were still alive. He started drafting the blond biker and stuck right with him through a two-lane swerve to bypass a drifting U-Haul straight-truck.

And then the traffic up ahead went into a dead stall. Two lines of traffic behind a big old truck, the driver lifting up the hood.

Royal would have died right there had it been left up to him.

His balls froze up inside him, he went totally rigid. But the blond cut a hard right, going straight for the sidewalk. He jumped over the steep curb and rode right into the busy afternoon crowd.

Royal followed.

People were scrambling out of the way, yelling. Royal flashed past them, having seconds only to notice a young woman grabbing a kid wearing a bright yellow T-shirt; a heavily muscled brother shouted. A second later, he ran over the toes of a fat old guy wearing a suit, but recovered his control just before clipping his handlebars into a parking meter.

That would've done me, he thought.

The two of them were hitting fifty at this point.

Something inside of Royal broke, and he screamed to the only one who had a clue as to what was in his head at that moment— the other biker: "Jack. Hey, Jack, how about this?"

They launched their bikes off the sidewalk and flew.

The traffic jam on the fifth block had kept the final stretch free of cars. Royal was digging in, making those years in the saddle pay. Aware now of the girl up ahead, the blond. He knew she was the dude's, but that made Royal work all the harder. If the fucker was gonna show off in front of his cheerleader, he had best take the consequences. . . .

Royal liked the sound of that in his head, and he put those words to work right on his pedals: Take—the—Consequences.

The blond guy had the inside, but just as they flashed by the woman, Royal took the lead. Royal felt a sharp burst of pride, wishing Lucine had been right there beside the bitch. But he shoved all that down and settled in for the curve ahead. He almost reached back with his foot to hit the rear tire, but figured he could take that corner if he laid the bike all the way over.

The tires were inches away from the gravel on the soft shoulder. The roofs of the houses below flashed by. Gonna make it, he exulted.

Then there would be the uphill to slow him down, the laugh he'd have at that blond bastard—the guy was a good rider, he'd give him that. He risked a glance over. The guy looked back.

Crazy eyes, Royal thought, then put his head down, concentrating on the win.

That's when the blond guy drifted into him.

It wasn't a hard hit, didn't have to be.

Royal suddenly found himself sitting straight up through the curve, surprised. He hit the gravel, slid, started to fall. He corrected by jabbing the wheel toward the guardrail, but that was just a reflex. He knew he was screwed. The front wheel hit the low fence and crumpled.

Royal and the bike flipped through the air until they landed on the roof of the stucco house below. The bike kept on tumbling and went over the edge. Royal didn't go as far.

At first, he thought the breath was just knocked out of him. And definitely that was true, he was gasping and flopping on top of that house, his body not his own.

But it was as if it was all happening to his upper body, his legs were twisted at an angle that would've made him scream if he had the air.

The voices above him, the sight of the woman and man looking down at him, those were things that came back to him later. Days later, in the hospital.

"We can't leave him," she had said. The lady was terrified. "He's hurt."

"People get hurt," the man had said.

"Not like this!"

"Just like this. I can't afford this kind of trouble. Not now. Neither can you."

Royal had tried to call out to them. To tell them to get an ambulance, to get him some frigging help. But the two of them took off. Left him to wait two hours with a compound fracture in his right leg, and a mess of splinters in his left. Left him to wait until the owner of the house came home and wondered aloud what the hell was a ruined bike doing on his driveway.

The bike. The least of Royal's problems.

Because Royal never raced a bike again.

Or walked, for that matter.

CHAPTER 2

It was Steve's turn.

The hull trembled. They were fifty feet underwater, taking the big wheel out of the cabin cruiser when they both felt it. She was beginning to shift.

Buddy spun for the cabinway and Steve headed for the shattered porthole.

Every bit of instinct, training, and knowledge told him to stop. The boat had been listing to port, the cabinway was more protected—he was putting himself in a worse spot.

But it was his turn.

The boat captured him by the knees as she settled. He screamed in his mouthpiece, but the pain was strangely remote. Buddy was there, his face concerned through the faceplate. But Steve could see relief in Buddy's face as well, relief that it wasn't him who was trapped. It shamed Steve to see that, because he knew it must have been on his own face when it had been Buddy's turn.

Buddy tried to dig him free. But it quickly became apparent that Steve was pinned to rock, covered by only a fine layer of mud. Buddy's dive knife did no more than make a sharp scratching sound. But Buddy fought for Steve, fought in a way that gave Steve pause, insight into himself, perhaps.

Even so, Steve knew and Buddy knew, it was simply Steve's turn.

And so Buddy left when it was his time to go. Steve rode the anger, the hatred for his best friend as he swam away to let him drown. He watched Buddy reach the silvery surface, and a part of him wondered if that meant Lisa would now be Buddy's too.

The air in his mouthpiece tugged against his lungs, that artificial shortening of breath that meant he was sucking his tank dry.

Here we go, Steve thought.

And then he began to drown. He watched his friend watch him from far above. Steve gagged and coughed, and beat his hands against the slick fiberglass. In his struggles, he knocked his mask askew and the water poured in, blinding him.

For a horrific moment, it was all true.

And then Steve broke to the surface—and woke up in his bunk alongside Lisa.

"Sssh," she said, holding him. "Again?"

He coughed and gasped. The air was close in their sloop. He had dogged down the hatches because it had been raining when they turned in.

"Yeah," he said when he could speak steadily. "I could use a new nightmare."

"You're all right," she said.

"I know I am." His heart was tripping.

Steve was very definitely alive.

He couldn't say the same for Buddy. As much as Steve's subconscious insisted, the truth was, it had been Buddy's turn, and always would be.

Steve stroked Lisa's back until she fell asleep. His eyes were wide open and he knew that after that particular dream he wouldn't be sleeping again for hours.

After a few minutes, he slipped out of bed and pulled on a T-shirt and shorts. He quietly made his way over to the icebox and pulled out a beer. It was beaded with condensation, and he touched the cold bottle to his forehead. He caught a glimpse of a photo of him, Alex, and Buddy over the navigation station, and he said, quietly, "Hey, I could use the sleep."

He climbed up into the cockpit of *The Sea Tern,* and was struck immediately with the beauty of the Boston skyline. He wondered, not for the first time, if they were making a mistake building their new home so far from the city. He checked his watch. Just after three-thirty in the morning.

He grabbed a seat cushion and quietly made his way forward. He settled back against the mast, thinking about the nightmare. It had been months since it had visited him. Years since the actual event. Steve thought it through . . . damn near twelve years. He was thirty-seven now. He and Buddy had just gotten out of the navy when they had bought the salvage boat.

Steve would guess that the dream revisiting him probably had to do with the move and the new job. Steve smiled wryly, wondering when the hell he had become such a weenie. He didn't deal in life-and-death decisions anymore. Profit and loss. Markets and share. Financially, Steve was moving from a decent income to a damn good income. Possibly a spectacular income, if he played the next year right and the executive vice president position for the corporation opened up, the way it was rumored. In fact, that could be what Carl Jansten, the head of the conglomerate that owned Steve's division, wanted to talk with him about. Jansten's secretary had called to schedule a breakfast meeting at Jansten's home. And if Steve *did* land the position . . . Jansten would most likely be retiring some time within the next four or five years, and Steve should be well positioned for the president and CEO position. All the money and power he could want.

Hell, probably more. And maybe that's why Buddy was coming to visit him now. Buddy, and others, had always looked for Steve to take the lead. Buddy had been as fully capable a diver as Steve, but he had followed Steve into that boat even though both of them knew damn well that it was balanced precariously. Their air had been low; they had been searching for days for the boat, and money very definitely had not been decent back in those days. Finding the cruiser with only minor damage meant their fledgling business could make it through the next few months, and they had been anxious to prize something free and go up and claim the salvage rights. They should have at the very least braced the boat, protected their exit.

But we were twenty-five, Steve told himself.

Sometimes that rationalization helped. But at three-thirty-eight in the morning, it didn't make a dent.

Steve downed his beer.

After a while, it became apparent that the city lights didn't have any answers for him. And an occasional sleepless night wasn't so bad, not as atonement went.

So he went below and started in on some paperwork.

He was still at it when the sun rose and Lisa awoke.

"You didn't," she said, "you didn't stay up working all this time."

"Insomnia," he said. "Secret to my success."

As she yawned and stretched, he smiled, just to look at her. She was five years his junior, thirty-two. Black hair, fair skin with a sprinkle of freckles. He enjoyed watching her emerge from her slumber, hair tousled, faintly cranky at the start . . . he always felt that as she awoke he could see the child she had been. It took no more than a few minutes for her to quickly become her normal self. And that self was good-natured, sexy, smart, and tough.

He loved her without reservation.

She said, "Do I hear wind out there?"

He looked up through the hatch, and indeed, the halyards were slapping against the mast. "Not bad. About ten knots."

She reached out for his hand. "Take a little sail with your wife?"

"You romantic, you."

"We can do that, too." She kissed him and pulled him down onto the bunk. He drew off his shirt. She said, "You're never home before ten, and you've worked every weekend since we've gotten here. So take a couple hours off, play with your wife, get some rest. You can be a little late one morning."

"Hmmm . . ." he said.

"Hmmm . . ." she mocked.

He pulled her close, burying his face in her dark curls . . . and ticked through the responsibilities of his morning: a conference call over the Blue Waters design budget, which he could perhaps postpone until later in the week . . . two short meetings with members of Jansten's corporate staff that he really shouldn't miss, if he was to keep after the executive vice president slot . . . he needed an hour or so to gear up for a briefing he was to give to the ad agency over a lunchtime meeting . . . there was just no way.

He gasped. The warmth of her bare skin against him was so pleasurable it was shocking. She had opened the old shirt of his that she had been wearing. He said, "How long's it been?"

"Ten days, but who's counting." She looked up mischievously. "I know you must be exhausted. . . ."

He stood up and kicked off his shorts, and she pulled him down to the bed and straddled him. He drew the shirt off her shoulders so he could look at her. She had been a competitive swimmer in college. And though he hadn't known her back then, he could still see the lean strength of an athlete within the ripeness of her body. Time had added faint character lines about her eyes and he loved that about her too—time was passing with them together. He only wished he had known her sooner. "God, you're beautiful to me." He laid his hand along her face and she held him by the wrist.

"You are too," she whispered.

Outside, the wind gusted, rocking their boat. As he entered her, Lisa's nipples stiffened and she grew flushed. There was a faint shiver in her voice as she leaned down, her lips moving against his ear. "We're going to do this . . . and then we'll shove this boat away from the dock, and I'm going to sail it while you sleep. You think you can make time for that?"

Those responsibilities flashed through his mind again, meetings and tasks fanning before him like a deck of cards. "No," he said. "But I will."

CHAPTER 3

Coming out of the terminal at Logan Airport, Geoff found a limo driver holding a sign bearing his name. Geoff handed the driver his luggage ticket and said, "Get me a newspaper first."

The driver tipped his hat and offered him tightly folded copies of *The Wall Street Journal* and *The Boston Globe* from his front seat. "I picked these up on the way, sir. However, I'll be happy to get you something else if you prefer."

Geoff shook his head. "The bags, and let's go."

After they were out of the airport traffic and heading into the tunnel, the driver cleared his throat. "Mr. Jansten said to offer you his welcome to Boston. He is occupied this evening, but if you are free, he would like to have you out to his home for breakfast tomorrow morning, along with Mr. Dern."

"Steve Dern?"

"Yes, sir."

Interesting.

Geoff didn't let the surprise show on his face. He kept his eyes busy on more important business, working his way quickly through the *Journal* back to the New York Stock Exchange listings. He scanned a few of his smaller purchases. Nothing much had happened. Then he focused his attention where it mattered: TerrPac.

His only reaction was to draw his breath just a tad more sharply. Just a little taste of additional oxygen to acknowledge what had happened to him.

He flipped to the front page and began to work his way back, paying attention this time. He found a lead taking him back to a more in-depth article on page twelve. TerrPac had lost a lawsuit charging them with copyright infringement. Their settlement would not be a record breaker for the pharmaceutical industry, but it would possibly be enough to put them out of business. Certainly enough to send their stock into a tailspin.

And certainly enough to be a nasty surprise for Geoff.

At thirty-four, he had amassed just over three million dollars, the results of hundreds of high-flying transactions in and outside of his own field of real estate development. Plenty of times he had taken hits, but never anything like this.

On TerrPac, he had leveraged everything to bet the pot. His inside informer was highly placed, and for over six months the stock had been climbing as expected.

Now Geoff had virtually lost the pot.

He went through a series of rapid calculations. For a number of good reasons, no one within the corporation knew of his personal investments; he had even conducted the transactions over the wire. Bob Guston, his informer at TerrPac, would keep his mouth shut. Geoff had sniffed out a sweetheart deal that Guston had put together, where he was buying real estate for TerrPac that he ac-

tually owned. He had been holding that over Guston for information for over two years now. The blackmail would work just as
well for silence.

Geoff's position at Jansten Enterprises would certainly give
him enough income to keep up appearances for the time being.
And there would be even more of that once he nailed the executive vice president job. He figured that Jansten's agreeing to let
him run his division from Boston was a sure sign of his favor. So
if everything went the way he intended, there would be plenty of
money.

But part of him wanted to tell the driver.

Part of him wanted to tell Jansten, tell everyone. He felt the
buzz of adrenaline. He wanted to *do* something. Bloody his
hands, with Guston to start.

Geoff glanced up at the vanity mirror and saw that his face appeared calm and relaxed. The seething impatience inside was well
in check.

Maybe it's time to try something else. Maybe Kelly had been
right. Maybe this was the start of his fall, his own tumble from the
saddle.

He closed his eyes, thinking of his parents, dead twenty years
now. They would have been flabbergasted to know he had
amassed such a fortune. Couple of losers, both of them. His
mother, pretty and weak—and a lush. His father, full of grand
schemes, but ultimately nothing but a lousy salesman who con-
tinually ascribed his own limitations to his son.

His father's voice spoke in his ear, *Big frigging surprise you
lost it, Jeff.*

He opened his eyes and thought about the money, about not
having it. Thought about how his father had crowed when Geoff
had changed the spelling of his own name. Jeff had liked the so-
phistication of "Geoff" and had informed his parents of the new
spelling when he was thirteen. Years later, he made it legal.

"You're too damn full of yourself, Lord Geoff," the old man had said. He had been sitting on the sagging back deck of their ugly little ranch house in Sacramento, drinking a beer. "I've tried pulling us up, but some shitter always comes along to knock you down. Saddled with you and your mom, I just can't get out from under. It'll happen to you someday. I was as good at running with the ball as you, and look where I am now."

Geoff had just looked coolly at his father, a going-to-fat ex-jock whose failure as a man was right there on his face for anyone to see.

"Bullshit," Geoff had said. "You were never as good as me."

"Watch that mouth!" His dad had raised his hand, but Geoff didn't even flinch. The old man had dropped it. "Get away from me."

Even then, Geoff could tell his father was a little frightened of him. Geoff was just beginning to realize the extent of the gulf between himself and other people. The way Geoff saw it, his dad still had a slight physical edge, but it wouldn't be long before Geoff could start calling the shots himself. And in four or five years, he would be out and away from them forever.

When that separation came only one year later, he felt no pain, just mild disappointment that he didn't have the opportunity to truly flex his muscles with them. Drunk, and probably in the middle of one of their vicious arguments, his mother and father had swerved into the oncoming lane and took themselves and a long-distance trucker out of the equation forever. Geoff had landed with his mother's parents, an old couple who didn't want him. Particularly after the first week, when he kicked the old man on his ass to show them both who was boss. He was able to squeeze cars, cash, and, ultimately, a college education out of them. Including the tuition for an MBA from Wharton. It took all of their retirement money to pull that off. And they did it while main-

taining the public fiction of being the doting grandparents of their
star-athlete grandson, as he demanded. He even kept a portrait of
them in his office for visitors, although they could be dead by
now, for all he knew.

As was often the case with Geoff, he found that he had arrived at
the answer while thinking about other things. He decided that as
long as he didn't have to endure the appearance of being a loser,
he truly didn't care. He told himself he didn't need the insulation.
In fact, he rather liked the idea of pulling himself back up to the
top.

Geoff thought of the bike messenger, his broken back. He
looked for some sense of pity or shame in himself, knew it should
be there. But it wasn't. Just a sense of revulsion for the damage
done. *Paralyzed.*

Then he realized the driver was talking and was holding something out for him. "I'm to show you to your apartment . . . and
give you these."

He handed Geoff a set of car keys with a BMW logo.

Geoff laughed quietly to himself. The car was probably leased,
just a gesture from Jansten to welcome him to Boston. But he
might as well take it as a sign.

People like me are never poor, he thought, pushing aside im-
ages of his father and mother. The bike messenger didn't know his
name and sure as hell wasn't going to crawl all the way to Boston
to embarrass him. And Geoff had taken care of Kelly.

Geoff gave himself two goals: He would become the next executive vice president of Jansten Enterprises as a stepping stone
to president and CEO. And he would put together another million
in personal fortune before the year was out.

He grinned to himself, already feeling much better. The way he
saw it, a goal named was a goal achieved.

* * *

A few minutes later, they pulled in front of an elegant brownstone in the Back Bay.

The driver said, "They unpacked everything for you . . . even hung all those pictures. I made sure of it myself."

Geoff paid attention to the driver for the first time: an intelligent-looking man with his personality carefully hidden by his manners. Geoff stared at him until the driver apparently felt compelled to speak.

"Certainly was impressive . . . some of the things you've done."

"Thanks." Geoff smiled, disarmingly. "You're good at your job, aren't you?"

The driver returned the smile cautiously. "I try to be."

"I expect you've driven for Jansten for some time?"

"I have."

"Know him pretty well?"

"He's been very good to me." Still the driver was being careful. Geoff's reputation preceded him, which was just the way he liked it.

"That's good. So you know his taste in restaurants, drinking establishments, and such."

"I could recommend some of the better establishments in Boston, sir."

"What I'd like is for you to recommend exactly the opposite for me."

"Sir?"

"I want you to find me a place where Jansten wouldn't go."

"Excuse me?"

"I think you know what I mean. And feel free to pass it along to Jansten when you next talk with him."

"I don't work for him in that capacity."

"Sure you don't." Geoff liked the worry he saw on the driver's face. If he was going to win the top job and pull himself out of his financial disaster, he wasn't going to do it playing nice. "Now find me that bar. But you can keep calling me sir. I like that."

The driver took him to a series of bars in the Back Bay. None were what Geoff had in mind. "You're cold."

"I think I know what you have in mind."

The driver took him through a tour of what remained of the Combat Zone. "Keep going," Geoff said. "This place is dying."

Just a few blocks away, however, he saw what he wanted. A seedy little place across from the Boston Common that was staving off gentrification on either side. A young blond woman Geoff took to be a hooker stood with her back to the street, looking at her reflection in the mirrored glass.

"This will do," Geoff said, as they stopped at the light. He got out.

The driver called out politely, "Shall I pick you up at seven for your breakfast meeting?"

Geoff didn't bother to acknowledge the man.

Just then, the hooker turned. She backed away abruptly, and, for a moment, Geoff was certain she was frightened of him. She looked past him at the limo, then forced a smile.

"Whoa," she said. "Thought you were somebody else."

Geoff waited for her to get out of his way. Under the bright blond wig, miniskirt, and stiletto heels there was a surprisingly pretty woman. Green eyes, flawless skin. Faint sprinkle of freckles over a straight and imperious nose.

She smiled awkwardly. "So, this is where I'm supposed to ask if you want a date."

Geoff sighed. Instant pauper or not, he still had his standards. "And is this where I'm supposed to think this is your first time and whisk you away from it all?"

She smiled ruefully and stepped aside. "I'd be yours forever."

In spite of himself, Geoff laughed as he brushed by.

* * *

It was an old dark wood tavern, with the smell of stale beer and cigarettes. Geoff asked the bartender for the phone.

"Back near the can." The bartender was a white-haired guy with a huge gut and broken blood vessels in his face. He looked at Geoff's impeccable suit as if it offended him.

Geoff dropped a fifty down on the bar. "Set me up with your best scotch. Give me some change, too."

Geoff went back and dialed Harrison, who answered on the third ring.

"Hey," Harrison said. "Figured you'd be about due in. Good flight?"

Geoff gritted his teeth. Harrison performed best if they maintained the fiction that he was Geoff's friend, instead of the ass-kisser that he was. Geoff told him the name and address of the bar. "Come on over and bring me up to speed," Geoff said. "Twenty minutes."

"How about this evening? Geena and I have plans this afternoon, but tonight, I could break free and we could hit the town."

"Twenty minutes," Geoff said and hung up.

Back at the bar, Geoff sipped his scotch and looked out the fly-blown window. He could see the hooker out front, but he was fairly certain she couldn't see him through the mirrored glass. Pretty thing, even with the ridiculous clothes and wig.

Kelly's hair had been the color of that wig. Of course, hers had been real. Geoff missed her, but only a little. It had been two weeks since he had broken it off with her, so to speak. She possessed a spectacular body. Honeyed skin, blue eyes, and model-perfect features. To walk in a room with her on his arm made him the envy of every man in sight. And she had truly seemed to enjoy Geoff's little adventures, more so than any of his previous women. She had been damned inventive in bed afterward.

He had wondered about that, at times. If that's why he had been escalating lately, taking greater and greater risks. Physical challenges. Rock climbing without any protection. Whitewater kayaking in rivers never meant to be run. Extreme skiing. Cliff diving.

He liked the audience, certainly.

But the real action was inside him. He loved the adrenaline, just like a junkie spiking his arm. When he had poured everything into the TerrPac investment it had given him a great buzz as the stock climbed. And now that the worst had happened, he was still alive and well, thanks for asking.

But the night after the bike messenger thing, Kelly had just lost it—and, to be truthful with himself, so had he. It had started with her standing just inside the glass doors while he sat out on the balcony, drinking.

They had just made love, and, unlike previous times, she had been cold and unresponsive. She kept worrying about the bike messenger. Worrying that he might be paralyzed, worrying that someone might have seen them drive away, or captured the license plate.

Geoff was normally too prideful a lover to let her remain unsatisfied. But after the incident, he had been too charged up to wait. The feeling that he was taking her for his pleasure alone added to his appetite. Afterward, he went out on the balcony. She followed him, whispering her fear. He quickly downed two shots of scotch. He became hard again, almost immediately, and figured he would drag her away from that door and take her back to bed again, thaw her out. Geoff couldn't remember being so pumped up.

Kelly had kept after him, though. "Geoff, are you listening to me?"

"He wanted to play the game," Geoff said, calmly. For the fortieth time that night. "And he lost."

"He didn't *want* to. He needed the money. You hurt people. You frighten them and bribe them into doing things they don't want—and for what? You hardly needed that boy's money!"

Geoff went to her. He put his palm against the small of her back and pulled her close. "I don't seem to remember bribing you."

She looked away. When she spoke, her voice was shaking. "Believe me, I know I played a part." She waved her hand around, taking in his penthouse apartment, the view. "We've got all this. We've got money. You've got power, and if this vice president thing works out, you're going to be set for life . . ." She laughed, tears on her cheek. "Hell, you're *already* set for life. Why do things like this to that boy?"

He kissed her behind the ear. He wondered how many of her tears represented genuine guilt and how many represented fear of getting caught. His gut reaction was to count heavily on the latter, but he supposed it could have been both. Either way, he had no use for the emotions. What he had use for was that she was beautiful and available. He was so full he was almost bursting. He let his robe fall open and stroked her back and ran his fingers along the swelling of her hips, along the smoothness of her legs. A part of him remained remote, watching. And that part of him decided he was going to break it off with her, no matter how perfect her body.

He whispered in her ear. "We needed to do it because I'm *bored.*"

Christ, Geoff. What a dive." Harrison laid his hand on Geoff's shoulder and squeezed.

Geoff smiled back lazily. His every instinct was to slap the idiot's hand away, even though Harrison worked for him.

Instead, Geoff said, "Geena let you break free. Tell her I owe her."

"Oh, I will. She will, if she sees you any time soon." Harrison called for a beer, his voice booming loud, his every mannerism saying, I'm-a-hearty-guy-meeting-my-good-friend-isn't-life-grand.

Fucking pathetic.

Geoff let Harrison prattle along, telling Geoff all sorts of specifics in which he had no interest. Geoff was president of the real estate division of Jansten Enterprises, a multinational conglomerate headquartered in Boston. Geoff had led the hostile takeover of the San Francisco–based real estate firm five years back, then managed to turn the successful independent company into an even more successful division of Jansten's empire. It had been a major coup, especially considering he had been just twenty-nine at the time. It also made Geoff one of the top-ten officers in the company.

Harrison was Geoff's age, but apparently he fancied himself some kind of combination adviser-protégé of Geoff's all at once. Which was a joke, considering the growing gut about Harrison's waist and the veiled fear in his eyes. But he was a natural politician, so Geoff had assigned him to represent the real estate division on an ongoing basis back at corporate.

In theory, it was just a liaison role to make sure the real estate division got its fair share of whatever corporate was handing out, and to ensure that they weren't saddled with what they didn't need. In truth, his job was to make Geoff look good—to the board members and to Jansten.

As such, Harrison had a lot of face-to-face time with Jansten, and Geoff could tell it made the slug feel like *he* was the man of the house. Patently ridiculous, of course. But Harrison had been efficient in setting up the invitation back to corporate headquarters once Geoff decided San Francisco was no longer good for him—what with the newspapers picking up the story about the bike messenger, and his friends riding around plastering a surprisingly accurate sketch of Geoff's face all over the place. When Jansten had called with the offer, he hinted rather broadly that Geoff could be in line for the VP job: "Your man tells me you might be willing to come to Boston. I'd like that. You can run your division same as always. I can tell you that you'll be in the top three or four contenders for helping me run the company into the next decade."

Top three or four. Neither Barry Lerner nor Phil Rudden were lightweights, but Geoff felt confident he could burn past them. If Steve Dern was now to be a contender, then that was a surprise, but surely one he could manage.

Vice president of a conglomerate with over sixty thousand employees in twenty-two countries, including half-a-dozen consumer brand lines, two high-growth electronics companies, Steve's boat line, and Geoff's own real estate division. The VP position would bring in a salary of over a half-million a year, plus stock options and perks, and a clean shot at the presidency when Jansten retired, which would be the genuine pot of gold. Yes, that would be entirely acceptable for a guy who hadn't yet reached thirty-five.

Geoff tuned back in to Harrison, who was saying, "So I told Voss, 'Uh-uh, you got the wrong idea. Try again.' Face went red as a frigging beet, I thought we were going to have to do CPR on him, and then I figured, what the hell? Maybe I should lock the conference room door, come back an hour later with a wreath." Harrison began to laugh.

Geoff said quietly, "What's for breakfast tomorrow?"

Harrison cocked his head. "I . . . breakfast?" He reached absently for his breast pocket and pulled out his pocket calendar.

Geoff said, "Jansten's called me out for breakfast. With Steve Dern. What should I be expecting?"

Harrison looked genuinely confused. "I don't know anything about it. With Dern?" Harrison's face was red, and Geoff thought of the story about Voss.

"I'm sorry, man," Harrison said. "I talked to Jansten just yesterday, and he said his secretary was making all the arrangements to welcome you into town. In fact, I thought the first time we'd see you would be at the executive committee meeting on Monday. There has been a rumor of one of Jansten's godawful team-building things. Going on a retreat."

"Tell me about Steve Dern," Geoff said softly.

Harrison lifted his shoulders. "Don't know him that well. Wish I could tell you he was a scumsucker, but he's a good guy. Smart, calm, knows his business."

Geoff sighed internally as Harrison slid into the background. Most of it was stock company propaganda about Dern's success with the Blue Water line. Jansten liked to brag about it. Probably figured it was one of the few lines Jansten Enterprises actually earned, rather than bought.

"Boats?" Geoff said, scornfully. "You think Jansten could be taking Dern seriously?"

"You've got no argument from me," Harrison said.

Never do, Geoff thought.

"Sure, boating is strictly a small-potatoes industry. But, if you go to any marina, you'll see that Dern's line has rivaled the best of Boston Whaler and Mako—and he's got a better price."

"What's he doing back here?"

Harrison grinned. "Dern's making us some money. No doubt about that."

"How's our boy doing himself, financially?" Geoff asked this, hoping that somewhere Dern wasn't asking some toad to pull up the same information on *him*.

"Got me. Probably stretched somewhat, though. He's just been in Boston the past two months, you know. Building a house out-

side of Route 495. He and his wife are living on their sailboat in
the meantime."

"What's that?" Geoff was genuinely surprised. "He's building
a *house?*"

"Oh, yeah. He's here to stay. Jansten pulled him out of
Charleston to run his division from here. Same as you." Harrison
winked over his beer. "Now you tell me it's the two of you for
breakfast. Rumor is that Barry Lerner slammed the door so hard
after his private session with Jansten that he broke glass. And
Phil Rudden hasn't attended a meeting or made a decision since
Monday. So maybe it's going to be neck and neck between you
and Dern. I'm counting on you coming through, buddy."

Geoff leaned forward and put his hand on Harrison's shoulder,
mimicking Harrison's earlier gesture. He said with quiet intensity,
"Then you better come through with some better information than
this. Next time I call you, be ready."

"Geoff . . ." Harrison shook his head, and started to sip his beer.
Geoff surprised both of them by slapping the mug out of his hand.
It crashed on the floor inside the bar, and the bartender yelled,
"What the *hell?*"

Without looking, Geoff took a twenty out of his change and
tossed it to the bartender. To Harrison, he spoke in a low whisper,
"Why didn't I know this two weeks ago?"

"None of it had *happened* two weeks ago!" Harrison kept looking at his smashed mug and back to Geoff, his face blotched with
color.

But Geoff was no longer in the listening mode. "That's what I
pay you for, you fat-assed shit. Now get out of here. Next time I
call you, bring me something I can use. Or tell Geena to start
packing for Des Moines."

Harrison started to speak—and then looked at Geoff more
closely. He shut his mouth and left.

* * *

Geoff sat breathing quietly after Harrison was gone. Feeling his heart beating harder than before. Pumped. Feeling it in his hands, how close he had come to hitting Harrison's plump face rather than his beer mug. Knowing that, his actions were inappropriate. Knowing that, once again, he had gone too far. Knowing that it was one thing to have the reputation for being a wild man, quite another to get a reputation as a nut.

But he enjoyed the power in himself anyhow.

He had enjoyed it with Kelly, too.

She had threatened him.

"You're bored," she had repeated. "Because you're bored that boy can't walk. You think you can't fall too? You think you can't land on the street?"

"I don't worry about it."

This had infuriated her. "You think you can't get hurt? Maybe I'll give you a taste of it. Maybe I'll just go to the police. Maybe I'll let them know who ran that boy off the road."

That had pulled Geoff up short. Kelly had smiled, thinking she finally had his complete attention. Geoff had suddenly moved into violence. Before he had known himself what he was going to do, he reached over for his jump rope on the nightstand, casually, and looped it around her neck. Before she realized what he was doing, he had hauled her off the bed and thrown the handles over the pull-up bar in his doorway.

Naturally, she tried to yell. But all that came out was a cawing sort of sound, nothing that would make it to the next condo. And within seconds, he had hauled her to her toes.

He spoke into her ear, feeling incredibly alive and excited as she clawed her throat. He said, "I've got some good news and some bad news. The bad news is that I really do not know if I'm going to let you down. I may just hold you up here until you stop breathing. The *good news* is that I know you better than you know yourself. You're weak. Your whole life has been nothing but easy, and it's all you know. So killing you is simply an option. If I decide to let you live, you will never, ever, carry out that silly threat, because you'll be looking over your shoulder for me the rest of your life. You understand?"

She tried to nod. He let go of the jump rope, and she dropped to her knees. She was terrified, gasping for air. He knelt down beside her and smoothed back her hair so he could speak into her lovely ear. She flinched.

He said, "Another thing. Don't worry about me landing on the street. Because I think I just might like it."

CHAPTER 4

Geoff was thinking about the hooker when he left the bar. He had never paid for sex in his life, but he was charged up thinking about that time with Kelly. And the money problem kept on intruding into his thoughts, worming its way past the mental barriers he had carefully stacked.

He would have missed her, had the man not raised his voice. "I said what the *fuck* you been doing?"

Geoff instantly decided the man was a pimp. Very muscular, white, long black ponytail. An angular, cruel face. Geoff started in the other direction. Not his business.

The girl cried out.

Geoff looked back and saw the man cuff her with an open hand.

"I've been working, I've been—"

The man closed his fist. "Shut your mouth." He knocked her to the ground.

"Hey!" an older man yelled from across the street, while his wife tugged at his arm. "Leave that girl alone."

"Shove it, you old fart."

Geoff saw the hooker touch her mouth and take away blood from her lips. The pimp took his walking stick that he had leaned against a tree and nudged her with it. "Get in the car. We'll finish this."

"No."

The pimp looked surprised.

Across the street, Geoff's eyes narrowed. This was getting interesting. He hesitated, thinking of his resolve of just a few minutes ago to rein himself in.

But he walked across the street. He had the sense of being a little outside of himself, thinking, *What are you doing here, what are you doing?*

Knowing by now that he wasn't going to stop, he kept just behind the pimp's line of vision.

"Get in the car," the pimp hissed at the girl. He snapped the stick against her head. Geoff winced for her, the noise it made.

"No!" She lashed out with her heel, those sharp heels, and caught the pimp on the thigh. He cursed and drew back his stick fully.

"She really was, you know," Geoff said.

The pimp looked over his shoulder, surprised. "Keep moving, faggot. I'm doing business."

"I'm *talking* business. She just did her job on me. Half an hour ago, just as I was going into that bar."

The girl looked more frightened. She shoved her bright hair away from her face, streaking her cheek with blood. "Jammer, he means I asked him. I did, that's doing my thing. But he said no. I didn't make any money; I would've given it to you if I did. Tell him what you mean, mister."

Jammer looked back at him, confused, and angered by it. "What's this shit?"

Geoff winked broadly at the girl. "I wouldn't call it nothing. Gave her five hundred bucks."

Then he looked directly at the pimp. "That's why she's working for me now."

There. Geoff felt the adrenaline pour into his veins as if he mainlined it with a syringe. Felt the rush, tasted the blood singing through him. Felt himself maintain control even as his heart beat faster, as the sweat trickled down his back. His balance was good, flowing down from him to the pavement through the balls of his feet.

Geoff wondered if the pimp had a gun and reveled in the absolute *confidence* that even if he did, somehow, Geoff would take it away.

Somehow.

What a great high.

Better than with that bike messenger, much better.

He saw the pimp was still thinking it over, wondering what was going on. So Geoff made it very simple by hitting the man with quick pop, bloodying his nose.

Eyes back on the man's torso. None of this bullshit about watching his opponent's eyes, the key was to watch the man's body, see where he was going with it. Geoff had taken years of martial arts lessons: kung fu, jujitsu, boxing. Mainly for conditioning, he had told himself all those years, but now that he was into it, he *knew* it was to be ready for this.

He laughed out loud, thinking of Jansten seeing him here, Jansten seeing one of the top contenders for his executive vice president position kicking ass in the Boston Common.

His laughter surprised the pimp, making him hesitate for a split second before swinging the stick in a whistling arc at Geoff's face.

Geoff drew his head back, and the tip missed his nose by inches. He stepped into the pimp and landed a right-left-right combination to the kidneys, turning his fist just so. Nice, short punches. Feet firmly anchored to the ground. From what seemed a great distance away, Geoff heard the hooker screaming.

His concentration was wonderful. He saw the pimp's face crumple in pain, saw the glare of assessment and hatred. Then the pimp jabbed his elbow at Geoff's face. Geoff moved back quickly, but still the man caught him with a glancing blow on the chin, jarring his vision.

Fair enough.

Geoff kneed the pimp in the groin, then cracked him on the back of the neck with his forearm.

The pimp went down to his knees.

Geoff drew a deep breath. It had been easier than he thought.

The man was crouching low, head just coming up, a murderous look on his face, but it took more than ugly looks . . .

The girl was screaming at him, yelling something Geoff couldn't quite understand, saying, *Jammer's got a board, Jammer's going to cut you, watch out, Jammer's* . . .

Jammer shoved glittering steel at Geoff. *It's a sword cane,* he realized, and he slipped aside like a dancer as the metal slid into the left breast of his suit coat. He wound his arm around the light blade and clasped it near the base. Jammer tugged, but Geoff held firm, then pivoted on the ball of his right foot and kicked Jammer in the face.

He split the pimp's lip. Jammer cried out and covered his face. Geoff picked up the walking stick just as a police siren began to howl in the distance.

The girl was up now. She looked scared and even younger than he had first imagined, a little over twenty. She said, "You better get out of here, mister. And I can't stay with Jammer. He'll kill me after this."

Geoff admired her fight. And now that her wig was knocked off, he noticed she had beautiful auburn hair, far richer than that ridiculous wig. "You want me to go with you?" she asked.

He was tempted. But he couldn't exactly see her fitting into his lifestyle. "Sorry."

"What am I going to do?" she cried.

He shrugged. "Make an adventure of it."

"But he'll kill me!"

Indeed, the pimp lowered his hands and glared at the sword in Geoff's hands and then at the hooker. Her spine straightened when she saw him looking, and Geoff liked that about her.

So he slashed Jammer across the forehead. Blood gushed into the pimp's eyes. "There," Geoff said to the girl. "That'll give you a start." He slid the sword back into the cane and walked away.

She took off her heels and started to run. She spun once, looking back at Geoff, and yelled, "Hey, mister! Thanks."

He found the right kind of woman an hour later at Daisy Buchanan's. He pursued her with his characteristic drive and skill. Regaining his lost millions was now firmly compartmentalized in his head, regulated to an important task to be accomplished no more. Not a serious obstacle for a man who could hold his own on the street as well as the boardroom.

The woman was a beauty, about twenty-five, with long black hair. Graduate degree in French studies. It took him most of the night to bed her, but he enjoyed himself, reveling in his strength, reveling in every element of the summer night in the city, from the scent of her perfume to the chateaubriand they had for dinner at a Newbury Street café.

But he was amused to find, even as he moved inside her that night, the walking cane propped up against the wall beside him, that he was thinking of the hooker with green eyes and hoping that she had run, but not too far.

CHAPTER 5

I think I can hear snare drums playing," Lisa said. "Big exec, waiting for the limo."

"If I were such a big exec, I wouldn't be waiting up here with a travel mug of coffee and my wife kissing me off." They were sitting on the rail overlooking the marina, the morning sun low on the horizon.

"Sending you off, not kissing you off." She stretched, and he watched her, savoring the contentment she brought him. She was wearing faded jeans and another one of his old shirts. "Don't I make enough for you to buy your own shirts?" he said.

"I'll be oiling the teak today," she said. "Paying you back for the style in which you keep me."

"Has the glamour worn off?" Until their move north from Charleston, Lisa had managed a successful real estate office and was accustomed to bringing in her own income. Steve had promised himself to make sure their new arrangement continued to work for her. Their plan was that she was to see them through both the refitting of the boat and the building of their new home. All preparation for their master plan of at least two children, if all went well.

"You know me, I love sawdust in my hair," she said. "Besides, I ran the numbers again yesterday. We can't afford to pay for any jobs I can do myself."

The limo turned into the marina lot.

"Here goes," he said.

She leaned over and adjusted his tie, which he knew it didn't need. "You be careful. Jansten's a tricky old bastard."

"I know that." He drew her close. "All he's got on me is thirty or so years and a hundred or so million."

"Mere details," she agreed, before kissing him good-bye.

You brought your own coffee, sir." The driver held the door open and said to Lisa, "You're going to put me out of business."

She laughed.

"I'll hide it before we reach Jansten's," Steve said as he climbed into the back of the limo. Indeed, there was a carafe of coffee and a bowl of pastries and fruit on the small table in front of him. "Kurt, you must want something."

The driver looked back into the mirror. "I'm waiting until your career really takes off before I spring it on you."

Steve grinned. "What's it going to take for me to have a big job in your book?"

"Well, I should be picking you up in front of a house, to start."

"We're working on it. So what's up today?"

"We're to pick up Mr. Mann. Did you know?"

Steve cocked his head. "I didn't. When did he get to town?"

"Yesterday."

"You pick him up yourself?"

"Yes, sir."

"I don't know Geoff, other than by his reputation."

Kurt smiled. "Yes, sir."

Steve pulled out the newspaper Kurt had left for him, knowing that to ask any more would constitute pumping.

They drove in comfortable silence until they reached Geoff's brownstone. The driver left the car idling and went into the foyer to call up for him. Steve enjoyed the silence, looking at the long hood stretching out in front of him. He couldn't help but feel a little foolish, as if he were playing a role: big executive, sitting in the back of the limousine.

It still surprised him, his rapid ascension. Even though he knew, objectively, that he had fought each step of the way to earn his position—starting with going back to school after Buddy's death and earning an MBA from Northeastern. He had bounced around the country after that in several different manufacturing and design management positions until he saw the potential of the Blue Water line, the floundering marine division of Jansten's huge conglomerate. Alone in his kitchen, Steve had penciled out a new line of boats that combined performance, utility, and a classic grace that he felt had been lost in the market in general—and certainly lost on Blue Water's existing line of poorly built "feature-rich" boats. The harder challenge had been turning himself into the combination salesman, manufacturer, financial analyst, and troop leader that it took to rally support from the company and dealers.

Luckily, the customers had been easier. They had recognized what a sweet line of boats the Blue Waters were. Steve was able to convince the dealers to offer a "no-haggle" pricing strategy. While the rest of the boating industry muddled through cutbacks and layoffs, Blue Water gained dramatic market share—and Steve found himself on the cover of *Business Week.*

That article and the others that followed were hardly luck. Once Jansten saw the success of the Blue Water line, he had the corporate public relations agency swing into action. But what was even more important was that Jansten allowed Steve to keep his division autonomous from the rest of the company and supplied enough marketing dollars to keep the momentum up. Jansten publicly praised Steve and had remained a solid supporter, if not a friend, ever since.

Steve turned away from his reverie to see Geoff Mann striding toward the limo, the driver two steps behind. Geoff's expression was unreadable, and Steve realized that perhaps the driver hadn't told him to expect Steve in the same limo. But when Geoff climbed in, he gave a dazzling grin and put out his hand. "Mr. Blue Water, I presume?"

"The Wild Man of the West?" Geoff's grip telegraphed hidden steel. Steve was immediately struck by Geoff's energy. It radiated off the man and made Steve feel tired, goddamn it.

Steve asked Geoff if he enjoyed his first night in Boston.

"Absolutely," Geoff said. "I got the driver here to drop me off at a dive where I met some of the locals. I think I'm going to like it here."

They settled into a few minutes of the outwardly friendly, but cautious conversation of two people who realize they may soon be adversaries. "I've been admiring your line of boats," said Geoff. "Chartered one in Tortola for some diving. That's your field, right? Ex-navy diver?"

Steve was flattered, as he knew he should be. It also made him feel flatfooted, as he knew it was intended. Mann had done his homework, and he had not.

"You've got the advantage on me," Steve said. "All I know

about you is that you're a terror in the real estate world, plus I hear rumors of some amazing athletics."

Geoff waved that away. "They don't call them rumors for nothing, believe me . . ." He paused and then looked Steve in the eye. "So what do you think Jansten has up for us this morning?"

Steve returned the frank, sincere bit, although he wanted to laugh. "I'd say anything from a casual welcome to Boston to full marching orders."

"Oh, it'll be marching orders," Geoff said, opening his newspaper. "I expect you've heard the rumors about Rudden and Lerner."

Steve nodded. Phil Rudden announced an unexpected vacation. Lerner had been sulking quietly for days, making no decisions, attending no meetings.

"Jansten doesn't waste time on being nice to the help," Geoff said. "The way I see it, one of us is going the distance. The other is hitting the sidelines sometime this morning."

Kurt looked in the mirror.

Steve said, "And here I am trying to build a house."

Kurt looked away, suppressing a smile. The three rode along in silence the rest of the way, although it was no longer companionable.

Jansten met them at the door himself.

"Welcome, welcome," he said. "Sorry to drag you out here so early, but I assumed you two are early risers." Jansten waved to the limo driver and called, "Why don't you try out that new diner, Kurt. Great hash and eggs. Give us an hour and a half." Jansten was dressed casually, in chinos and a blue oxford shirt. His face was ruddied by the sun, and his hair was a shock of white. To Steve, it looked as if he were striving for the image of a kindly old grandfather.

Not that Steve believed it for a minute. Jansten had a long line of hostile takeovers under his belt. He was a modern-day robber baron by anyone's definition, and Steve had seen him in action too many times to confuse him with a nice old guy.

Still, the house surprised Steve. He knew Jansten had bought it recently. But instead of the palace he would have expected for a man of Jansten's wealth, it was a relatively small colonial home, quite old. There had been a plaque outside the door with the date 1776. But the house wasn't a Revolutionary War showpiece. It had been updated here and there, with new windows, French doors leading out to a deck that overlooked a spectacular cove. A blue sailboat bobbed alongside a pier that had room for a far larger boat. The sailboat piqued Steve's attention immediately, not only because it was the same make as his own, but it was surprisingly small given Jansten's wealth. "A Hinckley thirty-five is it?"

"It is," said Jansten approvingly.

"I thought you had a Swan," Steve said. "Even down in Charleston we heard stories about you winning race after race."

"Things change," Jansten said, dryly. "Did I hear that you and Lisa are living on a Hinckley forty-two right now?"

"That's right. Until the house is finished."

Jansten chuckled. "Better get it finished before winter comes. Boston is not Charleston."

He moved them along slowly through the house.

In the office, Jansten was constantly surrounded by people and seemed to enjoy all the perks of his position, from the limo drivers to the barbers and tailors that would come to his office. Steve had expected to see a substantial staff at his home. Yet it became apparent, as Jansten walked them about the house, showing Geoff and Steve his place, that the three of them were alone.

He led them into the kitchen, which also offered beautiful views of the cove. "We're having omelets, gentlemen, unless you have some objections." He smiled. "Geoff, I know you're some kind of health nut, can you stand it?"

"I'm not that kind of health nut."

"Good. Then the two of you take the plates out onto the deck, and I'll get us going here. Coffee is in the pot, help yourself."

Geoff turned to Steve with a what-is-this? look. Steve smiled, bemused. He didn't mind schlepping dishes, but he too wondered what the old man was about.

Jansten lit the burners on a big, industrial-sized stove, and poured beaten eggs into a large pan. Cheese, mushrooms, peppers, tomatoes, and bacon were already prepared alongside. Steve and Geoff came back to watch the old man finish making their breakfast. He went about it slowly, whistling tunelessly as he checked and rechecked to see that the eggs weren't sticking. It struck Steve that Jansten didn't really know what he was doing, but he seemed to be enjoying himself nonetheless.

"Steve, make some toast, will you? And Geoff, I guess we'll need those plates back after all."

"Guess you better stick to your day job."

"Wait 'til you eat." To Steve, he said, "Did I hear you salvaged that boat of yours?"

"That's right. A friend who's still in the salvage business brought it up from fifty feet, and we've been pouring money into it ever since."

Geoff hesitated on the way outside. "Why didn't you buy a new one? I'm sure you're paid pretty well running that little division."

"Pretty well," Steve said, dryly.

"I love the thirty-five," Jansten said, as if Geoff hadn't spoken. "Got her set up with a clubfooted jib and self-tailing winches, and I can handle her all by myself."

Geoff brought the plates in and Jansten divided the omelet into three portions. "Let's go out onto the deck."

After they settled down, Geoff said, "Did I hear we have one of those team-building outings of yours coming up?"

"Hiking and rock climbing in the White Mountains around the end of the week. I hear that you both are quite experienced climbers. Something you've got in common, maybe you two should go off together sometime, get to know each other better. This thing, it'll be senior staff, about a dozen of us, with the wives who can make it. I'm counting on the two of you being there."

Both of them nodded.

Geoff said, "So, what's up this morning?"

"Breakfast," Jansten said, curtly, and began to eat.

Geoff and Steve followed suit. Steve noticed the old man glanced their way from time to time, apparently to see if they were enjoying the meal. Otherwise, he kept up the friendly but innocuous dialogue of before, talking about the Red Sox, asking about Lisa.

About her he listened intently. "She's a special one. Guess you know that."

"Certainly do."

He turned his attention to Geoff. "Did you ever marry that girl, Kelly?"

Geoff shook his head. "We've gone separate ways."

"Big mistake." Jansten looked over at Steve. "Absolutely breathtaking woman, this Kelly. Flirted with me once when I came into San Francisco. Did it just to help Geoff's cause, but who was I to object?"

Geoff smiled politely, but there was something behind his expression that Steve couldn't catch.

Jansten shoved his plate away. He winced as he adjusted himself in the chair to look at the two of them. "Okay, that's done. I always hated small talk and socializing. But now that I'm seventy-one, I find I'm beginning to like it. Just like I now like making breakfasts, sailing a boat not much bigger than the lifeboat on my last yacht, and confusing the serious, ambitious young men who come to my home."

He grimaced. "The fact is, I've got this thing inside. Malignant. Started in the colon. And so I'll be starting the song and dance with doctors and hospitals that people in my position start."

Steve felt a quiet stab inside himself. He realized he knew something like this was coming. "I'm sorry to hear this," he said, hating how inadequate the words sounded. He hesitated. "I really don't know what else to say."

"Course you don't." Jansten shrugged. "I've done my share of swearing and stamping around, but I don't know what to say either." He glanced over at Geoff and cocked his thumb at him. "Geoff here doesn't know what to say, so he's not saying it. He's thinking, 'What does this mean for me?' "

"And how would you know what I'm thinking?" Geoff said quietly.

"Because that's what I would've been thinking if I was your age and the old man told me he was about to cork off."

Geoff made a dismissive gesture. "That's what anyone would think. You and I just admit it. So tell me why I'm sitting here."

"Partly what I told you on the phone. I wanted you two to come back and help me put together a plan that will keep Jansten Enterprises thriving for the next decade—whether I'm here or not. What I didn't tell you is that when it comes to executive level management, you two are it. You two represent the future of this company. Rudden and Lerner have done some amazing things for me in the past twenty years. And they've done it just the way I wanted. They've ripped into other companies, gutted them, and drained every drop of financial blood out of them—at my request. Made both of them rich men in their own right, not to mention what they've done for me."

He looked at Geoff with an expression close to fondness . . . but not quite. "And Geoff, you represent the best example of that line of thought. You are the youngest, toughest Turk I've got. A year ago, you would have been my automatic choice to succeed me as president . . . if I ever became willing to let it go under normal circumstances. Who knows, maybe I would have in the course of the next five to ten years. But now I don't have that. I've got less than a year, if I can figure out everything I'm hearing in all that gobbledygook from the doctors."

"I'm ready now," Geoff said.

"I know you think you are. And maybe you are."

He shifted his attention to Steve. "And Steve, I've always admired you and your work. We've never been friends, not only because I'm in my goddamn exalted position—but because you and I are two very different members of the human race." He smiled. "Hell, I'm ex-marine, and you're ex-navy. It was hard for me to respect you right there. But really, it's a matter of personality. When I was Geoff's age, I would have tried to weaken your role and smash you because I would have been nauseated by this sincere form of business you try to promote. I would've seen it as a Boy Scout approach to a storm trooper's job. Yet, your business is thriving. Now that I've gotten to this advanced age, I've been not only publicly, but privately quite proud of having you and your clean little enterprise in place within Jansten Enterprises. And now that I'm dying, I tend to give it even more weight."

"You've found religion," Steve said.

"Something like that. I'm not wasting my time at church, but I do recognize there's going to be an entity with my name on it for at least a while after I go. I cut Rudden and Lerner free last week. They'll be drifting away on some pretty remarkable golden parachutes. That leaves you two. The youngest, and best, examples of two diametrically opposed ways of doing business at Jansten Enterprises. In three weeks, we'll be having a board meeting. I know that I can convince them to put either of you at the helm, and I know either of you would probably keep the company alive. Geoff, most likely running it as I would have. Steve, most likely running it as I should have."

"Just what are you saying?" Geoff said, his tone even.

Steve saw Geoff remain stone-faced, not the slightest hint of change as Jansten's words rolled over both of them: "What I'm saying is that assuming the two of you are willing—I'm going to recommend that Steve succeed me as president and CEO, and Geoff, you will become executive vice president and general manager of Jansten Enterprises. That's what I'm saying."

CHAPTER 6

Jammer was on the verge of beating Carly again. They were in their apartment on the edge of the Combat Zone, and he had already done it to her twice since hauling her out of the bus station the night before, blood streaming from his forehead.

She was just in from a hard day on the street, and Jammer had his eye on her just about every second so he knew damn well that she couldn't have his frigging sword cane. But that didn't stop him from working himself up again. "I told you to get it back. Today!"

"I don't know him." She said it quietly. Like she was talking to a little kid. Which was pretty much true. She had done enough baby-sitting before she ran away from home to know Jammer was about as patient as an infant and as cruel as a ten-year-old boy with a captured fly.

Jammer shoved her against the wall. He grabbed his belt buckle, a broad-faced plate, and she cried out, "Don't, Jammer, please don't!" Hitting the wall with her hands, hoping somebody would be a hero, but knowing they wouldn't. Also knowing that Darlene wouldn't be able to stop him if he really got going. Already she was trying her best, edging her body between them, saying, "Come on baby, let me calm you down, let me take care of you, don't baby, don't . . ."

But Jammer wasn't listening to her either.

He shoved her away, and put Junior—the short dagger attached to his belt buckle—right under Carly's eye. The blade protruded between his fore and index fingers, and she knew it was sharp enough to punch through metal, never mind her face. He said, "You looking to get messed up?"

"No."

"That's what you say, but not the way you're acting. The way I see it, you're begging me to rearrange that pretty face and put you on the street as a geekfuck." He pitched his voice high. "Screw the bag girl. Got a body that won't quit, but you take off that bag, you get the scare of your life." He lowered his voice, "I can market that, baby, you think I can't?"

Even with her heart pumping like it was going to jump out of her chest, even with Darlene wailing in the background, a little part of Carly noticed the "market that." Jammer was so fucking stupid. The idiot hadn't finished high school, but liked to talk as if he was some kind of businessman instead of a pimp in the dying Combat Zone.

Carly thought this, but what she said was, "You're scaring me. Jesus, you're scaring me. I'd tell you if I knew. I'll find him, but I just don't know this second. I just don't know who he is."

Jammer sighed.

Then he yanked her hair tight, making her scream. The blade winked past her eye, and she felt a tug on the side of her head, and then he shoved her to the floor. She looked up as he dropped a handful of her hair onto her face. "You find it. Or me and Junior are going to take you apart a piece at a time."

He left.

Darlene rushed over. "Oh, baby. You're okay. It's just a little hair, he didn't cut you. And he won't. Your face makes him too much money."

"Yeah. He won't do it right up until the moment he does."

Carly stood up, resting on Darlene a moment, then pulling away. She felt the reaction beginning to come over her. A tear slipped down her cheek. That made her angry with herself, furious. It was one thing to beg for mercy with Jammer, that was what she needed to do to make him walk away. It was another thing to be scared of him after he was gone, and Carly hated that she was.

Darlene followed her into the bedroom.

"I've got to get out of here," Carly said, her voice shaking. "I've got to get clean!" She took a picture out of her drawer, and Darlene moved beside her, leaning close.

"Look at you," Darlene said, putting her arm around Carly's waist as they looked at the picture. In it, Carly stood knee-deep in a mountain stream, her hair wet, her arms covering her breasts as she looked back over her shoulder. She was smiling in a way Carly herself knew she hadn't smiled in over two years. She wondered if she still could smile that way, if her face could ever be taught again to show such happiness.

"You're like the girl next door every boy wants to meet," Darlene said. "You'll get back there; you'll go for a swim like that some day."

"He always finds me."

Darlene rolled her eyes. "That's the truth. You never know

when that son of a bitch is watching." Darlene leaned closer, pushing herself against Carly. "Oh, baby, I wish I could take care of
you better." She kissed Carly on the cheek.

Carly slipped back. "Stop it. I'm sorry, but no."

Darlene looked hurt. "You want to get clean of everything,
huh?"

"Yeah, I do. I don't belong here."

"And I do?"

Carly looked at Darlene and her face softened. She put her
palm against Darlene's face. "Hey, thanks for trying to pull him
off. You've saved my ass more than once."

"Look, why don't you go find this guy and get the sword cane
back? You know Jammer's going to be crazy until he gets it. He
talks about it being his trademark—I think he's got it confused
with his dick."

Carly laughed. "Maybe you should explain that to him."

"Oooh, not a good idea."

"Yeah, well, I've got no clue where this guy is with the sword
cane. He was just a stranger. But even if I did, I wouldn't give it
to Jammer; he'd kill me with it."

"Naw. He gets it back, he'll be all right."

Carly shook her head. "Not when he finds out about Raul.
Jammer might kill you too, just for exercise when he finds out
about that."

Darlene paled. "What about Raul?"

Carly lifted a straight razor from her purse. "You know a couple weeks back, you were on that weekend call down at the Cape?
Well, he sent me down that way, too."

"You didn't tell me."

"I didn't tell *anyone*. And don't you either. Anyway, Jammer
said Raul might be 'a little rough.' But when I came in, he had a
video camera and tools set up like a frigging torture chamber. He

started hitting me, 'just to loosen me up.' He said I was going to be out of commission for a while, but that he'd make it worth my while."

"Oh, shit."

"He meant broken bones. He meant cutting me."

Darlene listened quietly. "So what did you do?"

"I cut the bastard first. On the arm. He'd sent his guys away for the night, and I got away."

Darlene eyebrows lifted. "And Jammer didn't do *anything* to you? Raul didn't send Strike or Lee around?"

"No. Nothing happened."

"Why?"

"I don't have a clue. Jammer doesn't know. I'd be dead by now if he did. As for Raul, I just don't know."

Darlene was shaking her head slowly. "This doesn't make sense, honey. Guys like him don't forgive and forget."

"I know. Believe me, I'm afraid of every car that pulls up on the street that they'll be inside." She laughed, bitterly. "A hooker afraid of strange men in cars. That's why I need to find the guy who cut Jammer for me."

Darlene was confused. "I thought you weren't going to find the sword."

"I'm not," she said. "I'm going to find the man."

CHAPTER 7

Geoff belayed the top rope as Harrison struggled up the rock-face. The fat boy was doing pretty well. Seems that there was some muscle under the flab after all. Harrison's face was pouring sweat, and he looked scared, but he was still climbing. Fighting the rock harder than necessary. Scrambling rather than setting his feet as Geoff had taught him, not leaning back much, not trusting his grip. But making upward progress. Harrison was nothing if not a climber, Geoff decided.

Or maybe it was just the top rope giving him confidence he didn't deserve. Geoff had free-climbed the rockface himself, with the coil of rope tied to his backpack. The two kids who were act-ing as guides—hell, as camp counselors—hadn't been too thrilled. But they had too many other people demanding their at-tention. And by the time one of them could have hiked up the back trail to the rockface, Geoff was already up and dropping down the line. Geoff knew he could climb better than either one of them, and they probably recognized it too.

He handled the rope for Harrison now, thinking of all the negotiating he should be doing, building his bridges with the other members of the "Executive Team." That's why Jansten had arranged the little outing. Plus the old man was an old-time jock himself. High school football quarterback, middleweight boxer in the marines, a half-dozen tennis trophies in his office, and an even more impressive array of sailing trophies.

Normally, Geoff would have been working those points, highlighting their similarities. But almost without knowing it, Geoff had crossed a bridge within the past few weeks. He was too weary of the nonsense to do all that. After what had happened with the bike messenger and Kelly—and then that pimp—Geoff recognized that his personal wiring had changed permanently.

He wondered briefly if he was going crazy. He knew some people would judge him so, maybe call him a psychopath, if they had followed his actions for the past few weeks. His grandparents certainly would have said so years ago, if they had ever dared.

But he wasn't sure himself. It was as if all of that cold ruthlessness of his earlier days was a prelude to a capacity that was now coming alive within him. And this "capacity" wasn't so cool. It wouldn't necessarily hold back for his own good. He looked at his hands, his muscular arms still gleaming with sweat. His belly was hard as a rock from thousands of sit-ups, his legs and chest layered with muscle from years of rock climbing, windsurfing, martial arts training.

His body, his mind, weren't meant for office politics.

The thought energized him. He wouldn't—couldn't—play Jansten's games any longer. Not even for the money. There were other ways a guy like him could make money.

Still . . . he had made one fortune within the company . . . could he really walk away so easily?

Geoff looked down at Harrison and then over at Jansten and Dern.

Steve Dern. His new boss.

Christ.

Geoff decided abruptly to give Jansten Enterprises one more chance.

If it didn't work, then the place truly wasn't his kind of company anymore.

Harrison had to claw over the last bit, his eyes wild. He rolled onto his back, gasping for air. "Oh, God. Oh, God." His face was beaded with sweat, and his white shirt was gray and black with dirt. His knees and elbows were flecked with blood.

Harrison had been acting as if the incident in the bar hadn't happened; maintaining the buddy fiction. Geoff had let that stand for a while, even to the extent of pouring on the charm to Geena, Harrison's wife. She was thin, dark-haired, and, Geoff suspected, an equal partner in Harrison's driving ambition. She had smiled gaily the whole time, her eyes searching Geoff's face sharply, trying to measure his intent.

Geoff slapped Harrison's belly with the back of his hand, inwardly repelled by the touch of the man's sweaty gut. "You wild man," he said. "You sure showed me something there."

"Yeah?" Harrison looked over at him, and Geoff could see wariness competing with gratitude in his eyes. "I appreciate that."

Pathetic.

"Well." Geoff looked away, feigning embarrassment. "It's true. And I owe you an apology anyhow, for the way I blew up."

Harrison sat up. Like a dog, but trying to show some dignity. "Yeah, you do."

Geoff sighed and was about to continue with his line when Harrison surprised him.

He said, "Hey. I got a couple of things for you."

"What's that?"

"Jerry Cahill was in from Dern's division."

"Don't know the man."

"No reason you would. He's a senior designer down in Charleston, got lots of years under Dern. I ran into him and got to talking about his old boss. Guess the word is pretty good on Dern."

"Has this got a point?" Geoff asked, sourly.

"One is that Dern's kind of quiet. Only has a few real friends. He's supposed to be crazy about his wife." Harrison sat up and looked at Lisa climbing easily up a rockface more difficult than the one he had just scaled. "Can't say I blame him."

"What else?" Geoff asked.

"Okay, next is a small point. One of his good buddies just moved into the area. Guy by the name of Alex Martin. Was with Steve in the navy. Runs a marine salvage business."

"So?"

"So Jerry told me an interesting story that is part of the lore back there. You know that Dern was a salvage diver after the navy, right?"

"Everybody knows that."

"Yeah. But does everybody know Dern and his partner got into a jam diving—and that Dern left him to drown? And that Dern quit diving professionally right after?"

Geoff cocked an eyebrow.

"I went to the library and read the articles. No real blame was assigned to Dern. Fact is, he probably did everything he could, and the other guy's luck ran out. But Cahill says Dern came out with a case of the shakes as far as diving in tight spots, caves and shit. Even that boat he lives on now, he supposedly did some diving on that salvage job, but it was his buddy Alex who was responsible for bringing it up." Harrison shivered. "I'm not saying you'd get me in one of those spots either, but, hey, maybe you can jab him with it someday. Guy like him, it probably still eats at him."

Geoff let his face communicate his appreciation for Harrison's work. In truth, Geoff was disgusted that Harrison wanted to be told he did a good job rooting garbage.

"That's good insight," Geoff said. "You're really coming through now."

He paused, letting the fool enjoy the compliment. Then he said, quietly, "I drive the people who work closely with me too hard, I know that. I push myself just as hard to deliver extraordinary performance. I expect the same from my right-hand man."

Harrison shrugged. "I'll give you that. Like climbing this rockface. I didn't think I could've done that."

Geoff shook his head. "I watched you. You could handle a lot more."

"You think so?"

"Sure." Geoff let the full weight of his attention rest upon Harrison. "I'm going to tell you something."

Harrison sat up slightly. Geoff could count on one hand the times he had confided genuinely important business to Harrison, and the man was flattered—just as he should be.

Geoff told him what Jansten had proposed.

Harrison grinned delightedly. "Holy shit. Number two man in the company! Hell, it paid off, everything we've been working toward." Here Harrison glanced sidelong at Geoff, checking out the reaction on the "we've."

Geoff kept his face blank while Harrison continued, stumbling a little now. "Hey, man, I know long-term that you had your sights on the presidency. But, shit, there's *going for* something and there's *getting it*. Really getting it. You shot high, and while Dern's going to be in your way, who knows what will happen in a few years after Jansten is gone? Dern fucks up, and you're right there. You've still got a good chance of getting the whole thing."

"I'm not waiting that long," Geoff said, lifting his binoculars to look at Steve and Lisa. Both were climbing the rockface to the right of Geoff. He had to admit to himself, they both looked good. Not in his league, perhaps, and they set chocks for protection—which, to him, missed the point. But there was no denying that they were strong, competent climbers. Geoff watched Lisa for a while, thinking that on looks alone, Kelly had the edge. Not by much, but there. Of course, she was a good eight or nine years younger. Nevertheless, he had to admit that he wouldn't mind having Lisa by his side. Those classic features, dark hair and blue eyes. A nice body, a little leaner than Kelly's. Holding herself well on that rock, sweat beading her brow. Strong woman. When Dern had introduced them before, she had shaken Geoff's hand firmly, looking him in the eye. "We want to have you out on the boat," she'd said. "I know you and Steve have a lot to talk about."

Friendly enough, giving him a chance. But he could sense a toughness in her, a wariness.

He switched the binoculars back to Jansten. The old man was sitting not too far away, looking up at some of the other climbers. Geoff saw him wince slightly, then rub his side. Geoff said, "I'm counting on there being something left inside that old guy besides the Pollyanna I'm seeing now."

Geoff put the binoculars down. Harrison was practically bursting, clearly wanting to ask what Geoff's promotion meant for *him*.

So Geoff told him.

Harrison's face went slack. He looked over at the steep wall across from them. "You've got to be kidding me."

"You wanted to go along for the ride."

"After all I've done . . ."

"All you've done earns you the right to win it. It's the difference between *going for it* and *getting it.* Now shut up while I show you how to rappel down."

Geoff sat beside Jansten and watched the others climb the easier rockface, the one with the guides.

"I heard our guides yelling at you some," Jansten said.

"I didn't ask permission."

Jansten smiled. "Never your strong suit."

Geoff kept his eyes on the opposite rockface, looking out at the small ledge that sloped down toward the ground. "I've got to ask you something."

Jansten smiled thinly. "I would expect you do."

"I've got to ask you if any of the man who has been running this company for the past forty years is still left inside you."

"I think so." Jansten's tone remained even.

"You're sure now? You're sure he hasn't been entirely consumed by nice breakfasts, sailing days, and all the sweet nonsense I heard out at your house?"

"I'm sure," Jansten said, comfortably. "And I can prove it by kicking your ass out of this company any time you want to continue this line of conversation."

"Not a problem," Geoff said, looking at Jansten frankly. "Because this second-in-command shit has nothing to do with me. I'm not staying here in that capacity—not for long anyhow."

"Well, that would be a shame. And I certainly realized this might happen, given your ego. But I thought that you and Steve might cross-pollinate, so to speak. The company would be all the better for it. Frankly, you would, too."

"The company is going to fail under Dern. You realize that, don't you?"

"I realize no such thing. His division has done remarkably well, better than your own."

"It's *grown,* yes, but it hasn't brought in a fraction of the total revenue," Geoff snapped. He waved back Jansten's response, and was pleased to see the old man keep his mouth shut. Geoff had no intention of quibbling on that level. "Steve is a nice guy, but you've got a company full of sharks. And he's going to make them soft. He'll turn Jansten Enterprises into some sort of matrix system, make sure everyone is happy and nothing gets done."

"I'm looking at what he's accomplished already," Jansten said in that infuriatingly mild tone. "And I'm looking at what you've accomplished. Admittedly, it's a tough choice. My plan, at this point, is to make the recommendation to the board as I described. I had dinner last night with McGarrity, and he agreed to go along."

At this point. Geoff smiled to himself as he looked back up at the wall. *McGarrity would go along.* An opening left. And if Geoff was hearing the code of corporate language correctly, McGarrity was agreeing only under pressure. Geoff had done more than a few favors for that old bastard, including sending two teenage hookers to his room one night out in San Francisco. He was sure McGarrity would pop back into line once Jansten let him.

Geoff said, "You know that fat boy I've got working for me?"

"You mean Harrison?"

"That's right. What do you think of him?"

Jansten lifted his eyebrows at the change of topic, but answered. "I don't know. Sort of a kissass. Does all right."

"Would you expect him to go beyond a day's work?"

"Not much."

"How about risk? Would he be willing to risk it all?"

"Not that I've seen," Jansten said, tiredly. "What's your point?"

Geoff pointed to the ledge. Harrison was now visible climbing up the rockface alone. There was no top rope. No one was belaying him from below. He was setting no protection.

He was free-climbing a rockface far beyond his skill. Even at that distance they could see that he was terrified.

"What the hell . . ." Jansten said, wonderingly. "Is this you? Did you put him up to this?"

Harrison's wife, Geena, approached them. She moved stiffly, looking up at the wall, then back at Jansten and Geoff. "What's going on?" she said, looking up at her husband and then back at them. She was struggling to be polite, trying to keep calm. "Michael!" she called out to Harrison. "Cut it out, honey, come on down." She moved closer to the fall line, and glanced back again at Geoff and Jansten.

When her attention returned to Harrison, Jansten said, quietly, "What the hell did you promise him?"

"My old job," Geoff said. "If there is any of the man I once worked for left inside of you, he'll recognize that Dern could never bring himself to push Harrison that hard. If there's any of you left in there, you'll recognize that you and this company have succeeded because you've hired people like me who can make losers like him succeed. And that's your legacy whether you like it or not. And that's why I should have the top job, whether you like it or not."

Jansten looked over at Geoff coolly, then back to Harrison. "All right, let's see how he does."

Geoff grinned. "I knew you were still in there."

elp him!" Geena cried. She turned back to Geoff and Jansten. "He'll listen to you, and you know he can't climb that."

"He may surprise you," Geoff said. "Besides, it was his choice."

She put her hand to her mouth, trying to restrain herself. Then her emotions broke through. "Like hell. He told me what you said in that bar. Like hell."

Others were coming at that point. Keiler, Jacobs, Barnaby,

Urlich, Nickerson, and Lane showed up, their wives trailing them. Geoff didn't know any of the men all that well, but Harrison himself had confirmed that not one of them would take a piss without consulting the others about their read on Jansten's opinion. So Geoff didn't expect any real challenge as long as Jansten was sitting there quietly beside him.

And indeed, after Keiler took in the situation, Harrison's climb and teary-eyed wife, he smoothed his black mustache, looked at Jansten, looked at his compatriots, and said, "Didn't know Harrison had it in him."

Dern was rappelling down the rockface behind them. Lisa was already down.

"What's going on?" one of the guides called from the top of Dern's rise. "What's that guy doing?"

Jansten smiled at the guide calmly, but didn't answer.

The guide turned, apparently speaking to his partner behind him. "One of these idiots is trying to free-climb a five-eight. Get your ass over there, see if you can hike up the back way and get him a top rope."

Dern was already down before the guide finished yelling. He and Lisa hurried over, coiling their rope. Dern stepped around Keiler and said directly to Geoff, "This is your guy. Does he know what he's gotten himself into?"

"We'll see."

Geena grasped Dern's arm. "They must have made him some offer. Believe me, he wouldn't do this on his own."

Dern looked at Geoff, who smiled back blandly. *Let's hear the speech,* Geoff thought.

Just then, Harrison slipped. He scrambled frantically, trying to regain his footing.

He did, but when he looked down afterward it was obvious he was wild-eyed with fear. He was over a hundred feet up from the ground.

"Belay me," Dern said to his wife.

He started up the rockface immediately. He trailed a rope and Lisa moved quickly, setting several chocks between boulders and crevices at the base. She hooked herself into these and then put his line through a figure-eight on her harness. Steve set his first chock just as he got past the ledge and continued climbing straight up.

Geoff watched Lisa quietly, noticing the skill with which she moved. He couldn't imagine Kelly being of any help in such a situation, and he had to admire Lisa a bit. But that didn't change the fact that the Derns were intruding in his plans. Geoff didn't mind all of the hysteria: Harrison's crying wife was perfect. But this competence on the part of Dern and his wife was a pain in the ass.

Geoff saw Harrison was moving again. Geoff wasn't surprised. He had Harrison's abilities—and ambitions—figured within inches. The man would make it to the top, hard as it was. Geoff felt a calm excitement inside. His point and his future would be proven by a man far weaker than he.

If Dern didn't fuck it all up, that was. Dern was moving up the rockface with a dexterity and assurance that Geoff knew would rival his own.

The first guide came running up to take over the belay from Lisa. He called Geoff and several of the other executives over. Jansten hitched himself up on a rock and said, quietly, "Go on, Geoff."

The guide was a big kid with a wispy beard. "Steve is looking good, and I hope to hell he can get this line onto Harrison. If he does fall, both of them are going—so we're talking upwards of four hundred pounds dropping on one line. Who knows if the protection will hold. But if it does, I'm going to need some help."

Harrison cried out again. Geoff stood back from the belaying line and pulled out his binoculars. He ignored the guide who was yelling, "I need you back on this rope, mister."

Harrison's legs were visibly trembling.

Above him was the final obstacle, a subtle outswelling of rock that required a layback to pull it off. Tough stuff for a newcomer. But even where Geoff was standing, he could see a small crevice within a foot of Harrison's right hand. A solid grip there. Geoff could see the moves, easily enough. Nothing that would have given Geoff a moment's pause—or even Harrison if he were well rested, and five feet from the ground—but from the way Harrison's legs were jiggling, the way his head was turning frantically one way and the next, Geoff could see he was just about played out.

Geoff sighed. He hadn't planned on being a coach, but maybe when all was said and done it would help his cause. After all, Steve was certainly making himself look the hero, climbing after the guy.

Geoff stepped back further from the rock and cupped his hands to his face. "Harrison, listen to me. *Calm down.* You're almost done. Just above you to the right is a great handhold. Man, you could spend the afternoon on that grip. You've got to put your right foot forward, catch that little nub and trust the grip you've got on the right. Put your left palm down against the rock and *climb.*"

Harrison seemed to be listening. His head stopped that foolish swiveling, in any case. He started moving up the rockface again.

Geoff exhaled. Dern was getting too damn close for comfort.

Geena moved beside Geoff. She said, "Keep talking. You got him into this, please help him."

"He's doing just fine himself."

Dern was alongside Harrison now and the tension Geoff had been holding in rein seeped into his belly. The fucking Boy Scout was going to ruin everything. He saw that Dern had a good grip himself with his left hand and was getting ready to snap a carabiner with the rope onto Harrison's climbing harness. Even if

Harrison finished after that, the victory would be Dern's for making it safe.

Geoff cupped his hands together again. "Harrison—you've got somebody trying to steal your thunder—and my offer—right beside you. I want you to do this on your own."

Harrison's wife gasped.

"You're going too far," Jansten snapped.

Geoff ignored them, focusing instead upon Lisa. She strode over from the base and said, "You listen to me, you son of a bitch. I don't know what you promised that man, but if he falls, my husband very likely will go down with him. So shut your mouth."

"Or what?"

She cracked him across the face, shocking no one more than Geoff.

It was a hard blow, leaving a red mark on Geoff's face.

Everyone went silent.

It took everything Geoff had to restrain himself. Jansten put his hand on Geoff's wrist and said, "Back away."

Geoff was flush with the knowledge that had they been alone, he would have killed Lisa Dern. He would have broken her neck. He would have wrapped his arm around her head, grasped her jaw, and twisted until her neck popped. "Keep her away from me," he said, hoarsely.

"Go on," Jansten said to Lisa. "Go back and help them with that rope."

Up above, Harrison's voice was desperate. "Don't. Don't snap it on. I'm going to finish this. I'm going to do it now."

Geoff wiped his mouth as he watched Lisa go back to the belay line. He closed his eyes briefly, centering himself, and then said to Geena, in a voice loud enough for all of them to hear, "You're going to like Michael's new job. He'll be more than tripling his salary."

He saw her look back at him, then back up at her husband. He was within reach of the top now. A weak smile crossed her face, and Geoff laughed inwardly. *Already trying to recover from the things she said.*

Geoff looked over at Jansten. The old man was looking up at Harrison still, his face unreadable.

And then the old man winced.

Harrison's wife screamed out, and Geoff looked up to see everything he had worked for fall apart.

Harrison was slipping.

His right foot broke free, and then, trying to recover, he jammed his foot hard against smooth rock and shoved his leg out entirely. He screamed, his words incoherent as he hung from one hand—and then he lost that altogether and began sliding down the rockface.

Dern reached out for him.

"No, Steve!" Lisa cried.

Dern caught him by the harness and tried to pull him close, tried to provide with his own body the purchase Harrison so desperately needed. And for a moment, it seemed he had succeeded. Harrison's downward slide stopped. He tried to find something in the rock, some support. But in his panic, Harrison succeeded only in kicking Dern's legs free from the rock.

The two of them began to fall.

Geoff watched the others around him—even Jansten—throw themselves onto the belay line. Above them, Harrison clung to Dern and their combined weight ripped away the first protection point. The two of them fell a good dozen feet before slamming against the wall. They both came away dazed and bloody, Harrison now hanging on to Steve's legs.

"Let it free, let it free," the guide was calling to the others as he paid out rope, trying to get Dern and Harrison down as fast as possible. Then the guide's bottom protection broke free. He and Lisa were hauled away from the others up the face themselves, kicking against rock. They quickly let themselves down and paid out more line.

The last chock broke free just as Dern and Harrison reached the ledge. The two of them slid down the last twenty feet, grabbing for whatever they could. Harrison fought the wall in pure panic; Dern kept his balance and shoved away at the last second so he could roll away from the boulders at the very base.

Harrison wasn't so successful. Geoff saw him hit a rock, and his ankle twisted flat in a way nature never intended. There was an audible popping noise, like heavy pottery breaking. The idiot tried to stand and then fell, clutching his ruined ankle.

He screamed like a girl.

Geoff shook his head. "Shit."

Harrison's wife wrapped her arms around her husband, crying his name. He shoved her aside, and yet, she came back to him.

Geoff looked around, saw them all staring at him. Dern, his face bloodied and white with anger. Dern's wife, all of the others. Harrison looking at him through the tears and trying to be manly about the whole thing and failing miserably. He said, "I almost made it, man. I almost made it."

"But you didn't," Geoff said.

"Neither did you," Jansten said. He was smiling coldly, the tough old bastard Geoff had always known. "You're out, Geoff."

CHAPTER 8

Later that day, Carly began her rounds. Out of the dying Combat Zone, down a few blocks to the bar, and then a turn around Berkeley Street. Back up Commonwealth into the Public Gardens, then back to the bar again.

Dressed in hot pink, offering love in fifteen-minute increments.

Most times on that circuit, something happened. She would get a signal, a wave from some guy, and she would service him as he drove around the Garden. Other times, she brought the johns back to the room. That meant more time, more risk, more games from the men, and more money for her. It also meant more conversation, too. Sometimes that was okay. Sometimes she just had a sense a guy was lonely and just wanted to be with somebody. Sometimes a guy had a fun attitude and talked to her as if she was along for the ride too, not just her tits and ass.

But, all and all, the rides around the Common with her head in some guy's lap meant the least time for the money and there was something to be said for that.

Nasty girl, she thought, as she approached the bar and saw herself in the mirrored window. She hated the silly blond wig and skintight bodysuit. Jammer's selection. She felt sweaty and her ankles were dirty from walking the beat. *Nasty, dumb girl.*

Jammer had told her to be on the lookout for a cabbie who liked to be called Mr. Boffo. He brought a lot of johns in, and so she had to service him for free. Work that Jammer usually relegated to Darlene.

Just a month ago, she had been off the street and taking only calls. She could do her work at the Ritz or sometimes on the arm of a visiting businessman wanting a companion for the night. Five hundred a throw. That was before she'd tried to run, the time *before* last. Hours after the incident with Raul, Jammer had found her at the train station, bags packed.

So Jammer gave her the punishment detail, back on the street. He said that Strike had called, saying Raul had been "disappointed with her performance." That's all Jammer apparently knew. If he had known what *really* happened at Raul's, she fully believed he would make good on his favorite threat of spraying her face with lighter fluid and lighting a match. She was pretty sure he had it in him to carry it out.

Why Raul hadn't told all, she had no idea. Maybe it would make him lose face to admit to the pimp that she cut him. Men were like that, posing for each other all the time. She was nervous every time a car slowed down for her, nervous that Strike or Lee would be waiting in the back to take her to Raul's.

Her White Knight had been adopting some sort of pose, she was sure. That's the name she had given the man in the park, just kidding around with herself. She knew he must have had reasons of his own for getting in the fight with Jammer. And her life had hardly become better for his interference.

Jammer had slapped her around again this morning when she had pointed out to him that she had been making more money for the both of them by working as a call girl.

"You think *I'm* gonna lose?" he said, his voice breaking with outrage. "You think *I'm* gonna lose money because you need your ass kicked? You make your five hundred, and I don't care if it takes one trick or fifty!"

No way she was going to do it, but if she brought in three hundred he might not hit her too hard. Dumbass pimp. He was losing out on all that cash just to make his point about the damn sword cane.

But she knew the real issue was that he was afraid of losing face. Afraid that Raul wouldn't let him in on the distribution deal. Afraid that if Raul heard some tourist in a suit took Jammer's weapon away, he would smile like he was pretending he was sad while Strike or one of his other lieutenants smashed Jammer's elbows with a baseball bat.

Carly could have told Jammer that Raul wouldn't have given a shit one way or the other about Jammer's sword cane or anything else about him. Jammer was only half smart. Strictly small-time, but with an ego big enough to fill a small castle. Good at skulking around, following people. Tough enough to slap around whores. Mean enough to earn his nickname by jamming his sharp toys into anyone stupid enough to cross him and look away.

But she knew Raul was just playing with Jammer. Maybe looking to suck up some of his cash and throw Jammer a dying territory. Carly sometimes felt the stirring of what she figured was the wife inside her. She wanted to tell Jammer sometimes what she saw; she wanted to let him know he was making a big mistake with Raul. But she always held back. Giving Jammer advice would only earn her a beating. Besides, she wasn't giving him anything for free.

Carly searched her reflection, not admiring her beauty, but trying to see if she was still *in* there, behind the whore's clothing and makeup. For the millionth time, she thought, *why me?*

She had grown up just outside Camden, Maine, a beautiful little town that attracted tourists from all over the world with its jewel-like harbor, complete with oh-so-perfect shops. But when she thought of Camden, she thought of the trailer park just outside of town where she had lived with her mother. And how, even at age sixteen, the boys had seemed to know about her.

She could never figure it out. Was it something about her face? Something about the plastic, aluminum, and Formica of trailer park life that made her seem less real, less flesh and blood than the other girls? What was it that made the boys expect her to come across? And worse still, that she would? Maybe it was that she didn't have a father around anymore to chase them away.

The only one who was different was Neal and that was just in the beginning. Even though he was the one who hurt her the most, she still thought about that summer, starting the day he had come up to her when she had a job at Friendly's. His family had a vacation house in town, and he was working a construction job between his freshman and sophomore years at Boston College.

He had been in the restaurant every day for weeks, always arranging it so he could sit at her table. Staying polite while his buddies—also out-of-towners—kidded and flirted with her outrageously. Finally, he asked her out to the movies. She went and was surprised to find he didn't touch her until their goodnight kiss. Even then, she could feel that he wanted to do more, but was holding himself back. It wasn't until he left her alone that night on the steps, her mother inside already finishing up her first bottle of Lancers, that Carly realized he was respecting her, treating her like she was special.

They had several more dates like that. Once she had seen some of the guys from the Cage coming up to her, and she had hustled Neal into his car. As they took off, Neal looked in his mirror and said, "You know those guys?"

"Just from school," she had said. And that seemed to be the end of it.

He picked her up to go hiking their third weekend together. They drove to Mount Chocorua. Hiking was harder work than she thought it would be. But when they made it to the top, he had kissed her and said he never had a girl like her before, and would she go with him? That they could figure a way to see each other when he went back to school.

"I know it's way too early, Carly. But I wish I could just take you with me. Maybe you could get a scholarship, you're smart. Or maybe work someplace close by. I want you with me."

She knew he meant it, and she knew in her heart he was nicer than she was. She didn't really deserve a guy like him, but she wanted him anyhow. He was strong, smart, and going places. Gray eyes, curly black hair, a bit serious, but he knew how to laugh. A little stiff, but that was something she could help him with.

He had held her and although it was wonderful and although she loved him in that moment, she wondered about what she had done with the other boys in the backseats of their cars. How she seemed entirely different now from the girl Simon Creed, cocaptain of the football team, called "a pretty little piece of nothing."

She knew she had to explain. She knew she had to be straight with Neal as much as she wanted to forget it all. And she almost had been, right there on the mountaintop, but somehow she had let the chance pass.

On the way down, they had come across the stream. They were

sweaty and grimy right then. And the way she was feeling about him, her clothes seemed just like so much itchy interference and she had slipped out of them, watching his eyes go wide. He had raised his camera and snapped a picture, the one she still had. She had teased him into jumping into the water with her. She had felt so good, so fresh and alive. She dunked herself repeatedly in the cold mountain water and felt she was emerging whole and clean, her past left behind. He had kissed her and touched her all over. And in spite of the shocking cold water, he was far from shrunken. They made love right there on the sun-heated rocks.

It was the best time for her, ever.

And in the weeks that followed, he brought her flowers, they took long walks . . . always she found herself steering them away from people who knew her.

She dreamed in those weeks about going away. About somehow being able to leave with Neal and never again see Camden or the faces of those boys who knew so much about her.

Carly pushed those thoughts away now, angry with herself. Forcing herself to see that she *was* still in there, behind the makeup. *Remember the swim. Remember the clean water and how fresh and alive you were. You can do that again.*

Why remember the coldness of his face? The harsh jerkiness of his little speech when he arrived hours late for their last night of the summer. They were supposed to talk about how they could be together more during the school year. She had a year left of school, and her grades weren't all that bad. He had an aunt who lived in Brookline that he thought she could move in with if she transferred. Her mother hadn't quashed the idea yet, saying that maybe this was Carly's chance to "hook him."

But when Neal finally arrived, he was clearly drunk and bloodied from fighting. He stood in the doorway of the trailer and said how her "high school friends" had showed up at the bar and asked if he'd had any good head lately.

She tried to tell him then, but the words couldn't come out, she didn't know what to say. First she denied it. Then she clung to him, begging him to take her away, telling him that she could explain.

"How? How can you explain it?"

She saw even then that he was waiting, he wanted an answer to make everything right. His voice was hoarse. "Is it true?"

She withdrew from him slowly. She felt herself go still, her arms and legs leaden. None of the explanations she had elaborately worked out seemed to make any sense now. She had dreamed of him listening, his face serious, but forgiving. Of him putting his arm around her and saying it was all right, and that they would leave and together they could start all over. But now, she felt the same as she had before: a pretty little piece of nothing.

"Is it true?" he repeated.

She simply nodded her head.

He had lost it then and struck out with his fist. "You're a whore!"

Always the gentleman, he didn't touch her, but left a fist-sized dent on the aluminum wall of their home.

Carly's mother had started screeching, and the lights had turned on in the other trailers nearby. Neal fled, tears in his eyes.

Carly's mother went on about it for hours, while Carly herself said very little. Early the next morning, she had left at the regular time, but instead of putting on her waitress apron, she had taken a bus to Boston.

Her money ran out within the first ten days. It didn't take her long to realize just how desperate her situation was, how quickly hunger came, how quickly lack of shelter sapped her strength. How quickly she realized she had virtually no skills. Even waitress jobs were beyond her, filthy and obviously homeless as she now appeared. Jammer had picked her up in the Boston Common and took care of her for about a week before telling her that she would be turning tricks for him. When she tried to walk out, he beat her and raped her repeatedly for another week and told her that not only were tricks all she was good for, but he was making it his job in life to watch her and see that she did what she was told.

After she recovered, he sent her out on the street for a few months to break her in before she advanced to the call girl status where, somehow, two years had passed. Some of the men on her calls were pretty well off. Maybe a few of them were rich. None of them were interested in her for anything but sex, but she quickly learned enough about clothes and making conversation to not embarrass herself too much at a nice restaurant.

Carly had just passed her eighteenth birthday and felt her eyes were open to the wide world. She knew her last two attempts to get away were pure desperation. Taking off at the bus station with virtually no money on her and no skills would land her in about the same spot on some other city street. If she was going to make it, she needed a better escape plan than that.

"You'll be back on the street . . . indefinitely," Jammer had told her, as if he were proud to know how to use the word. "First the train station, now your boyfriend cuts me. You're lucky I'm not killing you."

The way she saw it, he *was* killing her, one day at a time.

Either she got off the streets and out of Boston, or Raul would get to her. She turned away from the mirror, keeping her eye on the street for Strike or Lee. Because men like Raul don't forgive and forget.

The shadows were growing long on the Common when she saw her White Knight. And saw that he had seen her. He was jogging—running, actually. Moving faster than she was used to seeing someone out for exercise. She looked to see if he was being chased, and quickly searched the street to see if Jammer was nearby.

Safe on both counts.

She looked back at her White Knight, and their eyes locked. Carly raised her hand and said, "Hey."

Suddenly, she was dreadfully afraid that he would turn his head and just keep running—and for a moment, it seemed as if he was going to do just that.

But he didn't. He veered direction and crossed the street. She couldn't help but grin, watching him now. He flew!

"Hey, yourself," he said, stopping. He bent deeply, stretching as he regained his breath. Sweat poured off him.

She touched the back of his head. "Yuck."

He straightened up, and she let her hand fall along his cheek and then his chest. His heart was pounding furiously.

"You always run so hard?" she asked.

"I've had sort of a tough day. Working out hard clears my head."

She ran her fingers down his side. He was in wonderful shape. Muscular, but not a weight lifting freak. She was startled to find the stirring of physical interest in herself. How long has *that* been, she thought, amused.

He didn't stop her, but she didn't read any encouragement either. He said, "What are you doing back here? I thought I cut you free."

"Jammer got me at the bus station." She looked up and down the street again. "In fact, let's get off the street."

He shrugged and followed her into the alley alongside the bar. She flushed, embarrassed. He probably thought she had done tricks there, which she hadn't. And indeed, when she turned to face him, he was already looking at his watch and looking back at the entrance of the alleyway. "I'm not looking for anything," he said.

"I've been looking for *you*."

"Why?"

"To say thanks, first of all. I don't know why you did what you did, but it meant a lot to see somebody kick Jammer's ass. He's still wearing the bandage on his head."

"Yeah, well, I've been a little out of control lately." He looked upward, as if making fun of himself. She thought he was pleased, but he was hard to read.

She smiled. "Jammer wants his sword back."

"Tell him life is full of disappointments."

"Uh-huh. *I* know that, but he has a hard time hearing it."

"Has he been beating you over what happened?"

"Like it's his hobby," she said, looking him in the eyes. She didn't see much of a reaction, but she was happy he was still talking with her. Not that he seemed all there. He seemed interested and distracted at the same time, the way he would look away and then focus back on her.

"Can I ask you something?" she said.

"Sure."

"Why *did* you do it?"

He laughed shortly. "Damned if I know. I've been getting myself into all kinds of trouble lately."

"That's all?"

He smiled at her coldly. "It wasn't love at first sight, if that's what you were thinking."

She looked away, briefly, so he wouldn't see the hurt on her face. She knew better than to expect anything, but it seemed like a part of her still did.

"I will say I was impressed the way you were taking him on," he said. "Even when you knew you couldn't win."

That warmed her, and she told him simply, "I've just had enough."

She leaned forward and kissed him on the cheek. He started to pull away, but then let her. She moved closer, pressing herself against him and whispered, "Take me to your place. I'll do anything you want, won't cost you anything."

He pushed her back. "No."

She was surprised the way the word kicked the breath out of her. She usually took rejection with nothing but relief, but this bugged her. She had really wanted to thank him, in the best way she knew how. "You like girls, don't you?"

"Just fine. I just need to keep healthy. I've got a lot of things to do."

"I'm clean! No drugs, no HIV. Tested just last week. That's why I need to break away now, while I still can."

"Uh-huh." He looked at her silently, and, instinctively, she shut up and waited.

"I don't know that much about hookers," he said, after a moment. "This whining about getting away—is this just a pipe dream all of you talk about for entertainment, or are you really trying to make it happen?"

She held back her immediate answer. She let her eyes rest on him until the count of five, and then said, quietly, "I will get out somehow. The question is whether or not I get out with most of my skin. Jammer has promised to ruin my face if I run again, and I believe he'll do it."

The guy paused, looked away, and then came back to her. "Well, if you want to thank me, there may be a way."

She went silent. Her heart quickened but she settled back, looking at him closely. His distraction wasn't so much nervousness because of the situation, being in an alleyway with a hooker. There was something else. No matter what he had said, she decided their meeting was not just a coincidence, or her keeping her eyes out for him.

He had come looking for her.

"What do you want me to do?" she asked, quietly.

He pulled her closer, and she could feel his breath on her cheek. She inhaled the scent of him, his sweat was clean. "I'm not sure exactly at this second," he said, quietly. "I've taken kind of a setback in my career today, but I recover fast. And I'm going to be making some plans. I might need a friend who knows her way around Boston. Someone who can put me in touch with people who can get me things."

"We working girls know a lot of people." She smiled up at him. "It's in the job description."

"How about for passports?"

"Sure, I know somebody."

"And guns?"

"Even easier." She looked at him curiously. "What exactly do you do?"

"Until this morning, a corporate officer in a Fortune 500 company."

"So you're rich?"

"Not anymore. As of now, I'm probably Boston's newest member of the street. The question is whether or not I stay. I could land a new job tomorrow, but I'm not sure I want that for myself anymore."

"What is it you want?"

He shrugged. "I'll start with paying a few people back for what they did to me. And I need to put my hands on some cash, a lot of it. From there I'm going to do some traveling. See the world without the kind of timetable I've been keeping. Carve out a life that's more in keeping with who I am." He laughed suddenly, and the smile lighting up his face made her soar right alongside him. "I feel a lot better than I should, under the circumstances."

"Okay," she said. Her mind was racing, and she was seeing at least one point where their needs met. "I think we can help each other. My name is Carly, by the way."

He hesitated, then told her his.

"Geoff, let me ask you something."

"What's that?"

"Do you consider yourself a nice guy?"

He grinned. "No one has ever asked me that before. No, I'm not a nice guy. Not at all."

"That's good," she said and meant it. Because she had come to firmly believe in the past two years that you only get what you deserve.

Diagonally across the street, from the back of an old van, Jammer put down the binoculars and touched his cousin's shoulder. "Follow that guy," he said. "I told you that bitch was up to something."

CHAPTER 9

Alex knelt down in the cockpit, looking into the warm glow of the cabin. He said, "The tables are too close and the headwaiter looks sort of churlish. But the chef is radiant, and I have high hopes for the wine I brought."

"Ah, you Boston boys talk so smart," Lisa said, sweetening her southern accent by a few thousand calories. She stepped up on the ladder to kiss him. "Welcome aboard, Alex."

Steve was right behind her, and he and Alex shook hands, both grinning hugely. Steve said, "Took you long enough to get down here. We've been in town coming on two months."

"Just got here a few weeks ago myself. Going after that cabin cruiser I told you about." He looked around the boat, taking in the new woodwork, the teal cushions, the gleaming cabin sole. "My god, this lady came back from the dead, didn't she? Last time I saw her, you were shoveling mud and seaweed out of the bilge."

Steve inclined his head to Lisa. "The yard did the bulk of the refit before we sailed her here. Lisa oversaw it all and has been doing all the finish work herself."

"Boggles my mind how you got so lucky," Alex said. His gaze stopped on the picture of Buddy along with the two of them. He rubbed his chin, and said, quietly, "I have a copy of the same photo. Still gives me a jolt to see it here."

Steve saw Alex's eyes well up briefly, and he felt Buddy's absence himself, a tightness in the back of his throat. Alex had been their divemaster in the navy. Back then, he had been an old man in his early thirties. Now, there was more gray than black in his hair, and time and sun had deepened the wrinkles about his mouth and eyes. Still, his eyes were as bright and cheerful as ever, his handgrip as strong.

Lisa kissed each of them on the cheek. "The best part of moving to Boston is right here. Now, Alex, sit down, and tell us about the latest job."

Alex opened the bottle of wine and told them about the cabin cruiser that had tangled with the tow cable of a string of barges in a deep fog. "Everybody got off. Damn lucky there. And me, I've got my line of credit, I've done enough dives to feel like I can bring her up and turn a few bucks. Hull isn't bad at all—she's a big Egg Harbor—looks like she rolled and sank before the barge came over her. I won't actually start the salvage until next week. I'm still pulling my crew together." He looked at Steve. "I need a first mate if you want a break from this high-priced life of yours. Try a little adventure for a change."

Steve smiled wryly. "We've got all I can handle."

"We never knew the corporate life was so dangerous," Lisa said. She told Alex about Geoff.

Alex sat back, listening carefully. When she was finished, he said, "This guy sounds like a lunatic."

"I thought he was going to murder me on the spot when I slapped him," Lisa said. "But I guess he was afraid of Steve."

"I don't think he's afraid of anything," Steve said, mildly. "Certainly that's his reputation. And even this stunt might have worked for him."

"How so?" Alex asked.

Steve made a face. "For all his talk about a new leaf, Jansten admires winning above everything else. So if Geoff had succeeded in motivating Harrison to achieve a climb that was well beyond his skill, that would have meant something to Jansten."

"You think so?" Lisa said.

"Jansten was hardly calling him or Harrison off."

"Even though 'motivating' was nothing more than a bribe?" Alex said.

"Success is success, in Jansten's book."

"In that case, I guess you're a hero today for getting that guy off that rockface," Alex said. "So your position is now solid."

"Seems that way. Jansten announced to everyone there that I'm the acting president until the board makes it formal at the end of the month—complete with pomp and circumstance, reporters, the whole bit."

Alex shook his head, amused. "And I knew you when."

Later that night, Alex joined Steve on the deck. They stood at the mast looking out over the skyline of Boston, just as Steve had a few nights before. The dream slipped up from his unconscious, as if Buddy were trying to join the party.

Alex looked back at the twenty-five-foot Blue Water in the slip beside *The Sea Tern*. "Jesus, that would make a sweet dive boat."

"It's on loan from the company. I keep it around and test it, enjoy it."

"Give it to me. I'll put it to work."

"You give me an honest rundown on how it works out, we may do just that."

Alex grinned. "Can't beat that. I'll give you a written report in triplicate." He paused. "You do any diving lately?"

"I've got my gear, but I haven't done anything up here in Boston yet. I've been too busy." That was the truth, but it sounded like an evasion. He added, "Besides, you know diving isn't the charge for me it once was, particularly in cramped spaces. You saw how much help I was bringing up *The Sea Tern*."

Alex shrugged. "You pulled your weight. Besides, there's not much need for cave diving as the president of a major corporation, the way I see it. Look how things have worked out for you." He pointed to the deck, toward Lisa.

"Like you said, I'm a lucky man."

"When it comes to her, yeah. Everything else, you've worked for. So when do you move into the big house that goes with the big job?"

"About four months. They've got the roof up and they'll be finishing the inside. We should be in by Thanksgiving. In the meantime, we'll rough it here, bring in electric radiators. Assuming we can afford them. We managed to sink every dime into the house, so I'm in the weird position of being on the verge of a huge new job with empty pockets."

"Huh. That's good, actually. You've been getting too soft. All that cold air will keep your head from swelling. Being low on money will keep you hungry. Probably the last hard thing you'll have to do before all of that money comes pouring in."

"You think this job is going to be easy?"

"Naw," Alex said, shaking his head. "I think it's going to be murder. Leading all of those people. Not much privacy. For you and Lisa, I expect that's going to be hard. And you'll be dealing with problems all over the world, some of them I can't even imagine. But if I know you like I do, you'll be loving every second of it. What you might miss is that you're not going to be physically tested in any way. Keeps me young, doesn't it?"

Steve smiled at Alex. Indeed, though his skin was leathered by harsh sunlight and wind, there was the same vitality about him that Steve remembered from the first year of his enlistment.

Alex said, "You're smart, tough, and good on your feet. And that last bit sometimes makes everything else work out. Hell, you nailed your competition this morning rock climbing, didn't you?"

"That's the way it worked out. And that's probably the way Geoff thinks about it."

"Count on it. I bet that nut is sitting at home right now, grinding his darts down to a needle tip to throw at pictures of you. Beating his butt by climbing that rockface is probably the last time you'll ever be tested, physically. So enjoy the cold winter, enjoy being short on cash a little while longer. You're going to be fat and happy all too soon."

Geoff was not having such an uplifting moment. He had been working out for hours: push-ups, pull-ups, sit-ups. Lifting weights. At last, he took a break, falling to the floor. He tasted blood in the back of his throat.

The pictures on the walls seemed to mock him. Pictures of himself rock climbing, extreme skiing. A shot of himself skiing off a small cliff. Another of him racing a motorcycle, laying the bike down for a hairpin turn. The karate competitions . . . he closed his eyes.

He was sliding into a depression.

He saw the depression as something that tinged his vision with gray. That put everything under a fluorescent light that highlighted only what was banal and mundane. That made him see himself not as an adventurer, but as a fool. A man dangerous only by virtue of his ego.

He suspected that the depression simply allowed him to see reality. The depression forced Geoff to see how most of his troubles were his own creation. It had been crazy to expect Harrison to make that climb. Crazy to count on Jansten sticking with him.

And it had left the door wide open for Steve to take advantage of the situation.

That thought sparked a little heat within Geoff.

Steve had taken advantage. He and Lisa. The bitch. Slapped him in front of everyone.

The anger made Geoff feel a little better. Stronger.

He thought about the hooker, Carly. Cute thing, but tough. He couldn't help but admire her. Every day she walked the side of the street where people didn't try to *persuade, convince, motivate* others—she worked the side of the street where the strong took whatever they wanted from the weak.

If he and Dern worked that side of the street, Dern wouldn't have a chance against him. Of that, Geoff was certain.

Carly had said she could get him a gun. He had been toying with the idea of shooting Steve and Lisa. Hell, he had been toying with a lot of ideas, but the two of them figured into most of them one way or the other. Jansten, too. Everyone else, Harrison, even fucking Guston, had pretty much been following Geoff's lead. Not that he intended to let any of them go unscathed. But Lisa and Steve had thwarted him directly, and, damn it if they hadn't succeeded.

Geoff had to admit he had underestimated them.

Which only meant he wouldn't the next time around. The trick was doing it so he wouldn't get caught.

Geoff pulled out his hiking gear and started filing the edges on his crampons and ice axe, keeping his hands busy while he analyzed his situation. He was virtually broke. He was unemployed and alone. His apartment and car were leased by the company; no doubt both would be gone soon.

He hated to admit it, but he had become dependent upon the company. He had joined Jansten Enterprises shortly after getting the MBA from Wharton.

He was dependent not only for his salary, but for the occasional loan when he wanted to cover an investment or make a substantial purchase. Loans that, in fact, had been the basis of the wealth he had just lost. Loans that had been requested, reviewed, and authorized by himself.

Loans that he never actually paid back.

Three "vendors": three obscure—and fictional—consultants who sent Geoff invoices on an occasional basis. Geoff made sure not to be greedy, with no single vendor billing over fifty thousand annually.

The loans were just seed money, the way he saw it. They were also far below Geoff's signatory authority and too small to interest the roving audit teams that Jansten kept employed year-round.

The way he saw it, Geoff brought in so much money for the company, they owed it to him.

And yet, without so much as blinking, Jansten had fired him. In front of all of them. "You're out, Geoff," he had said.

Geoff hated to admit even to himself that he needed his own brand of security. With the dozens of life-threatening risks he had taken in pursuit of his adrenaline fix, he knew he could always come home to a nice apartment, free to have a hot shower and relax. Free to lord his adventures over some beauty. He was used to wearing good clothes, to limos, to being treated with respect.

He wasn't into poverty.

And yet, that's what he was facing. He looked over at the mirror, saw himself sharpening the ice axe. His hair was matted with sweat, his body was alive with muscle. He knew how to do the résumé and interview bit, he knew he could pick up a phone and probably land a job within a week or two. Nothing like his role with Jansten Enterprises, but enough to keep him afloat in a reasonable style.

But he just didn't seem to have it in him to do that anymore.

Geoff exploded suddenly, throwing the ice axe into the wall. Plaster rattled all over the floor. What he had in him was the overwhelming urge to pay back that smug bastard, Dern, and his cornpone wife.

The sword cane had been propped up against the wall and it fell to the floor. He felt a quickening of interest, felt the sudden rage center with a bit more focus. He stood and drew the blade, suddenly feeling a touch of exuberance. He sliced the air in his apartment, the whistling sound evocative. He didn't believe in past lives, but he knew beyond any doubt that if he *had* lived in the past he would have been a warrior, not a goddamn merchant.

The steel in his hand truly made him feel better.

He thought about Steve, thought about visiting him with the sword cane right then.

Better still, visit Lisa. The idea loosened a warmth inside him that spread through his belly and downward. Rape and pillage. The way to hurt Steve was through her. The guy was obviously crazy about her.

The idea felt so right. He needed more than a test of speed and balance, he needed some of what he got in that fight with the pimp. And Lisa and Steve deserved his attention.

He hesitated, knowing that attacking them without any sort of plan would land him in jail.

And he could not do jail time. That was one thing he truly feared. He couldn't be penned up like that.

But equally compelling was the need to act. The walls of his apartment were damn close to a cell right then. He couldn't stay there a second longer.

He sheathed the sword and left.

CHAPTER 10

What do you think that BMW of his goes for?" Jammer asked his cousin. "Thirty, forty K?"

They were in the van across the street from Geoff's apartment.

"At least," Ball said. The baseball cap that had earned him his name was turned backward, the easier for him to peer out the window. His heavy brows furrowed. "Hate those yuppie sewing machines. And we'll never get that kind of money for it. We'll be lucky if we get ten."

"All adds up."

"How'll that do against the total for Raul?"

Jammer looked at his cousin. His father's brother's kid. Tough lot, all of them. Ball was about six feet tall, thick-chested, arms like a gorilla. About as smart. Jammer played with the idea of telling him that he had accumulated over fifty thousand dollars.

Knowing the word would spread throughout the family that Jammer had finally made something of himself.

Jammer said, "Barely make a dent." Ball and his side of the family would kill each other for that kind of cash, never mind him.

"Yeah?" Ball stared at him. "What are your cunts doing, crossing their legs on the job?" His laughter filled the van.

"Shut up, dickhead," Jammer said, casually.

Ball went silent and that made Jammer's mouth go dry. He never knew what would throw Ball off. Jammer put his hand on the Beretta in his pocket, thinking that the idiot might go nuts on him.

"When am I going to get a gun?" Ball asked finally. The faint whine in his voice told Jammer he was going to cave this time around. "Put a forty-five on Raul and fucking take his shit and his cash."

Jammer groaned. "For the four thousandth time, Raul's got Uzis, forty-fives, he's got Glocks, he's got sawed-off shotguns . . . but most of all, he's got about thirty guys on the street willing to turn me and you into hamburger if we piss him off."

"I know that."

"Then how come I've got to repeat it? You worry me. You've got this attitude . . . talk about putting a gun in his face. *We're* buying into *his* game. *If* he lets us. Once I get that start, that first two hundred K together, then prove to him I can turn the shit around fast enough, then, maybe, we'll get a chance to make some real money."

"I know that."

"So stop talking about putting a gun in his face, willya? We've got to show him that we respect him; we've got to show him that we've got balls. Talking big doesn't do either."

"And sitting in my van following your bitch's boyfriend does?"

Jammer would've liked to pull the Beretta and pop the dumb bastard behind the ear right then. But he was going to need some muscle once he had the shit. And though Jammer barely admitted it to himself, he also knew he needed some help taking down this blond scumbag. The guy was simply too fast to mess with, one-on-one. It would have been easy enough to just shoot the guy, but he figured the prick was worth some money, and it would take a little time and muscle to work it out of him.

Hold on to him for a day, get him to clean out his checking account. Not to mention taking a little time and energy to teach him what happens to guys who try to steal Jammer's best whore. Teach him to try and cut Jammer.

The pimp sighed. If Raul ever heard how this guy had taken away his sword cane . . . And Ball worried him, too. The guy's mouth had a direct line from his little pea brain. If any of that shit came out in front of Raul . . .

"Hold up," Ball said, rubbing the window clean. "That's him." Jammer leaned forward.

Ball said, "That's him. Look, he's coming under the street-light."

"Yeah, you're right."

"Course I am." Ball grinned at Jammer. "And he's got your stick."

Geoff figured he would most likely get some action going down into Roxbury. Action with the sword cane. White guy, good clothes, alone. He figured if he couldn't get mugged there, he wasn't going to get mugged anywhere.

The thought that someone might simply shoot him didn't faze him. Already he was feeling too good to worry about that. The depression had been lifted, at least temporarily. He would figure out how to get his hands on some money later. This was like loosening his muscles. This showed that he could control the depression at will. So what if he had blown his career? So what if he was virtually penniless?

He could start the action.

He could do anything: make another fortune, rob a bank if he wanted. Hell, he could kill someone.

If only someone came through tonight.

The fear behind his already-pumping adrenaline was that after a few hours of walking around the toughest streets of Boston, he might be left alone. Untouched. Safe.

He started down Massachusetts Avenue, past Symphony Hall, into Roxbury. Already the few faces he saw on the street were black. So were the models on the billboards. Up ahead, he saw a small gang of teenagers sitting on the steps of a brownstone. Rap music pumped through a boom box.

Three guys.

Good chance, he thought.

Where the hell is he going?" Ball said. "There's not going to be enough left of him for us to squeeze out a dime."

"Don't know." Jammer was behind the wheel. They were hanging two blocks back. "He's one crazy bastard. Thought for sure those kids back there were going to nail him."

"Fucking angel on his shoulder."

Jammer had to laugh. Big ugly baboon like Ball talking about angels. A guy who had broken the arms of the other kids at school for lunch money. "You're going to have to do it on your own. If he sees me, he'll spook."

Ball snorted. "Yeah. Sounded like he spooked last time."

Jammer bit his lip. "Remember what I told you."

"Yeah, yeah. I'll make him give me your precious sword cane first." Ball rolled his eyes. "Your trademark."

"He's fast."

"Not after I'm finished." Ball slammed his fist on the padded dash, and Jammer could feel the vibration through the steering wheel.

Ball put out his left hand, palm up. "Gimme."

Feeling like he was losing something, Jammer handed him the Beretta. Ball checked to see that it was loaded, sighted it out the window at the back of the guy's head.

"Jesus, pull that in here!"

"Take it *easy.*" Ball turned his cap forward, then pointed at the corner in front of Geoff. "Right there, cousin. I'll get him, you be waiting by the side door. Then we'll pick him clean."

Geoff noticed the big man's hand was inside his coat as he got out of the van. The driver was moving back into the back. The big guy looked at Geoff, his eyes shadowed by the baseball cap. His hand was still inside his coat as he took a step closer.

Geoff pushed the little button under the knob of the sword-cane. His mouth was dry; his heart was pumping hard.

"Hey, buddy," the big guy said. "Got the time?"

"Late."

The big guy was close now. Just outside of lunging distance.

"Late? That's your answer?" He pulled out a gun and held it at arm's length so Geoff was staring down the barrel. "Guess I'll have to check your watch myself; you're so frigging rude."

The side door to the van slid open. Geoff recognized the pimp, Jammer.

Geoff hesitated. The big guy would obviously know about the sword cane.

As if he could read Geoff's mind, the big guy held out his left hand, still keeping his distance. "Gimme the stick."

Wordlessly, Geoff stepped forward and offered the cane to the man, holding it by the handle. The man took the bottom end. Geoff drew breath quietly and set his legs.

"Not like that!" the pimp yelled.

The big guy jerked his head to the right. When the gun barrel moved, Geoff grabbed it with his left hand, then drew the sword, letting the other man hold the empty cane. The blade glittered before he plunged it deep into the man's chest. A round exploded and flame flashed against Geoff's sleeve. The man's breath hit him in the face in a hot gust. Geoff shoved the blade deeper still, until the man's face was in his own. Then he twisted the handle, making the man scream as he fell to ground, his legs scrambling on the pavement.

"Ball!" the pimp yelled.

Geoff grabbed for the gun. The gun was clasped tight in the dying man's hand, and Geoff had to peel a finger away at a time.

Jammer took that in, and without another word, he slid the door shut.

Geoff got the gun free as the van's engine revved. He shattered the side window with the first bullet, then the back window as Jammer spun around in a tight turn. The van hopped over the curb and headed up Massachusetts Avenue, tires screaming.

Geoff breathed the city air deeply, while his heart tried to pound through his rib cage. He nudged the big man with his foot. "Hey."

He kicked the man, hard.

The guy was dead.

"Jesus Christ," Geoff said, pulling the sword out. "What a day."

CHAPTER 11

Geoff walked all the way back to the MIT Bridge and threw the bloody sword cane into the Charles River. His legs were tired from all of the walking by the time he returned to his apartment, but his head still buzzed with the excitement.

He knew who he wanted. His lust made him feel both weak and strong. Out of control. He told himself that she might have diseases. He told himself that as Jammer's whore, he surely couldn't trust her. That, if anything, he should be trying to establish an alibi in case the police ever found their way back to him.

But his need was greater than any rational thought. He put the gun under the bed and went looking for Carly.

Detective Lazar pushed the baseball cap with his toe and said, "Ball is way the hell out of his territory. What's a punk from Southie doing here?"

"Doing what punks like him do best," Bannerman said. "Getting their guts ripped out."

"Heart."

"Huh?"

"Heart ripped out."

"Guts were just a figure of speech," Bannerman said. "Want to be factual about it, I'd say his heart probably has a hole poked in it, rather than ripped out."

"Guess we'll have to wait for the medical examiner to set us straight." Lazar was a black man in his early forties. Heavyset, with a round moon face. His powerful shoulders and beer belly were winning against his slouchy sports jacket. The sleeves on the jacket were on the short side, and he couldn't help but notice Bannerman still looked smooth and unrumpled.

Bannerman was white, about thirty-five, and wore a nice suit. He was more of a comer in the department than Lazar and prone to give advice. In spite of that, Lazar liked him.

A small crowd had formed around the body. All of the faces were black. After the initial questioning that the two detectives and uniforms had conducted—*just got here, man, didn't see nothing*—the group had simply watched the body and detectives. Lazar heard someone say, "Whose black ass this gonna be pinned on? Gonna happen."

Lazar sighed.

From his days as a beat officer in Southie, Lazar remembered Ball. Lazar had been assigned to the tough white neighborhood in the late seventies for a three-year stint, right after forced busing. Top brass had deemed it politic to have a few black cops working

Southie, but it had been very, very tough for those cops to do their jobs.

Ball had been one of Lazar's first arrests. Back then, Ball was a teenager. A massive, brutal, and dangerously stupid seventeen-year-old with close-set eyes and a permanent scowl. He had already been arrested a few times for burglary and was a suspect in a number of muggings. This time they had a complaint sworn out against him. Ball had threatened to torch a local grocery store unless they came through each week. When Lazar had knocked on the door of Ball's house, he had come out to the stoop with his hand slightly behind his leg. He said, "A nigger cop? You can't be serious." A half dozen of the guy's brothers had been looking out the window at Lazar. All of them smirking, insolent, and looking a shade too eager. Ball had turned his back on Lazar. It had looked a little too easy to Lazar, the guy virtually begging to be cuffed and rolled down the stairs in front of the whole brood. Lazar had followed, but not too close.

Sure enough, Ball had spun around with a spring-loaded sap.

The department had backed Lazar up, put it in writing that Lazar's use of force was justified. Ball wasn't really that keen on pursuing the brutality charges. Embarrassed, probably, that his nose and two front teeth had been broken. Ball had made threats about his friends taking Lazar out, but nothing had happened. Lazar was fairly certain Ball had never been really connected. He was too much of a flake. He and his crazy family.

Now, he was definitely out of place, lying dead in Roxbury. Lazar figured the most likely scenario was that Ball had been trying to score some drugs, possibly by force. Ran into someone faster and tougher than him, someone good with a knife. Bye-bye, Ball.

It was truly hard to give a damn.

Nevertheless, there was something about Ball that he couldn't quite remember, and the thought flickered off to the side of his brain. Lazar let it alone.

When the medical examiner finally arrived, a bald guy named Dr. Vincent, he opened Ball's shirt and said, "Knife wound." Lazar tried to make a connection there. A known associate of Ball's who carried a knife? Big deal, so did all the people Ball *didn't* know, as far as Lazar could tell.

Dr. Vincent chewed bubble gum while making his cursory inspection of Ball.

To Lazar, the sweet scent of the gum added a surrealistic element to the grim scene: the white, cold body bathed by flashing blue lights of the police car, the circle of black faces.

"Help me roll the body, will you?" Vincent said.

What they found surprised them all. A pool of blood had formed from a hole in Ball's back.

"An exit wound," Vincent said.

"Thought you said the wound was made with a knife," Bannerman said. "You mean he was stabbed in the back first?"

"Why would I say 'exit wound' if he was stabbed there first?" The doctor looked from Bannerman to Lazar. "Don't I usually say what I mean?"

Lazar took over. "So what you're saying is that it's an exit wound . . ."

". . . that's exactly what I said."

". . . meaning whatever it was went all the way through the chest and out the back. Like a very long knife."

"Like a sword," Vincent said.

"Jammer," Lazar said.

"Huh?" Bannerman said.

"His cousin, Jammer. Pimp who carries a sword cane." Lazar laughed. It had come to him at last. "The shithead tells people it's his trademark."

Geoff waited for a half hour outside the bar on Boylston Street. He wanted to leave, but nevertheless, he waited until he saw her get out of a car and wave to the man behind the wheel. The guy looked like a businessman, late forties, driving a Chevy. A john.

Geoff supposed that's what he now was.

Before she saw him, Geoff slipped back into the bar. He ordered a beer and a glass of white wine as she came in and headed for the ladies' room. She hadn't noticed him. The ridiculous aspects of the whole thing were not lost on Geoff: She was wearing a tight black miniskirt, a black top that was little more than a chemise, and bright lipstick. Such blatant, cheap sexuality usually held little appeal for him. Now he was hard as a rock.

When she came back out, he was sitting at a table. Her eyes slid over the crowd, over him, then snapped back. She quickly checked out the rest of the room, presumably looking out for her pimp. Not seeing him, her expression changed from sulky invitation to a bright smile. A smile that was totally out of keeping with her whore's clothing. He smiled back at her, feeling it a little inside, too.

"Tell me you were looking for me," she said. "Make my night."

He stood and held a chair out for her. "I ordered you a glass of wine. Chardonnay all right?"

"Sure. I guess." She sat down, crossed her legs, and saw him noticing. She smiled. "Really, did you come looking for me? Or is this just luck?"

"Little of both." He sipped his beer and watched her. She drank some of the wine. She winced at the taste and tried to hide it.

He smiled, gently. "You don't like it, don't drink it."

Inside, he was raging. His body was so pumped up, he thought he might explode. Her long legs, the taut softness of her . . . it was all he could do not to pull her to him right there in the middle of the bar. He didn't care what she had been doing before with that businessman in the car. He wanted her with a heat that made him as nervous as a teenager. He knew his hunger was all tied in with killing that guy on the street, but that didn't feel bad. Hell, it felt fucking incredible.

He waved the waitress over. "Get her whatever she likes."

Carly ordered a Kahlúa sombrero.

"Jammer around tonight?" he asked after the waitress had moved on.

Carly shook her head. "Haven't seen him since this afternoon. But you never know with that guy." Her eyes left Geoff, searching the bar carefully. When her attention returned to him, she casually reached over and took his hand. It was a gesture that was unexpected and surprisingly appealing. "Tell me why you're here. You want me to make those connections you asked about? I can do that, maybe sometime tomorrow. But I'm getting other vibes from you here. Normally, that's great, taking care of those vibes is what I do. In this case, Jammer would kill me if he saw us together. So I've got to know what's going on before I sit here much longer."

The waitress dropped off the drink, and Geoff waited until she was gone before answering. His voice was hoarse, partially with embarrassment. "To start, just what any guy who calls you over wants."

"I thought you were afraid of diseases."

"There's protection for things like that. And afterward, I want to talk about what we discussed on the street."

"Sure," she said, smiling warily. "You're due a freebie, you don't have to spin a big story."

"You want money, I'll give you money." He couldn't believe he was saying those words, but he was shaking he wanted her so badly. He wanted his hands around that slim waist, he wanted her heat against him.

"I can't take you back to my place. Jammer might be there."

Geoff figured his own place might not be safe either. "I'll pay for the night. You must know a place."

"Sure. What's in it for me?"

"What do you want?"

She looked at him levelly. "I want it to be my last night as a hooker. I'm not asking to get married, just help getting free."

He squeezed her hand. "We'll be able to work something out."

His touch seemed to surprise her, please her. "You think so?" Her voice was small.

"I know so."

Up in the room, he couldn't control himself a second longer. He slid his hands up under the chemise and felt her firm breasts, hard nipples. Her answering sigh was probably false, but he was past caring.

She started to slide out of the miniskirt, but he pushed her hands aside, pushed her onto the bed and raised her skirt. Saw the patch of dark on her white skin, felt between there, felt her moistness. Smelled the scent of baby oil. The voice in his head that was saying, *she's a hooker, greased and ready for anyone,* didn't slow him down. He slid into her seconds later, thrusting hard, his hands all over her body. He groaned as he came instantly, coming so hard that he was practically crying.

Minutes later, he fell asleep lying on top of her as she ran her fingers along his back, saying, "Hey, hey, hey," softly, looking up at the ceiling over his shoulder.

CHAPTER 12

When Lazar and Bannerman showed up at Jammer's apartment and told him Ball was dead, Jammer said, "Christ, I knew I was gonna hear something like this someday." He had a big scar on his forehead, a pink, clean cut. A washed-out blonde he introduced as Darlene sat beside him on the couch. She stared straight ahead as if she were alone in the room. Both of them were fully dressed even though it was after one in the morning.

"Ball wasn't what you'd call a nice guy," Jammer said. "But his mama's gonna be screaming. You told her yet?"

"No," said Lazar. "We came to you first."

"Me? I was just his cousin."

"Where's your sword?"

"My what?"

"Your trademark," Bannerman said, grinning. "Lazar told me about it. I always wanted to meet a pimp with a trademark."

"I'm not a pimp." Jammer was indignant.

"She's your girlfriend, huh?" Bannerman gestured at Darlene. She stared back at him, but said nothing.

"That's right. Prove she isn't."

"I go looking for a sheet on her, I bet I'll find one saying she's been arrested for soliciting. We know there is one on you, man. Pimping."

"History," Jammer said. "What do you want right now? Because if that's all you've got to say, I'd just as soon get some sleep."

"Told you," Lazar said. "Your sword."

"I used to have a cane, but it was solid wood. I don't know anything about a sword. I don't even have the cane anymore."

"You offering us a chance to look for it?"

"You offering me a warrant?"

"If I have to," Lazar said, evenly. "But taking the time to go get one is going to piss me off. I have to warn you of that."

Jammer shrugged. "Hell, I was just asking. Knock yourself out if you want."

Lazar looked around the dingy, three-bedroom apartment while Bannerman continued the interview, saying, "So let me guess— you cut your head shaving?"

Jammer said he fell down. The blonde then provided Jammer with an alibi for the night.

The place had wall-to-wall shag carpeting and smelled of perfume, sweat, and roach spray. One bedroom had an aquarium on the dresser, with two turtles inside. Beside it was a picture of Darlene that looked as if it had been a high school photo. The other room held posters on the wall of mountain scenes, pictures of the ocean. A couple of the posters had inspirational phrases. Pathetic shit for a hooker's bedroom. Lazar didn't know whether to laugh or cry. There was a picture of a surprisingly pretty young woman standing in a stream, naked, but covering her breasts.

The largest bedroom, apparently the one Jammer used, had a big waterbed, mirrors on the ceiling. The whole place had been cleaned recently. There wasn't so much as a match in any of the ashtrays, not a speck of coke or pot in the dresser, the tank behind the toilet, or the kitchen. The nap of the disgusting rug still showed vacuum cleaner marks.

It looked as if the blonde and Jammer had just cleaned the place, getting ready for them.

Lazar went back to the living room. "Let's get some fresh air, Bannerman."

"About goddamn time," Jammer said.

Lazar winked at the blonde. "Be gentle with Jammer."

"What?" Her forehead wrinkled.

"He's suffered a grave loss. He may be a bit tense from now on."

Bannerman grinned at Jammer on the way to the door, but took the lead from his partner and talked to Darlene. "Lost his sword and his muscle in one day. And stepped into a big load of shit all by himself."

Down at the car, Lazar said, "You check out that cut on his forehead?"

"Nice and clean, huh? No jagged edges."

"Does seem like a lot of knife wounds for one family, doesn't it?"

Bannerman yawned. "Maybe not. What you told me, it's a goddamn miserable family. Could be as simple as it looks, that Ball got himself mugged in Roxbury."

"Awfully long blade, awfully long coincidence." Lazar leaned across Bannerman to open the passenger door. "Your turn to buy the coffee. We're going to stake this bastard out."

* * *

They spent the rest of the shift in the car. The lights up in Jammer's apartment went dark within the first hour. From there, time just crawled.

Bannerman tried to start up a conversation about Charlotte. "You're coming up on a year soon, right? When are you going to file the papers, make it official?"

"Dunno." Lazar kept his voice mild. "When are you going to stop asking that question?"

Bannerman let it go. After a while, he fell asleep. As three o'clock rolled past, Lazar settled into the watchful calm that was the best he could hope for in a stakeout: He wasn't particularly sleepy, and his patience was strong. He was aware of the breath coming in and out of his lungs. And other than the movement of his eyes to the pimp's apartment, and to the side and rearview mirrors, he moved not at all. When he was doing a stakeout, when he was on the job, his separation from his wife was ancient history, almost a whole year old.

At seven, Bannerman woke up and stretched. "Anything?"

"No."

"Then I'm hitting the sack. This shift is *over*. You want to keep watching this piece of garbage, you are on your own."

Lazar felt exhausted himself. Much as he hated being lied to, he didn't take it personally. Good thing, seeing as people lied to him all day long. "Yeah, I'm beat, too," he said. "I'm going to call in, get someone to stick with him today, and then we'll stake him out tonight. If nothing comes of it, we'll call it a simple mugging gone wrong. It was just Ball."

Bannerman grunted. "What you call a win-win situation."

CHAPTER 13

Geoff awoke to the sound of the shower running. He sat up against the headboard slowly, stiff from his battles the day before. He rubbed his left bicep and shoulder slowly, blinking in the harsh morning light. His nose wrinkled faintly as he breathed in the mingled smells of disinfectant, damp plaster, and cheap perfume.

He ticked through the last twenty-four hours. Harrison falling. Dern and his wife screwing him over. Jansten firing him. Then those two men . . . Geoff sat up straighter, taking in his new status in life.

He had killed a man. Pushed a sword into him, felt it shudder in his hand.

"Jesus," he said, his brain fully engaged now. He focused immediately on the past night, trying to remember everything he had done, and what he had said to the girl. For almost two minutes, Geoff remained stock still, his concentration complete.

Finally, he settled back, releasing a deep breath. The situation was far from perfect, but he figured if he made the right moves, he could walk away unscathed. He hadn't said anything incriminating to the girl, he was sure of it. He had wiped the sword cane clean . . . and even if the police thought to search the river and were lucky enough to dredge it up, Geoff couldn't see how that would lead back to him. Even if he had missed a print, he had never been in the military or arrested, so his prints weren't on any record.

No, the only person who could directly link Geoff to the dead thug in Roxbury was the pimp. Jammer most likely knew Geoff's name, or at least where he lived. Geoff didn't imagine it was a coincidence the pimp had found him alone on the street the night before. And while Jammer most likely wouldn't run to the cops with his troubles, Geoff surely couldn't trust him to keep such a dangerous secret. Guys like him were always looking to trade something.

The question was . . . the girl. Was she for real or had she set him up? Did Jammer know where Geoff lived because she had followed him home?

Geoff flashed through his options, limited pretty much between beating her and killing her. He now knew for certain that he had the capacity for either.

But she stepped out of the bathroom before he had committed himself to a course of action. And that was a good thing. Partially because she cleaned up so well, standing there with a towel wrapped around herself. The wig was gone, and her own hair was short and thick. She was free of the garish makeup, and her coltish beauty made his mouth go dry. He felt as if he could look at her all day long.

She gestured to her clothes. "You caught me before I put on my armor."

"You won't be wearing those after today."

It's just the sex, he told himself. "Drop that towel and get over here," he said.

She stepped closer, teasing. Leaving it to him to pull the towel away, to pull her to him. Her body was still damp and hot from the shower. "This what you had in mind?"

He didn't answer. The truth was, he wasn't used to feeling the way he did, and he was damned if he was going to feel that way because of a street hooker.

Happy.

At first it was a point of pride.

He took his time with her, even while knowing that it was probably a waste of time. Trying to turn on a hooker was an idiot's game, he told himself. She was probably dead to men. And he could tell she was acting at first.

But by the time they reached the point where he could no longer tell, he no longer cared.

Her heart pounded against his.

That much he knew.

Afterward, they lay in bed talking. She seemed eager for him to listen, and he found that he was still interested in spite of being momentarily sated. He lay there, his eyes half closed, listening to her talk about her former boyfriend, Neal, and the mistakes she had made that had landed her on the street. She told him about the mountain stream.

"That's where I always look at where it went wrong. You know, the moment I could have gone either way. I could have told Neal the truth then. We were alone, and we weren't so far gone that maybe if I said it the right way, he would have given me a chance."

"Doubt it. Sounds like a pious little prig."

"Yeah," she said, sadly. "I guess he was. He probably would have streaked down that mountain. Maybe I could have handled that. Better that I told him myself, than for him to have heard it from the boys at a bar."

"At least you would've had that," Geoff acknowledged. He didn't care much about honesty himself, but he was willing to believe she did. "So that's what you would do now if you had the chance? Tell him the truth?"

"Doesn't make any difference. He was the wrong type of guy for me. I know that now. What matters to me is that I get back to where I went wrong and do it differently. Get to that very same mountain stream, get myself clean. Start over. That's not too much to ask, is it?"

He didn't say anything.

She paused, then rolled up against him, companionably. "Tell me what you want. You told me a gun, maybe some new papers. Passport?"

"Uh-huh."

Her lips twitched.

"What?"

" 'Passport.' I even love the word. I've never even been out of New England. Hell, not even past Providence. But I'd love to go places. Have you ever been to Europe?"

"Lots of times." He looked her in the eyes. "And I need money. Don't forget about money."

"Sure. Are you crazy for it?"

"No. But I'm used to having it, and I'm used to getting what I want."

"So you think you're a bad boy."

"You wouldn't believe," he said, grinning.

"Are you willing to do bad things to get it?"

"Absolutely. Are you?"

She nodded. "Oh, yeah. I wouldn't kidnap babies or murder innocent people. But I know where there's some cash, and I wouldn't mind taking it from the guy and hurting him along the way."

"We're talking about Jammer, right?"

"Yeah."

"I thought you just wanted to get clean."

"I do. But I can't be clean with him still walking around. I'd always be worrying that he would be showing up to cut me or burn me. Besides, I made most of the money, the way I figure it."

"How much are we talking about?"

"Fifty thousand." She said it with a curious mixture of pride and shame. "Money he's been setting aside toward a drug deal with a guy named Raul."

"That would be a start," he said.

"A start!" Her eyes widened. "That's a lot of money."

She truly looked her age at that moment. He said, "Until a few days ago, I was worth just over three million. And I was on my way back to that and more when a couple of people screwed me up."

"Three million!" She looked at him warily. "What kind of job in a big company pays that kind of money?"

"Not many," he said, agreeably. "Especially if you stick exactly with the job description."

"And with the law?"

He hesitated, then figured, what the hell. They had already been discussing murder. "That's right."

"So you were stealing from them?"

He grimaced. He didn't think of it in those terms. "What's your point?"

"Well, I just don't get it. Why would a business guy like you take the kind of chances I'm talking about? Why don't you go back to that big company of yours and start working the angles?"

"Good question." Geoff got out of bed and padded over to the window, naked. He looked out onto the street, seeing a hooker already plying her trade at eight in the morning. A dozen yards away from her, a big black man stood in a doorway, watching her. Geoff opened the window—noticing that the hotel was old enough that he could actually open them himself—and took in the smell of the street, the faint whiff of garbage, of morning coffee and automobile exhaust. He said, "Taking chances is who I am. Even as a kid, I'd do things that would terrify everyone else. And it just didn't bother me. Jump off a bridge, race a car—hell, walk up and punch the biggest bastard in the school right in the face—it was fun, I'd get a rush." He turned to look her in the eyes. "I just don't get scared like other people do. I don't know why, it's just not in my makeup. The way I figure it, if embezzlement was kind of a sneaky thrill, armed robbery should be a blast."

"And you're willing to kill Jammer to get it? Because that's my price for telling you where to find him and the money. We split it, fifty-fifty. Deal?"

He grinned, ruefully. Still feeling good in spite of the fact that his share for killing a man would have amounted to pocket change a week ago.

"Deal," he said. "And if my car hasn't been repossessed yet, I'll even throw in a swim in the mountain stream of your choice this afternoon."

Her hand flew to her mouth. Then she was off the bed and when she pulled him against herself, her kisses were artless, enthusiastic, and very genuine. He laughed in spite of himself as she pulled him back to the bed. He said, "A lady friend of mine told me not too long ago that I'd end up on the street. I thought I'd like it."

"I can see you do," Carly said, touching him. "I'm liking it a lot more now that you're here." She took him in her mouth, teasing him, bringing him close to climax within minutes. Just before he lost it, she pulled back, squeezing him so he would hold off. She said, "As for your lady friend, you tell her that I carry a straight razor."

He rolled Carly onto her back. "She's already history."

"Good," Carly whispered. "Now hold tight and I'll show you how good the street can be."

CHAPTER 14

It had been one of the best days of Carly's life. It was like that angry little ball that had been burning inside since she had first arrived at the Greyhound station two years ago had been stuck with a pin and some of the acid had drained.

They were standing outside a doughnut shop on the edge of the Combat Zone. Just down the street from all the theaters. She had felt so far away from the Zone all day and was now seeing it with different eyes. Sure, it still had the same signs. ALL NUDE COLLEGE GIRL REVUE, up in lights, XXXXXs across the marquees. Pale and hopeless hookers working the street, occasionally chattering among themselves.

But instead of seeing the Zone as an inescapable trap, Carly saw it for what it was—a seedy little block of sleaze that would probably be history in a few years, what with the zoning ordinances that were slowly shutting the place down. The prostitutes would move to some other street, but Carly knew she didn't have to move with them.

She knew in that moment that it was truly possible to get away. Geoff had power to spare and being with him made her feel her own. Even though he was slumming being with her. She knew that. She knew he didn't think the cold swim in the mountain stream made her all new. Hell, she could see he had been laughing at her some when he waded into the water with the bar of soap, his dingle all shrunk up in the cold.

But the shocking water had been everything she had hoped.

It made her feel different about herself just to get something she wanted. To be treated as if what she wanted mattered.

And then they had taken each other shopping. He took her to Lord & Taylor and went through pulling out clothes, saying, "Try this, this, try this . . ." And it was like he knew just what was right for her. It was amazing. She had to figure the sizes, but the styles he picked out for her were just right. She couldn't believe herself now. She looked at the mirrored reflection in the doughnut shop window and shivered with pleasure. She was wearing a simple pinstriped shirt. Nice pleated jeans that fit right instead of the ridiculous skintight pants that Jammer made her wear. The new wig Geoff had bought her, the black one, made her look different enough with her sunglasses and clothes so that she wouldn't have recognized herself . . . except she *did,* in the sense that the woman in the mirror was the woman Carly had always known she could be.

What a day.

After that, it had been her turn. They had gone to see Louis, and he had taken their pictures and promised them each a new driver's license and passport by the end of the day. Louis had grinned at her. "You're beautiful, just like I knew you could be. Don't worry about me, keeping secrets is my business." But Jammer had once beat Louis, so Geoff gave him a fifty and they decided they could believe him.

It all seemed so easy, during the afternoon. But now the tension was beginning to creep in about what she and Geoff still had in front of them.

She peeked around the corner.

"Not yet?" Geoff asked.

"No." She looked at the gold watch he had bought her. Eight-twenty-five. "Five minutes. He's very regular when it comes to food."

Jammer.

Waiting for him now made her stomach twist and roll. She still felt the euphoria, still felt she and Geoff could do anything. But if she looked at it square, she had to admit she was worried about actually killing the pimp. She wouldn't mind seeing him dead, but she wasn't so sure she and Geoff had to be the ones to do it.

They might get caught, for one thing.

And while Boston might not be safe, now that she was with Geoff she knew the power to move away from Raul and Jammer was her own. She could move someplace else, and they would never find her. Geoff was talking as if he would take her with him. She hadn't told him about Raul, she figured she would mention that as if she had just thought about it once they hit, say, the Connecticut border. She would just look over casually and say, "Did I tell you about this guy who wanted to put me in movies?"

She knew that for some reason he admired her life on the street, instead of just seeing it as stupid and scummy. Who was she to set him straight—if she'd learned anything as a hooker, it was to let the guy live whatever fantasy he wanted.

"There he is," Geoff said, backing around the corner beside her. "Which booth again?"

Carly snapped out of her reverie. "The one by the window to

the left. The owner knows to keep it open for him, eight-thirty, and to have his food ready."

"We'll give him a second to get seated." Geoff slung the strap of the athletic bag over his shoulder and put his hand inside the open bag. He grinned at her, leaning back against the glass. "This is going to be fun."

She could see the reflection of the pretty, classy woman in the mirror turn to that of a scared hooker. "We don't have to do this," she said, knowing he wasn't going to like her saying it. "Let's just get in your car and go."

"Don't be stupid." His face darkened.

She bit her lip and let her stomach do its leaps while the minutes ticked by. Her hands were shaking.

Abruptly, he swung around the corner, walked up half a block, and walked into the restaurant. By the time she had followed him into the dark, hot gloom, Geoff was already seated across from Jammer, the gun under the table, trained at her former pimp's balls. "Have a seat, sweetheart," Geoff said. "Jammer's invited us to dinner."

The pimp handled it pretty well, Geoff had to give him that. He finished chewing his mushu pancake and then said to Carly, "I'm going to twist your head off, bitch, and feed it to Darlene's turtles."

"Don't you think you'll be a little preoccupied, what with having your balls blown off?" Geoff kept his voice quiet and pleasant.

Jammer started to say something, and Geoff gave him a glimpse of the gun. "Think about it."

Jammer's face went white. "There are cops all over the Zone. All I have to do is raise my voice. You'll be identified. Get you for what you did to Ball, too."

Geoff nodded, smiling agreeably. "Absolutely. They'd roll you up to testify in a wheelchair, wearing diapers."

"What about Ball?" Carly said.

"Later," Geoff said.

Jammer's eyes flickered between the two of them. "You don't know?" he said. "This guy stuck Ball, killed him. The cops came by to tell me."

She drew breath sharply, then regained herself.

Jammer said to Geoff, "What do you want?"

"I hear you've got a little cash stockpiled. About fifty thousand in a floor safe."

The pimp gave Carly a disdainful glare. "You cunt." He grinned at Geoff. "You believe that? I keep some cash there, a few thousand. But fifty thousand with sluts like her bringing johns in? You must be crazy. The rest is in my safety deposit box. You gonna hold a gun on me all the way there? What happens when we get to the cage, I gotta sign in, show my ID? They don't let you bring your friends back for a party, you know."

Geoff looked over at Carly. Her lower lip was trembling. She looked at him, scared. "He's lying!"

"We'll see," he said, nudging her with his knee, telling her to calm down. He didn't want her calling attention to them, especially now that he was thinking that maybe he should go back to his original plan, shoot them both up in the pimp's apartment, make it look like a murder/suicide. Not that he particularly felt like shooting the girl, but it sure seemed like she was beginning to be trouble. And if the police had already found their way to Jammer, maybe it was in Geoff's best interest to simply clear the thing out, pop Lisa and Steve in their sleep, and then hit the road. "Let's go take a look," he said.

Across the street, Lazar said to Bannerman, "That guy had his hand in the bag when he walked into the restaurant, too."

"You think?"

"I know."

"Kind of funny, whacking a guy with a chick along for dinner, isn't it?"

Lazar shrugged. "Big city, you see lots of things."

"You want to save his ass?"

Lazar looked at Bannerman.

Bannerman grinned. "We don't *know* a crime's being committed."

"Damn straight. Let's give them a few minutes, go upstairs, and say hello."

Jammer was quaking deep inside, but he tried to keep his face blank as they stepped into his apartment. Darlene was out. There was something so cold about this guy. He looked like a goddamn yuppie, the clothes he was wearing, the white smile. But the gun was rock steady in his hand, and Jammer believed the guy had it in him to pull the trigger.

Jammer swallowed deep, looked over at Carly, and wished he could smack her across the head.

Dumb, dumb cunt. She had always been a dreamer, and now she was going to get them both killed. She couldn't see that this guy was playing her.

What Jammer had said about the cash was true. He had five thousand in the floor safe, the rest in the bank. He also had a gun in the bag with the cash, for a situation just like this. Now he didn't know if it was such a bright idea. He wasn't sure if he could draw it in time, or if he should just try to reach in and shoot through the bag. . . .

He licked his lips. Best not to show he was scared. That first. *Think.*

The guy figured himself a player. That was obvious—how

many business types got in fights over whores, could disarm and kill a guy like Ball?

Maybe the guy would deal.

Jammer said, "You're a pain in the ass, buddy. You're gonna set me back a bit, the five grand in my safe. But it's like killing the goose, you know? The chick here tell you what I'm setting up? How I'm gonna get behind the scale?"

"She mentioned something."

"Yeah. Guy who's the big distributor around here in the trade, you know?" Jammer tapped his nose. "Coke, crack, heroin, you name it. He and I got an arrangement. Most guys work their way up through the trade as sellers, pushing on the street, working for suppliers. That's nickel-and-dime shit; you never get ahead until you're a supplier working behind the weight scale, running the teams. Well, I got an agreement with the distributor. Guy who deals right with the fucking cartels, you know? I can scrape up two hundred thousand for my first weight, I can skip all the through-the-ranks shit, and he'll set me up behind the scale for the whole Zone territory. He says it'll show my commitment, scraping up that much. See, I'm a natural to take this over; I've got the contacts. Say you're a john coming to the Zone to get his tubes cleaned, and you want a little coke to make it memorable, right? I'm going to be supplying all the hookers. We're talking millions the first year."

The blond guy smiled skeptically. "We are, huh?"

"Definitely. Give you an example—Raul, the guy I'm telling you about—he carries about a million around in a briefcase just for payoff money."

Geoff paused. "That's what he says."

"That's what I've *seen*. Two, three times, I've been there when he's opened the case, tossed some more in."

"And I'm supposed to hold a gun on you for the next year while you earn this kind of cash?"

"Don't even listen to Jammer," Carly said. "Talking is one of the few things the man is good at."

Jammer ignored her. "Shit, no. I'm talking investment. Hell, the reason Ball and I were gonna rip you off—besides the fact you cut me—was to raise some money. Figured you'd be worth another fifty to a hundred grand, easy. I'd be that much along on the two hundred."

He looked the blond guy straight in the eye. Jammer couldn't tell what he was thinking, but he appeared to be listening. "You want in?"

The guy kept staring back, that cold little smile on his face. That steady gun. Ignoring the bitch who kept on yammering how he shouldn't listen to Jammer, that Jammer could confuse the hell out of anyone.

Funny thing, that. As he had been talking, Jammer had started to listen to himself. And the fact was, for a goddamn tourist, this guy was as hard as anyone Jammer knew. And Jammer didn't have any muscle now that Ball was dead, and the guy probably did have money. A partner like him might be handy for a while, and once the cash really started rolling in, Jammer could always hire somebody to take him out. He sure as hell didn't feel confident trying to pull the gun on him now. So he took a deep breath and said, casually, "I'll unlock the safe. You should have the bitch here get the money out. There's a gun inside the bag."

Jammer held his palms up. "Now, I wouldn't have told you that if my offer wasn't real, would I?"

"You would if you were a chickenshit," the guy said. "Now open the safe."

They followed Jammer into the bedroom, and the guy kept the Beretta to Jammer's head while he pulled away the carpeting and did the combination. Then Carly pulled the bag out. She reached in and brought out the .38. She shuffled through the cash quickly.

"How much?" the guy asked.

"I dunno." Carly flashed a look of pure hatred at Jammer. "I guess about what he said. Five thousand."

The guy took the revolver and waved both of them into the living room. Jammer's heart was beating a mile a minute. The cunt just seemed to realize that she was standing beside him now. The blond guy had both guns and he was smiling at the two of them. She started toward him and he backed away. "Hold it. All that Jammer said, was it true?"

"Don't listen to him, Geoff—"

"Hush. Just answer the question."

"Yeah, I told you. Jammer's got this thing about getting into the trade. But Raul would chew him up, and he'd do the same to you."

"Chew me up?" Geoff said. "Is that right?"

"You're scaring me!"

Jammer figured his only chance was to shove the chick in front of him, let her take a few, maybe give him time to dive for the window. If he made it to the fire escape, there was a chance the guy wouldn't be willing to shoot outside with people watching. . . .

That's when the guy's face eased up and he tossed the revolver into the black bag, threw his own gun in there, too. He said, "Let's talk about this partnership."

Jammer almost threw up, he was so relieved.

"You ought to consider a job in sales," the guy was saying, his voice quiet and friendly. "Selling me a deal while I'm holding a gun on you."

Right about then, the cops started pounding on the door.

CHAPTER 15

Geoff's first reaction was to think that Jammer had someone backing him up, bluffing their way in. So he grabbed the Beretta from the bag.

But the way the pimp's face blanched, Geoff figured maybe the cops were for real. He took a bunch of bananas off the table and threw them into the black bag, then stuffed the two guns underneath the sofa cushions.

"Let them think you're just a john, got it?" Jammer hissed. "You're still wearing clothes—they've got nothing on you. Just shut up and look scared. Both of you, sit at the table." He went to the door and unlocked it, yelling, "All right, all right, don't break it down!"

The cops seemed to fill the room, just the two of them, a big black guy and a white guy. Both had drawn guns. "Hands on your head, all of you. Clamp those hands together now!"

Jammer, Geoff, and Carly did as they were told.

The white cop covered them.

The black guy walked through the apartment quickly, while Jammer shouted, "Hey, where's the warrant? You got your free look last time, now show me a warrant!"

Geoff put a surprised expression on his face. Carly closed down, her face blank and eyes slightly averted from the cops.

"What? What?" Jammer was saying. "I have a couple of friends up, and I get the goddamn militia in here."

"Doing okay, Jammer?" the white guy said. "We've been worrying about you and your family troubles."

"Yeah, well, don't. Where's that warrant? Let me see it."

The black cop went straight over to Geoff. "What's in the bag?"

Geoff started to reach for it and found the cop's gun in his face. "You first," Geoff said, mildly.

The cop reached in and pulled out the bananas.

"Ah, Jesus," the white cop said.

The black cop looked at Geoff, smiling a little. "You're a funny guy, huh?"

Geoff smiled back. "Just a little hungry."

The cop cuffed Geoff in the face.

It surprised the hell out of Geoff.

"Leave him alone!" Carly cried.

"You're about to get your ass up on brutality charges, man," Jammer said.

The white cop shoved Jammer against the wall and told him to shut the fuck up.

"What's your name, funny guy?" Lazar said.

Geoff wiped the blood from his mouth and told the cop his name. "And what's yours?"

"Detective Lazar. Now let's see some ID."

Geoff showed him his California driver's license.

"Local address?"

Geoff gave it to him.

"Where were you last night?"

"I was with her," he said, nodding to Carly. "And what's it to you?"

Lazar looked at Carly. "You friends on a professional basis?"

"No," Geoff interjected. "She's my girlfriend. Period."

Carly looked up at Lazar, a slight smile forming on her lips. "That's right," she said, almost shyly. "That's exactly right."

"Huh," Lazar said. "You may look it, but you held yourself like a pro when we came in here."

Geoff said, "That's it. Anything more, I want to see a lawyer."

"I haven't arrested you."

"You're damn right you ain't arrested anybody," Jammer yelled. "You got nothing. Now get out of here."

"Let's go," the white cop said. "I'm sick of holding this shitbird against the wall, Lazar. He stinks."

Lazar nodded. "All right, I can understand that." He backed to the door, and Bannerman shoved Jammer aside. Lazar winked at Geoff. "See you around. I like a guy with a sense of humor."

"Yeah," Geoff said, touching his jaw. "Me too."

In the street, Bannerman said, "That's it. Call this case, a closed case. Ball was mugged. Got himself into a little more trouble than he could handle. Nice ending for a guy like that. I don't mind doing a little roust now and then, but breaking into that guy's apartment, guns out, we got absolutely no probable cause—especially since our report gave his place a clean bill just yesterday. What are you going to tell internal affairs if that pimp brings us up on brutality charges? You saw that blond guy feeling up his bananas in the bag?"

Lazar looked up at the apartment window. The pimp was looking down at him. "I thought I was seeing something else."

"Yeah, well, that shitbird, Jammer, he's probably not smart enough to figure he can have us for lunch on this one. But I'm not pushing it."

Lazar sighed. Bananas. He looked at Geoff's name in his notebook. "I'm running this guy through the computer. Nothing comes of it, I'm with you. Ball's dead, and that's one for the good guys. Nobody else is getting hurt."

Jammer crowed as he watched Lazar and Bannerman drive away. "They're pissing in their pants, man. We want to, we could get a court order telling them to keep a frigging half mile away from us."

"We're going to drop it," Geoff said, rubbing his jaw. "Bad enough that the bastard has my name." He was irritated with himself. He shouldn't have moved on Jammer until he had those fake IDs in his pocket.

Jammer nodded. "Oh, yeah, sure. Don't want to bring down any more trouble. I'm just saying we could." He looked worried, but kept his mouth shut, as Geoff took the two guns out of the sofa and put them in the black bag.

Geoff pulled up a chair. "All right, let's talk about this Raul."

"You're working with *Jammer*," Carly said. "Are you crazy?"

Geoff just looked at her. "How about you sit down and listen this one out."

Her face flushed, but she sat.

Jammer held his arms wide. "What do you need to know? I've got the contact."

"I want to meet him."

"Wrong. We meet him when I've got the cash, the full two hundred thousand. That's the agreement. What you and me have gotta talk about is getting the rest of it together. You got it in the bank? Or are you going to have to sell something?"

Geoff shook his head. "I don't have that kind of lump, not any-more."

"What? No stocks? No investments?"

"Plenty. Worth shit right now." Geoff grinned. "Part of the rea-son I'm sitting here talking to you."

"How about the condo? Get a second mortgage on it or sell it."

"It's an apartment."

Jammer looked skyward. "Start by dumping that car of yours. You've got thirty or so right there."

"Leased by the company."

"Jesus Christ!"

Geoff held up his hand. "Relax. I know where to get it, take us less than a week. Sometime in there I want to sit down with Raul."

Jammer waved the bit about Raul away. "What do you mean, 'us'?"

"Yeah, us." Geoff grinned. "It'll take a little planning, but it'll be fun, you'll see."

"Fun?" Jammer looked at Carly. "What's he talking about?"

She didn't answer him.

"You still have that van?" Geoff asked.

"Hell, no. That was Ball's. I dumped it in a downtown garage, wiped it for my prints."

"Well, I expect you'll know how to steal another." Geoff hefted the bag with the five thousand dollars. "And this should take care of us for seed money to set the thing up."

"That's mine," Jammer snapped. "Your cunt girlfriend here earned it on her back."

Geoff kicked Jammer in the balls, sending the pimp to his knees.

Geoff slipped out of his chair. He wound his hand in Jammer's ponytail and jerked his head back. Geoff put his own face inches away and said, "There are rules. For a start, you don't talk about her like that. Next, what's yours is mine. And finally—you will do what I tell you or I will hurt you, then I will kill you. Understand?"

He shoved the pimp's head forward and back, making him nod. "I thought so." Geoff looked over at Carly, who was standing beside him now, a cold little smile on her face. She laid her hand on his shoulder.

"Cheer up, sweetheart," he said. "We're going shopping tomorrow. Starting at the junkyard."

"Oh, I'm cheered up," she said. "You don't know how much."

CHAPTER 16

Two days later, Lisa left the boat and headed up the dock toward the marina parking lot. She held a clipboard with a list of things to do, starting with a visit to the construction site. The summer breeze was warm on her face and when she glanced back at *The Sea Tern,* the boat was trim and beautiful against the Boston skyline. If Lisa had been a different person, she might have felt smug. As it was, she felt very good and just a little scared. *It's going to be even better,* she told herself.

She hadn't been brought up for this kind of life, of sailboats and new houses. She had been the oldest of three, her parents divorced. She had put herself through college on a partial scholarship on the swim team in Baltimore before moving down to Charleston, where she had bounced around from job to job before landing in real estate.

She smiled to herself, noticing how already those years in Charleston were taking on a sepia cast. How she had first met Steve as a client, when the local office of his own company—Geoff's division, as a matter of fact—had been unable to find Steve a new condo to his liking. She had decided to handle his placement herself instead of leaving it to one of her salespeople, in the hopes of securing some of his commercial work as well. Blue Water's success was already good local news.

But instead of the demanding executive type that she expected, she had found a quiet, likable man who simply knew what he wanted and wasn't willing to settle for less. He wasn't handsome in the traditional sense; his features were a bit too irregular. But he had lively blue eyes, sandy hair, and a very appealing crooked smile. She could tell he was physically strong. More like a workman than a weight lifter. Her dad had been a builder, and she appreciated the difference. Indeed, when she shook Steve's hand, it was hard, callused.

They had started out after a cup of coffee and a quick discussion at his office. She found herself talking more about herself than she did about her listings, which was frankly remarkable. She wasn't by nature flirtatious. She had also just ended a three-year relationship with a child named Paul, who masqueraded as a thirty-five-year-old architect. She was most definitely not in the market.

But the fact was that she liked Steve.

At that first meeting, driving through the city in her car, she couldn't help but speculate about the intensity and humor she saw in those blue eyes.

"Did you grow up around here?" he asked.

"Baltimore. But I've been here long enough to have a good feel for the town."

"If you can find me a view of the water that I can afford, I'll

be a happy man," he said. "I can put up with about anything during the day if I can spend some time staring out at the harbor in
the evening."

She showed him a half-dozen places and agreed that they
hadn't found what he needed. She let him off, promising to pick
him up the next day.

She made the rounds with him over the weekend and then
again on the following weekend. It was late on Sunday afternoon
that she admitted to herself that she was taking longer with him
than necessary. The knowledge embarrassed her, but there it was.
She had been stalling simply because she enjoyed being with him.

"I think I know just the right place." She drove him to the property she had earmarked for herself and Paul.

"The place is a pit right now," she had said, walking them up
to what had once been a former sail loft. Together they had to pry
the door open. "But the zoning just changed so this can be used
for residential property." She found herself telling him everything
she had once envisioned for the place: how she would put in sky-
lights and new bay windows, as well as expose the brick for the
kitchen area. She walked him out onto the small porch that overlooked the harbor. "And I think this is what you had in mind."

"God, yes," he said, looking at her curiously. "It's perfect."

"I guess I should have shown it to you earlier. I think you'll
love it." She couldn't hide the wistful tone as she looked over the
harbor. She drummed her fist lightly on the rail.

"But I couldn't take it from you."

"What?"

He smiled his crooked smile. "This place means something to
you. I'm not sure what, but I can see it."

"Sorry." She waved that away, feeling herself blush. "Ancient
history."

"Why don't you find me something else? After you receive

your commission, come back and make a deposit yourself." He smiled. "Winding through the city with you isn't the hardest thing I've ever done."

"That's a possibility," she said, smiling. Although she didn't know that they were to be married, it was suddenly clear to her they were going to have something. "Another is for you to make me dinner in your new kitchen. And then I'll forgive you."

Two months later, the sale had gone through. Eight months after that, he asked her to marry him. Wonderful years, three of them in a row.

Now all this.

Steve as president of a major corporation. Money reaching into the millions within the near future. Responsibility—and visibility—beyond anything she had truly expected. She knew from her microcosm as branch manager the way people looked to the boss. And now her husband was to have upwards of sixty thousand employees in twenty-two countries? And the way it happened didn't feel as clean as she would have liked it. Jansten's failing health. The problems with Geoff.

She had known of him from her days as a competitor, had seen his picture in the national trade magazines, closing one huge deal after another. Obviously he had a screw loose now, the thing with Harrison. Still, Geoff had once wielded significant power.

Steve and she had talked about it the night before. He had said, "I wouldn't be surprised if Geoff comes back with some sort of suit. Wrongful termination or something. The company has enough lawyers to do battle, and I can't see that Geoff would have a leg to stand on. But I can't imagine him just crawling away, either."

Fortune, intense responsibility, and visibility. Maybe a lawsuit or two. Add to that both Steve and she were committed to starting a family. The way she saw it, life as they knew it was going to be very different. Aloud, to make it true, she said, "It'll be even better."

In the parking lot, there was a van parked close beside her car with the passenger door wide open. Lisa frowned. She wasn't particularly picky about her Toyota, but even as she walked between the two vehicles, she could see a nasty scratch. "Ah, come on," she said under her breath.

"Oh, I'm sorry," a voice said behind her.

Lisa turned, surprised. She hadn't seen the woman before, a tall, pretty girl with long blond hair.

The girl said, "Did I scare you?"

"You surprised me."

The girl made a face. "I'm sorry. My boyfriend just flew out of here, he was late to meet up with some of his fishing buddies and I think he banged your car. I can't believe him, he didn't even close the damn door . . ."

As the girl got closer, Lisa realized that the blond hair was a wig.

And then there was a slight movement within the van itself, settling on its springs, as if something—someone—were moving inside.

In a glance, Lisa took it in that she was at the far end of the lot, and she was all alone as the girl started crowding her in against the open door, talking nonsense.

"Excuse me," Lisa said, trying to step by.

But the girl moved over, a tight little smile on her face. "No, excuse *me*."

The sliding door opened.

Lisa didn't even look. She tried to shove past the girl.

But the girl shoved right back.

Two men wearing masks were inside, and Lisa screamed once

before the closest one clamped his gloved hand over her face and wrapped his arm around her waist. The other one grabbed her legs and though Lisa continued to fight, the two men lifted her inside and the girl slid the door shut.

Lisa screamed and threw herself to the front of the van, but the girl was climbing in the passenger side and pushed her back. The girl got behind the wheel, started the van, and threw it into reverse. She said, "Do it to her, honey, use it."

And then a white cloth was shoved into Lisa's face.

Grotesque, bleeding faces. One man knelt on her legs, the other had her from behind. Masks, the men were wearing horrid masks.

She tried not to breathe. She knew if she screamed again she would have to breathe in, but she also knew at the speed the van was moving they must be near the parking lot exit now, there might be people nearby . . . .

The one holding her from behind shoved the cloth harder against her and held her tight at the waist. "Breathe deep, sweetmeat, breathe deep."

Already her lungs were burning for air.

She let herself go limp.

Both men shifted to regrip, and as soon as Lisa felt the pressure lighten, she reared her head back into the face of the one behind her and yanked her right leg free. She kicked the man before her in the face and lunged for the side door, determined to jump, no matter how fast the van was going.

She had the door open when they pulled her back. The mask of the one she had kicked was askew. She suddenly recognized him. "Geoff!" she cried, momentarily stunned.

"Shouldn't have seen that," he said, sliding the door shut.

He hit her. It was a short, hard punch to the stomach and it knocked the breath right out of her.

The cloth was shoved back in her face. She gasped for air,

gasped for the words to question the terrible mistake. She tried to talk to Geoff through the harsh, chemical smell.

But he didn't answer. He simply put his mask back in place.

She awoke with an excruciating headache. She was lying face-down on a linoleum floor that smelled of old grease.

She gagged, and just as she started to vomit, someone lifted her from behind and shoved a yellow plastic pail in her face. "Told you," a man's voice said, amused. His voice came from right behind her, he was the one holding her.

"Gross," a woman's voice said.

When Lisa finished, she looked up. She felt an unreasoning shame about the mess—and then was instantly furious. Geoff knelt beside her, shoved the pail away, and handed her a paper towel. "Clean yourself up. That's no way for the new First Lady to behave."

She tried to hit him.

He just laughed and batted her hand away. He stood up, towering over her now. "Empty that pail, will you, honey?" he said to the girl. "Place stinks."

The girl was wearing a mask now, a Cinderella mask.

Lisa tried to stand, felt dizzy, and sat back against the wall. She looked about the room. It was a small, dirty kitchen. Empty, with the smell of old food, sour milk. Beside Geoff, there was a big man, strong-looking. He was wearing a terrifying rubber mask of a man who had been badly beaten.

"Just what the hell are you doing, Geoff?" Lisa's voice was hoarse and shaky.

Geoff said, "Obvious, isn't it? We kidnapped you."

She stared at him, trying to comprehend. Waiting for the bad joke to become clear. "Why?"

He shrugged. "The usual. Money. And a little revenge thrown in."

She hesitated. She handled their personal accounts, she knew just exactly how cash-poor they were. Quietly, she said, "Geoff, have you lost your mind?"

Geoff swung himself up onto a big floor-mounted freezer. "Years ago. I've just been hiding it well, up until now."

She met his eyes. "Stop this nonsense. Untie me and let me go."

"And you'll do what? Simply forget the whole thing?" He laughed. "I don't see that as an option."

"What have we done to you? You blew it yourself, you know that! And Steve and I are not rich. Maybe we will be in a few years, but right now we've sunk everything into the new house!"

The other man groaned. "You fucking yuppies."

"We don't need 'rich'," Geoff said. "We need about a hundred and fifty thousand."

"We don't have that. Almost everything we've got is tied up in the house."

"Well, then, I've got another plan for Steve." Geoff tapped his forehead. "I've always been good at scaring up venture capital."

Lisa felt her lower lip start to tremble and forced herself to stop. The fact that Geoff had no fear of showing his face could only mean one thing. She remembered knocking his mask aside, the way he said, "Shouldn't have seen that."

She fought back panic, tried to keep her face calm.

"You know, I'm in no particular hurry for the money," Geoff said. "But I bet you and Steve will be once he hears from you." Geoff took a small handheld tape recorder from his top pocket. "I want you to read the newspaper headline and date, then this little statement I've prepared."

The blood drained from Lisa's face as she read the note.

She looked over at the white freezer, the one Geoff was sitting on. The guy with the mask began to laugh. Geoff grinned at her.

The girl stepped back into the room and said, "What?" and then looked at Lisa, the blank Cinderella face staring at her.

The freezer had holes drilled into it.

Air holes.

CHAPTER 17

Steve was not particularly surprised that night when he got to the boat and the lights were off. He had left a message on the answering machine earlier saying that he wouldn't be home for dinner.

Steve *was* surprised that she hadn't left a note. She usually left one in the galley, saying where she would be. Sometimes she just had dinner by herself up at Lawson's Landing, the little restaurant at the marina.

As he changed into jeans, he listened to the answering machine. There were several calls: a stockbroker pushing for a sale, an interior decorator offering her services, and the dentist's office.

And then one that gave him pause. It was Gary Bishop, the contractor for their house. "Lisa, it's Gary. Thought I was going to see you this morning. We've got a lot to go over. Give me a call."

There were two more calls that day from Gary with essentially the same message: Where are you?

Steve checked his watch. It was nearly midnight. "Jesus," he muttered. He finished dressing and headed up to the restaurant. The owner, Rick Lawson, was just closing up when Steve rapped on the window.

Rick opened the door. "Hey, Steve. Did I hear a good rumor about you?"

Steve was confused for a moment, then realized that Rick was talking about Jansten Enterprises. "Did Lisa tell you? I was looking for her."

"Yeah, it was Lisa that told me, but she's not here now. This was a couple of nights ago."

"Did you see her today?"

Rick thought for a moment. "I did this morning. I was setting up and saw her coming up the dock."

"Heading toward her car?"

Rick shrugged. "Maybe. Everything okay?"

"Yeah, I'm sure. I'm just looking for her."

Steve saw faint amusement pass over Lawson's face, and Steve turned away before he took his growing unease out on the man. "Thanks for your help," he said, curtly, and left.

As he was leaving the restaurant, he looked out across the parking lot.

Her car. Her car was still there. He walked over to it, and found it was still locked. "What the hell . . ."

He started to flip through the possibilities. She had gone out for dinner, maybe with Claire. They had taken a cab. Or maybe she had simply gone out for a walk. . . .

He hurried back to the boat and searched it again for a message, looking for a slip of paper that had blown aside.

After a half hour, he checked his watch again, sighed, and got out the address book and called the contractor's home phone. A woman's sleepy voice answered, and Steve apologized for the hour and asked for Gary.

"Yuh."

"Sorry to call this late, Gary. Lisa isn't home yet, and I heard your messages. Did you ever connect?"

"No," Gary said. "Tell you, I was surprised. She's normally right on time. Hope she's all right."

Steve thanked him and hung up. He flipped through the pages of their address book. It was the same one they had had since Charleston, and he couldn't help but notice that it was full of names; full of Lisa's friends back there. Here in Boston, there were listings of tradesmen, a host of people that Steve knew from Jansten Enterprises. But as for friends there were exactly two: Claire Bowden, a college friend of Lisa's, and Alex.

Steve called both and reached only answering machines.

"Damn!"

Steve paced in the limited space, growing more worried by the minute. It wasn't like her to forget to call. It wasn't like her to get wrapped up in what she was doing and lose all track of the time. That's what he did—and he couldn't shake the gut feeling that he had let her down somehow.

And then he heard someone step aboard.

He grinned with relief and started up the stairs to the cockpit. "You scared the hell—"

He stopped.

There was a dark shape of someone sitting behind the wheel.

He heard a sharp click and into the silence he heard a faint hiss and then a recorded voice speaking quietly. Lisa's voice. "Steve, I've been kidnapped. He says he'll kill me and I believe him."

There was a sharp, mechanical snap, then a whirring noise.

"Listen close, now," the man behind the wheel said. "I'll

rewind it so you can hear her again. And if you don't do what I say it'll be for the last time."

It was Geoff. He moved into the faint light from the cabinway and Steve saw the gun. "Get below," Geoff said.

Steve hesitated. What he was seeing made no sense. "Where is she? You can't be serious."

For an answer, Geoff reached out and put the tape player against Steve's ear, and hit the button again. The voice was clear, undeniably Lisa's—and it was also undeniable that she sounded frightened.

Geoff pressed the gun against Steve's breastbone. "Lisa is depending entirely upon you. Now get below."

Steve backed down the stairwell.

"Now sit at the table, lay both your hands out in front of you where I can see them." Geoff pushed the Play button on the recorder again. The tape hissed and then her voice came on again.

Steve's hands began to tremble.

". . . My kidnapper told me to read you this headline from today's *Boston Globe.* 'Small plane crashes on Cape, three dead.' I have been given a note to read: 'The clipping is a good example of how easily people can die.' "

Steve heard a catch in Lisa's voice, could tell she was trying to stay calm. Then she continued. " 'You are to raise a hundred and fifty thousand dollars, immediately. Until you do, I will be waiting for you in a box that normally stores dead meat. It's a big freezer, one of those floor-mounted ones, like a big white coffin. There's not enough room to lie down straight. My air is limited and the freezer will be padlocked shut. The man in front of you is my lifeline. You're to remember that.' "

The recording snapped off abruptly.

"She's tough," Geoff said, grinning. "Refused to read it at first, then tried to sneak in little clues."

He leaned forward and put the gun to Steve's temple. "I had to hit her once to get her to do it right."

Steve was shaking, and it took all he had to keep himself in check. "How far gone are you, Geoff?"

"I'd say pretty far, wouldn't you?"

"Why are you doing this?"

"Lots of reasons. I need the money, for one. But the fact you screwed me over ranks way up there."

"If you harm her in any way, I will kill you," Steve said.

"Kill me, kill her. But your attitude is understandable. Predictable, even. So I'm going to show you what you're up against."

Geoff walked Steve at gunpoint up to the vacant lot underneath the bridge. The place was full of rocks, pipes, construction materials. The streetlights gave just enough illumination for them to see. Geoff put the gun on top of a big metal drum and said, "Do your best."

He held his arms out wide.

Steve hesitated. Regardless of his every impulse, it had been fifteen years since he had been in a fight. And though the navy had trained him well in hand-to-hand combat, he had been using his head all his life, and his head was telling him that he should bargain, that this was the man who held Lisa's fate in his hands.

Geoff grinned mockingly. "You choking?"

"There's nothing to be accomplished here," Steve said.

"Sure there is." Geoff punched Steve in the stomach. It knocked the breath out of Steve and he bent over, gasping. Geoff stepped in grinning. "What's to be accomplished here is that *you do what I want.* And I want to kick your ass right now."

The heat pumped through Steve's chest and arms as he regained his breath. He let himself appear more winded than he was, backing away as Geoff advanced on him. And then, when he could draw enough air, he set his back leg and snapped off a kick at Geoff's right knee.

Geoff pivoted, swung his leg out of the way, and caught Steve's foot. He pulled Steve along, making him hop, once, twice. Steve dropped to his back, hitting the ground hard. He shoved his free leg behind Geoff's foot and rolled over onto his stomach to bind Geoff's legs. Geoff hit the ground with a surprised grunt. Steve kicked out hard, going for Geoff's face.

But Geoff blocked the kick and rolled to his feet. He came back at Steve with a rock the size of a grapefruit. Steve dropped to one knee, and, as the rock whistled past his head, he grasped Geoff's legs and threw him over his shoulder with a simple wrestling takedown.

He was all over Geoff in an instant. Kneed him in the groin, butted him in the head. Took a couple of short punches in his stomach, but he was too close for Geoff to deliver much power. Steve got his hand around Geoff's throat and pressed down while grasping for a rock off to the side.

Geoff went totally relaxed.

Steve stopped, the rock held high over his head. Geoff's face was bloody, he was momentarily defenseless. But there was no mistaking the victory on his face, even though he was on the bottom. "Go ahead, Steve."

"Where is she?" Steve shook him.

"Use that rock, and you'll never know." Geoff spit blood away. He whispered. "Maybe the gun. Maybe the gun will scare me."

Steve looked over at it on the drum and figured Geoff's gambit was to beat him to the gun.

So Steve hit him on the head with a rock. Not too hard, not hard enough to knock him out. Just enough to slow him down.

Steve went over the past few seconds in his mind as he got up to pick up the gun. He looked back at Geoff, who was touching his head where Steve hit him.

"Jesus Christ," Geoff said. "It's painful teaching you something."

Steve looked for some hint of fear in Geoff's eyes. He couldn't see any, certainly nothing like what he knew could be found in his own.

"Do it." Geoff stood slowly and ripped his shirt open. "Right there, put a round right there."

Steve pulled the hammer back. "You want to die?"

Geoff shrugged. "Not particularly. But I can't be pushed."

Steve moved the gun down to Geoff's knee. "We'll start here."

"You better hope I don't go into shock. She's got less than an hour left."

Steve repeated his threat.

Geoff shook his head. "You still don't get it."

Steve felt his hand move.

Suddenly Geoff's face was out of his line of vision.

Steve was barely aware of what happened, that Geoff had nudged the gun with the back of his wrist. Steve backed away and fired a round near Geoff's ear, trying to shock him into submission. But before Steve could pull the trigger again, Geoff had his hand around the gun and twisted it away. He kicked Steve in the stomach and then knocked him to the ground with his forearm.

The gun spoke four times in fast succession, big gouts of orange flame lit the underside of the bridge as Steve scrambled away on his back. Bullets slammed into the ground around him, at his head, his sides.

In the sudden silence that followed, Geoff towered over him and said, in a calm, cold voice. "That leaves one round." He spun the revolver's chambers and put the gun to his own forehead. "When I die, she dies." A bead of sweat slid down his jaw and Geoff shouted as he pulled the trigger.

Steve cried out too.

"Jesus, what a rush," Geoff said. "What a goddamn rush." He spun the chambers again, put the revolver back to his forehead, and this time Steve jumped to his feet and knocked the gun away.

"Don't! For God's sake, tell me where she is!"

Geoff nodded. "You're beginning to get it. And in my own time, I'll tell." He held the gun out for Steve, butt first. "Do it."

Steve's breath shuddered in. He broke the gun open, checked the cylinder. There was indeed one bullet left. He dropped it into his hand. The slug was heavy, soft-nosed. It had been cross-hatched.

"Enough to take off most of your head." Geoff took the gun, loaded the bullet and spun the cylinder. He handed it back to Steve. "Lisa's got forty-five minutes left. So I better get back. And I'm not doing that until you prove you love her more than yourself."

Steve's breath rasped out loud in the night air. He mentally scrambled for another answer, searched for another way out that left him and Lisa with a chance. Go ahead and shoot Geoff in the leg? Call in the police? Everything came back to whether or not Geoff could be forced to talk.

Sirens began to wail in the distance. Geoff smiled, almost gently. "Listen to me. I've got a timer set up. If I'm not back in time, it starts pumping water. If the police pick me up, I'll keep my mouth shut until it's too late. You understand?"

"Yes." Steve's voice was dull, but inside he was shaking, ready to vomit. Flashes of Buddy drowning came back to him, pounding on that slick fiberglass.

"You don't want that for her, do you Steve?" Geoff's voice remained soft, concerned. "I heard about your dive partner. How you let him drown. You wouldn't want to do that again, would you? Let your wife die the worst death *you* could imagine?"

Steve looked at the gun, made his decision and moved on it.

He put it to his forehead and snapped the trigger.

The hammer striking the firing pin was deafening. Steve cried out and threw the revolver to Geoff.

"That's a boy," Geoff said, putting the gun inside his coat. "Now if I get so much as an inkling that you've brought in the cops, I will walk away and let her drown. Do you understand?"

"Yes."

"That's good." Geoff patted Steve's shoulder companionably. "As for the money, how fast can you pull a hundred and fifty thousand together?"

Steve rubbed his eyes. "Not quick enough. Maybe thirty or forty if I cash in our stock. We're overextended because of the house. I could get a loan, but that would all take too much time."

"You can't involve officials like that. They'd ask questions. And you can't go to Jansten. He has the cash, but I don't want you running to him on this."

"What do you care?"

"Oh, I care. Like I said, how you act has everything to do with whether or not you see Lisa again." He took an envelope from his back pocket and handed it to Steve. "I've even figured out how you can get the money. Read this." He grinned. "Hell, I've got a contingency for everything. I would have made a great president and CEO, you know that?"

CHAPTER 18

Hard rock played in Geoff's head all the time now. Fast, hot, strong. It made his every move a pleasure. He had even spun Carly around in the kitchen a few times when he got back to the house in North Quincy that morning. Made her laugh behind her Cinderella mask, which was a switch. She had been so quiet since they had picked up Lisa.

"Did he recognize you behind the mask?" she asked, touching his bare cheek.

"Of course not, honey," he lied with a pretty effective soft southern drawl. "Not when I talk liked this." He did a drumroll with his hands on the freezer top. "Our little Popsicle been any trouble, dear?"

Lisa cried out inside.

Carly walked away, her back rigid.

He took the key from his pocket, opened the lid, and stood back. Lisa came for his eyes with her fingernails, and he parried her bound hands aside easily. She fell against the side of the freezer.

"Tough when your hands are tied, isn't it," he said.

She rubbed at her leg, half standing now.

"Pins and needles?" he asked.

"Go to hell." Her voice quavered, and he could see how she tightened her jaw. She hated being scared in front of him. He admired that.

"Just been talking with Steve." He gestured to his face and body, showing the cut on his head, his torn jeans. "Hell, I look worse than him. I was careful not to mark up his face so he can still go to work, play the corporate kingpin for a few more days."

She asked him the same thing Carly had—did Steve recognize him?

"No," he said. "I'd have had to kill him if he knew."

"And since I've seen you, you're going to kill me."

He said, "I'll let you know. In the meantime, you've got something else to worry about. I was struck with an idea that I figured would really motivate him. You being in the box is bad enough, considering his claustrophobia. But what was missing was so obvious . . . water."

He watched her then, felt the satisfaction right behind his breastbone the way she blanched.

"Tomorrow, I'm going to hook up a water pump. Make the threat real."

"You think you're so damn tough," she said, her voice shaking. She held up her bound hands. "Cut these and give me a chance."

"Oh, you're going to take me on yourself?" He grinned. "Good attitude, poor judgment." He put his hand on her shoulder and shoved. "Get down now. I've got to get some sleep."

She knocked his hand away. "I have to go to the bathroom. And I'm hungry and thirsty."

He shrugged, walked over to the refrigerator and took out a bag of doughnuts and a bottle of orange juice. "Have a feast. Piss into the jar when you're done."

Her lower lip trembled, but she held firm. "There's not enough room. I can't sit up or lie down."

He drew the gun back showing her that he would hit her with it. "I'll knock your teeth out," he said, quietly. "And you'll still be going back in the box. It's your choice."

"I want a chance," she said. "Before I'm too weak, I want a chance."

"Sure, I'll give you that. One way or another."

She crouched down and he locked the lid. And then he went in to join Carly, whistling.

———————————

Why are you doing this to her?" Carly said. "What did she do to you?"

They were lying in bed, having just finished sex. It had been like the first time. Geoff had ripped open her blouse and almost attacked her, his need was so great.

She didn't think he was going to answer her at first.

Then he said, "She and her husband got in my way. They derailed everything I've been working toward."

"Still . . . what we're doing to her isn't right. We could tie her up, cover her eyes. Let her lie on a bed or on the couch. I don't mind taking her to the bathroom. That box is awful." She rolled over and looked at Geoff. "Are you hot for her? She is pretty. My experience, a guy slaps a girl around, it turns him on. Are you like that, Geoff?"

"Are you psychoanalyzing me, little girl?"

Even though she was scared of him, she wasn't willing to drop it. "Maybe."

He rolled on top of her, clamped his legs around hers, and held her head in his palms. She froze. His control of her was total. Touching his nose to hers, he looked into her eyes. "What do you see? Homicidal maniac? A blood drinker? Axe murderer?"

She shook her head, just slightly between his tight hands.

"You're sure?"

"Yes."

He shifted his legs so he was between hers. She could feel that he was hard again. He entered her slowly, gently. "Well, *I'm* not sure." He nibbled at her earlobe, his day's growth of beard rasping slightly, tickling. "I'm conducting experiments." His voice was mock solemn. His chest felt good against her breasts. "I'm trying things out. Feeling high. Feeling hot and hard all of the time."

"You like hurting her?"

"No. . . ." He shook his head and leaned away. She ran her hands over his chest, felt his heart pounding. His stomach rippled with muscle.

She was aroused. He was the first man since Neal who had made her feel that way. She didn't know why. Geoff wasn't the first handsome man she had been with. He certainly wasn't the first to talk sweetly, to lie to her. And he was a freak, like Raul. "You do like hurting her," she murmured.

"No. It's what he's going to do. It's the game we're going to play."

"What?"

"It's what Steve's going to do to get her back."

"You're going to kill her." Tears slipped down her cheeks. "You're just like all the rest."

"Maybe. Maybe not. It depends what he does—and what I do to stop him."

Geoff continued on from there, leaving Carly behind.

Lisa tried to control her thoughts. She told herself it was the only way she could make it through another five minutes, never mind how long this ordeal would take. She was sitting down, her legs drawn up near her chest. There was just enough room for her shoulders to fit and only about six inches over her head. The only light was from the air holes, little peepholes into the kitchen.

Her muscles were cramping so much she wanted to scream.

"Take it slow," the girl had said when Geoff had gone to see Steve. "I haven't got the key so it's no use begging me. And the other guy here would hurt both of us if I did. Just imagine you are someplace else."

That had been worse, knowing there was no one close who *could* open the freezer. What if there wasn't enough air?

Now, she tried to measure each breath, tried to push back the memory of that panic. She thought about being out sailing on *The Sea Tern* under the stars. What was experience, but the five senses of sight, sound, taste, touch, and smell? For an insane moment, she wondered if she could re-create those sensations in her head, could she actually make them become real . . . and, if so, perhaps this was all a terrible dream and she would wake up to find out that Steve was beside her, and she was simply sleeping too close to the bulwark, and maybe the hatch was dogged down for rain and the air was tight . . . and it was her turn for a horrible nightmare.

She laughed a little, the sound ridiculously loud in the small box.

Because the reality was, she wanted to scream.

The reality was, she wanted to stretch her legs and stand. She wanted to see daylight, breathe deeply—those were the things she wanted so badly that she felt she should be able to break through the box, that soft metal box—but she couldn't.

Reality was that claustrophobia had entered her body like a demon.

She thought about Steve. One part of her desperately pleaded for him to find her, entertained fantasies about him breaking open that lid, that his would be the first face she would see. Another part of her raged against him, irrationally, she knew, but *that's what happens when you stick a person in a box.* She raged at him because claustrophobia was what frightened him most deeply, and now his hell was hers.

She tasted her tears, didn't even know until then that she had started crying again.

Her bladder was painfully full.

God, she wanted to get at Geoff. She felt at that moment she would be able to tear his eyes out, that he wouldn't be able to hold her back. She felt what his skin would be like under her nails, she would rake that smile off his face for the rest of his life—

Think. She pinched herself hard on her inner thigh. The pain made her eyes water even more.

Fantasies about starry nights would do her no good and neither would mindless thoughts of revenge, she decided abruptly. She needed a plan.

Lisa sipped the orange juice, taking the nourishment even though she would have to pee that much sooner. She ate one of the doughnuts and started thinking about what she would do if Steve didn't come. She was certain he would be trying for all he was worth, but he might not succeed. That's the way she had to figure it.

What did she have for a weapon? One bottle, a bottle cap. Her shoes. A belt.

And her hands were tied, her muscles cramped.

The bottle was fairly heavy, she supposed she could hit Geoff with it. But he was fast and clearly had been ready for her last time he opened the lid. The metal all around her was soft, flexible.

She reached up. There were two bolts coming through the lid, probably holding the padlock hasp. She tried to turn the nuts, but they were screwed on tightly. She used both hands, pressing the thumb and forefinger of her left hand tightly with her right and twisted until warm blood began to trickle down her wrist.

As the sun began to rise, a muffled noise woke Geoff. He got out of bed and padded into the kitchen. The freezer was still shut, the lock in place.

He went back to bed.

CHAPTER 19

Steve arrived at Geoff's apartment at five in the morning, wearing a long coat. A ski mask was stuffed in the coat pocket. After he pushed a few buttons at random, someone buzzed him in.

He went up to Geoff's apartment door quietly, took the sledgehammer out from under his coat, and swung it right over the doorknob.

Forty seconds, in and out, and then he pulled on the mask and strode down the stairs, past a man with gray hair who stood at the bottom saying, "You can't do this, you can't do this."

Forty seconds. That's all it took to see Lisa wasn't there, and that the apartment was empty except for an ungodly amount of sports equipment and photos of Geoff on the wall.

* * *

Steve found Alex's salvage boat an hour later, docked in Salem.

"What in God's sake am I seeing?" Alex said, coming out of his wheelhouse. "Aren't you supposed to be at the helm of corporate America around this time?" His grin faded as Steve got closer.

Steve said, "I've got problems, Alex. Are you alone on the boat?"

"Yeah. Sure." Alex said.

Steve followed him back into the wheelhouse, spoke low and fast. "It's about Lisa."

"What about her?"

"He's taken her. Geoff Mann." Steve told Alex what had happened. He watched his friend's face go through the same stages he had felt: surprise, disbelief, explosive anger.

"That son of a bitch! You've got to get the police in on this. Let them put electrodes on his balls or whatever they do these days."

"No." Steve shook his head firmly. "He's . . . *detached* from reality. Saying he's crazy doesn't quite explain it. He really did have a bullet in the gun when he put it to his head. All the police can do is arrest him and try to intimidate him. And he's not going to scare, not in the time that it would take to save Lisa. He would just sit there laughing while someplace she drowned."

"Well the fact he's not hiding his identity doesn't sound too good either. Seems to me he's planning on killing you anyhow."

Steve nodded shortly. "I'd say so."

"So what are you going to do?"

"What I'd do with any negotiation. Try to make him happy, but on my terms." Steve took out the list Geoff had given him. "He's given me three vendor names here. Consultants for Jansten Enterprises. Bogus ones, I assume, but with real vendor codes. I'm guessing that he's been embezzling for years, and now he wants me to pay off by wiring money to these accounts. Soon as the money hits these accounts, I expect the money vaporizes to offshore accounts that only Geoff can tap into."

"You do that and you've got no way of making sure Lisa comes home."

Steve started to say something and then his voice caught. He wiped his face and said, "You're right."

"How are you holding up?" Alex asked.

Steve's face was gray. "Just about like you'd think."

"There's no way you could've known."

Steve shook his head, holding the rail tight. "I knew something was coming from him. I told her that . . . but I thought it'd be a lawsuit, or something directly at me."

The pain was so naked on Steve's face that Alex wanted to look away. But he didn't.

Steve said, "I left her alone so much. . . ."

Then he regained himself with visible effort, closing his eyes briefly. When he opened them, he said, hoarsely, "Let's get back to it."

Alex nodded. "How much does he want?"

"A hundred and fifty thousand."

"Huh. Doesn't sound like as much as you'd think."

"Geoff's got the company figured to a T. Until I formally take the president and CEO role, that's the amount that I can authorize and still get out the door on short notice without much in the way of procedures."

"Why does he want it so fast?"

"He didn't confide. But it's clear that playing with me is a good part of his motivation. Getting me back for screwing him out of the job, the way he sees it."

Alex shook his head. "Fucking nut."

"So I've got to play him right. If I just send the money to his accounts, he'll fade away. If I have the money in hand, he has to deal with me. And if he wants the money, he's going to have to give me Lisa."

"Okay . . ." Alex looked Steve in the eye. "I'm in." He opened the locker behind him and pulled out a rifle with a scope. "Shooting sharks is part of the job. Got a revolver in there, too."

"Good. It may come to that."

"Where else do I come in? You're welcome to all the cash I've got, but it's not going to be more than about ten thousand."

"You'll be worth a lot more than that soon. At least another hundred thousand."

Alex lifted an eyebrow. "Yeah?"

Steve's new secretary, Monica, was ready with coffee and her checklist when he came in. Already their routine was established, and Steve forced himself to go through part of it, to keep some appearance of normalcy. She checked through a number of meeting requests, budget requests, and other agenda items.

"Basically, everyone wants to be your friend," she said, smiling. "Virtually every division head has called within the past few days looking to have some one-on-one time with you."

"Keep them at bay for the next week or so. And I'll have to assign someone to take over the day-to-day on Blue Water, but I'll hold on to it until we find the right person."

Steve listened to himself answering Monica. His decisions sounded well reasoned, his voice, calm and unhurried. Inside, his chest hurt and he felt short of breath, thinking of Lisa, cramped in some box while he was free to drink coffee and talk to his secretary. Free to steal money. He watched Monica as she continued on, knowing he had to use her and others, knowing that there was a wall Geoff had forced between Steve and the people around him. He was certain that was part of what Geoff wanted.

For a moment, Steve was so overcome with rage he couldn't

trust himself to speak. He felt, quite literally, like he might explode. That he might just sweep off everything on his desk, tear apart the big office that he had once wanted so much.

The big office and position that had put Lisa in Geoff's sights.

Lisa was Steve's anchor. He had done just fine by himself before they met. But once they had, everything changed. He couldn't envision life without her, simply couldn't see it. *Wouldn't* see it.

He exhaled carefully, telling himself, *This is an indulgence Lisa can't afford.*

Embezzlement required a cool head.

"Steve?" Monica said. "Are you all right?"

"Uh-huh. Fine." Steve sipped his coffee. "Listen, let's talk about Blue Water for a bit."

"Sure." She flipped to another page in her notebook.

"I'm hiring a salvage consultant I met up here to do some design recommendations on the twenty-five-footer, and I need you to do a wire transfer to get him going immediately. He's going to rip up the decks of the one I've got at my marina and rebuild a prototype of a commercial dive boat from the hull up, including putting in an inboard/outboard configuration. We've estimated he'll need a hundred and twenty thousand." He gave her Alex's name and bank account number.

"Okay . . ." She looked a little concerned. "Still designing boats yourself, are you? They're going to kick back at the factory. We still need to reschedule that conference call on the design budget, and I presume this comes out of that budget?"

"Yes."

"Who from down there should be coordinating with Mr. Martin?"

"No one. I want to see fresh ideas."

"I expect you'll get a call from J.C."

Steve smiled, as he knew the situation required. "I expect I will." J.C. was his head boat designer and would have no compunction about kicking and screaming about having his budget pulled away for an anonymous freelancer.

Steve said, "It's important this be done today. This morning."

She looked doubtful. "Well, I'll talk with Accounts Payable right away . . . but if this Alex Martin Salvage doesn't have a vendor code with us, then it might take a little time to set up some of the paperwork. Are you sure you want to simply transfer him the money? Wouldn't a purchase order be acceptable? Then he can just bill us. That would be a little more standard in——"

Steve leaned in so she felt the weight of his eyes. "Monica," he said, gently. "If you're to stay on with me as I run this corporation I can't have you questioning me on such explicit instructions."

Her face blanched. "It's just that an advance like this is somewhat irregular and I will be asked——"

"Wire-transfer him the money," Steve said. "Do it now so he has it by the end of the day. Is that clear?"

"That's clear," she said and headed for the door. She looked back over her shoulder and smiled quickly, a frightened smile meant to regain herself a little face.

The sort of smile Harrison used to give Geoff.

CHAPTER 20

You should've let me make the threat to this Steve guy," Jammer said that night. "It's nuts, you going to meet him like that."

"I kept my mask on the whole time," Geoff lied. They were at the door of an after-hours bar in Roxbury.

"I don't know what the frigging rush is. Raul's gonna be pissed, with us coming in with only fifty. But it's way too much to lose, man." The pimp looked nervous, as well he should with fifty thousand of his own money in a bag over his shoulder.

"Say what I told you."

Jammer didn't hide his nervousness all that well, Geoff thought, as he pounded on the door. A young black kid opened the door, stared at them.

"Hey, it's me, Jammer," the pimp said.

"Hey, it's me, the guy who don't give a shit," the kid said, but he backed away, letting them in.

Jammer laughed, a hollow, scared sound. He called out and waved to some of the young black men in the bar. Geoff was amused to see that none of them even responded.

At the bar, Jammer started whispering to Geoff again about Steve. "Still, the guy might have recognized your voice. How good do you know this guy?"

"Not that well."

"We're gonna have to do that chick, you know," Jammer said. "Before we do, I'm gonna put it to her once. Classy chick like that, if you could turn her, put her on the call girl circuit, she could make you rich."

"I think she'd be a tad difficult to convince," Geoff said. The pimp's pretensions toward business were laughable.

"Oh, yeah, sure. And she knows you. I can't take the chance on the cops finding their way back to you."

"You think I'd talk?" Geoff kept his voice low too. Conversation had stopped around the room. Geoff felt his heart start beating faster. He felt the tangible animosity with something close to pleasure. But he didn't want to start anything, exciting as it might be.

Jammer said, "I think my mother would give me up for more food stamps."

Geoff didn't admire Jammer, but he did find him amusing, the way the guy was scared of him, but kept trying to bluster along. Geoff knew Jammer would stab him in the back any chance he got. It added to the tension of the day, kept Geoff's adrenaline flowing.

He wondered how Steve was dealing with his day.

Lisa sure wasn't dealing too well. That morning, Geoff had unlocked the freezer to find her covered with blood from her hands. Apparently she had tried to undo the nuts on the hasp bolt, then broken the juice bottle. She had cried and begged him to let her go to the bathroom. He let Carly bring her in to use the toilet, and then he watched her himself while Carly cleaned out the old freezer like it was a dirty hamster cage.

Maybe he was wrong about Lisa's strength. She had fooled him the way she had come on strong the night before. But in the morning, sitting on the edge of the tub, she kept crying about how she had almost peed in her pants and that if he had to lock her up, why couldn't he let her out more often?

He had grown bored with her. He left Carly with the key and strict instructions to let her out no more than once every four hours, and to keep the gun on her at all times.

To Jammer, he said, "Just keep your hands off Lisa until I say so. The second Steve thinks she's dead, he'll call the police. I've got to keep those tapes going."

"What's to keep him from calling the cops anyhow?"

"I've convinced him." Geoff told about using the threat of the water pump to convince Steve.

Jammer looked worried. "That was a lot of talking. You sure he didn't recognize your voice?"

"Positive."

"Think he'll come through?"

"I'll see if the money has hit the accounts tomorrow."

" 'The accounts?' " Jammer's brow furrowed. "What's that mean?"

Geoff hadn't told him about the delivery system. He moved closer. "Now keep your voice down. The money will be wired to some accounts I've got set up. And then it's going to travel around the world a few times, including the Cayman Islands and Swiss accounts. It's going to come back laundered through a guy I know in San Francisco who owes me a big favor."

Bob Guston at TerrPac had clearly been frightened when Geoff called him. "Where are you?" was the first thing he had asked.

"Lucky for you, on the opposite coast," Geoff had said. "Now shut up and listen how you're going to start to recoup this mess you got me into."

Guston had blathered at some length about how he couldn't do it, but in the end he agreed he could.

Now Jammer was pissed, though. He leaned close to Geoff, his voice a harsh whisper. "Listen, *partner,* you talk to me before you do all this complicated shit and cut somebody else in. I thought we were just gonna go get the cash from this Steve guy, pop him, then come back and pop the chick. Now you're telling me we're getting paid with a *check,* for christsakes."

"It's safer this way. Picking up the cash is where we're vulnerable, where Steve could nail us if he does bring in the cops." It was the truth. It was also the truth that Geoff wanted Steve to feel what it was like to be a liar and a cheat. Feel what it was like to be an embezzler. Probably make a Boy Scout like him puke.

Jammer sighed. "Okay, I guess this makes some sense. But I don't get why you're so hot to see Raul now. Why don't we just wait until we've got the full amount?"

Geoff let his pale blue eyes rest on Jammer. "Because I want to know who I'm dealing with before I walk in with all the cash. And I want him to know the same."

Jammer shook his head and then took a deep swallow of his drink. He signaled to the bartender, a bald, heavily muscled black man with a large belly. He ignored them for a good minute or two, and then walked over, his face impassive. "What?"

"Raul," Jammer said, handing the man a rolled fifty-dollar bill. "Get word to him that Jammer and a friend want to meet with him tonight."

The man stared at him. "Don't know no Raul."

"Sure you don't. That's because I didn't explain myself." He handed the man a hundred. "The fifty is to get the message out. The hundred is to remember to ask for safe passage."

The man walked behind the curtain.

Jammer began to whistle between his teeth. He said quietly to Geoff, "Raul might be busy. Might tell us to try another night."

The bartender came back. The smallest of smiles touched his face. "Buy everybody a drink while you wait."

Jammer put another hundred down. The bartender began serving and around the room, Geoff felt the animosity go up a few degrees. The drinks were left alone. After a moment, the bartender came back.

"Guess you boys ain't too popular," he said, in a southern sheriff drawl.

Jammer laughed it up with everyone else, acting like he was in on the joke instead of the butt. Geoff smiled pleasantly.

A half hour later, a young man came in. He wore black denim jeans, a two-inch fade haircut, and a black leather jacket. On his left hand he wore a gold ring with raised letters spelling "Nike" flanked by two guns. Even though he appeared to be only about twenty, he held himself erect, looked at Jammer and Geoff with open contempt, and said, "Jammer, don't you know the fuckin' sixties gone, man? When you gonna cut your hair, walk like a man?"

"Hey, Strike," Jammer said, fawning. "You ain't reading your fashion mags. All the models are wearing their hair long now."

"Your faggot mags," the kid said, laughing. He jerked his head at Geoff. "Who the fuck is he?"

"I'm the guy that's banking Jammer."

"Uh-huh. You two homeslices wouldn't be wasting the man's time, right? You got what he told you?"

"Yeah."

"Awright. This is what we be doing. We go out to my Baby

Benz. I like what you show me, we go. I'm not happy, I put Lee on your case."

Inside the little Mercedes a few minutes later, Jammer opened the pouch, let them see the loosely stacked bills.

Lee, a huge black wearing gym warm-ups that barely contained his massive chest and arms, leaned forward and said, "Uh-uh, Strike."

"That the amount?" Strike said.

"That's a lot of money, and we're ready to give it to Raul."

Strike ignored him. "I said, is that the amount, Jammer? It looks way light to me."

"It's fifty. We'll bring the rest in a day or two."

"That ain't what the man *told* you. I heard him."

"I know." Jammer looked at Geoff. "But I got a new partner."

"And before I hand over the balance I want to know who I'm dealing with," said Geoff.

Strike rolled his eyes. "What you think, Lee?"

"Maybe they figure Raul's an insurance man, huh?" The big man's voice was a deep rumble. "Wants to meet him. New partner. Shit."

Strike nodded as he started the car. He headed off in the direction of the Southeast Expressway. "Okay, man, you want to meet an insurance agent, you'll meet him." He grinned back at Lee. "Maybe we're gonna rewrite these dudes' life insurance, hey?"

CHAPTER 21

They drove to Duxtable, on the South Shore. Geoff had never been there before, but even in the dark he could see it was a wealthy coastal town just a short distance from Jansten's home in Sea Crest. The houses were large, with expansive lawns. "Gotta have a Benz to get in this town," Strike said. "You should see them looking at us brothers in the daytime. *Word.*"

They turned down a private drive of crushed sea shells and went about a quarter of a mile toward the shore before coming to an iron gate. Beyond it was a large, modern home. The grounds were lit with bright lamps. A tall metal fence surrounded the property on three sides, down to a small cove. Coils of razor wire shimmered atop the fence. Strike reached into the glove box and opened the front gate with a remote control.

Once inside, they started up a walkway to the front door. Midway there, an overgrown grape arbor formed a narrow path that would force them to go single file. Strike slowed so that Geoff and Jammer would go ahead. Geoff tensed, but continued on.

A gun was put to his head midway through the arbor.

Jammer yelped behind him.

Geoff held his coat open. The gunman took Geoff's Beretta and patted him down. Behind him, Lee was checking Jammer out as well.

"This one is carrying, Strike," said the gunman.

"Yeah, he the new hotdog coming to meet Raul. The man still up?"

The gunman grinned, white teeth showing. He was a strong-looking Hispanic man. "The two chicks he's got out on the boat now, I'd say he's still up." He nodded to Jammer's backpack. "You check that out? He doesn't want a flake, you know that, man."

"Yeah, they's got cash. Nothing wrong with that." Strike slapped Jammer's head. "You tell me, man, you got any personal stash on you? You got so much as a stick of dope, you tell me now. The man don't allow no drugs on his place."

"Nothing," Jammer said.

"Never touch the stuff," Geoff said, amiably.

"He's the fucking comedian." Strike shoved Geoff. "Come on, Lee, I'll be thinking the man's looking for a laugh tonight."

Strike opened up the big outboard on the Mako so they were flying along in the dark toward a power yacht anchored at the mouth of the small cove. "Yah!" he cried back at Lee. "Fucker's fast!"

The yacht was about fifty feet long, with a high bow and wide beam. "Man, crime do pay, don't it?" Strike said to Lee. "I want to cream in my jeans every time I see this thing."

He shoved Jammer, in a not totally unfriendly way. "That what you dreaming about, man, you so hot to talk to Raul?"

They climbed the ladder off the yacht's stern.

Sitting in the sportfishing chair was a young black woman wearing a man's bathrobe. Even in the poor light, Geoff could see she was naked underneath. She held a handkerchief, dark with blood, up to her nose.

"The man be screwing your brains out, girl?" Strike said.

"Don't bother him now," she said, in a small voice. "He's auditioning Cindy."

Lee grinned. "What's the matter, honey, you didn't pass the screen test?"

"I went limp," she said. "He just slapped me around, got bored."

Strike said to Jammer, "Hey, maybe you bargain real good, Raul let you take her, huh? Put her on the street, the man figures she's no good no more."

Jammer nodded uncertainly. "Sure."

Lee and Strike laughed.

They all waited.

Geoff looked over the boat. It was a big sportfisherman, with a tall flybridge. He figured the fifty thousand in the backpack truly wouldn't mean that much to the man who owned this.

They heard a woman cry out.

"Shit," the girl in the chair hissed. "That sick bastard."

"That right?" Strike said. "I tell him you mad at him, girl. Tell him you got a problem with the *director.*"

"No." She laughed, scared. "Don't do that."

"Why not? Give me a reason." He tugged his balls. "Good reason."

She sighed, then threw the handkerchief away. She knelt in front of Strike and he laughed, looking over his shoulder at the others. "Take me a pause that refreshes, guys."

Jammer smiled and looked at Geoff. "Little different from where you come, huh, man?"

Inside the cabin, the woman's voice cried out again, and Geoff could hear the slap of skin on skin.

"Carly couldn't walk for a week the time I sent her over to him," Jammer said. "Starts shaking every time I mention his name."

Geoff looked at him. "Have you ever sent her back?"

Jammer shook his head. "That was just a few weeks ago. He hasn't called for her again."

"But you would have?"

Jammer looked at Geoff as if he were stupid. "That's what she's for."

Lee was chuckling, watching Strike with the woman. "Ooo, ooo," Lee mimicked.

The kid climaxed minutes later. He patted the woman on the head and said, "Long's you remember what I remember and service me good like that, you be okay."

Geoff had begun trembling. He couldn't figure it, his heart was pumping hard. He was angry, suddenly sick with fury that Carly had been used like that. That she couldn't walk for a week afterward.

He didn't think for a second how he was treating Lisa himself.

The emotion surprised him, as did all his feelings for Carly. He had never cared about anyone before and he certainly was under no illusions about Carly.

But Geoff could still see Carly splashing in that stream, thinking in her naive way that it made everything different. And the way she fought back at Jammer, that first time in the Boston Common. So strong on her own, yet so eager to be transformed by what Geoff could teach her. For the past day or so, Geoff had found himself considering following through on his promise and actually taking her along with him. For a while, anyhow.

At that moment, a man came out of the cabin. He had a blond

woman by the hair and he dragged her out to Strike and Lee. "Hose this cow off before you send her home. She was boring, I'll be dropping the Betas over the side."

He was a big man, soft-looking. About forty. His face was pale, with a baby petulance about the mouth. When the first woman helped the blonde away, he grimaced. "Both of you, get out of my sight before I have you drowned. Waste of good skin." He waved the men below.

The cabin was brightly lit with battery-powered camera lights. A video camera was mounted on a tripod and directed toward a big bed.

Geoff envisioned Carly damaged like the blonde was, with her pretty face ruined by a split lip, perhaps a broken cheekbone and nose. Obviously, Carly hadn't suffered anything like that kind of damage. But why hadn't she told him about Raul?

Geoff took a good look at the man. His clothes were casual, conservative. Good quality. His hair was black, short. He didn't look Hispanic. If anything, he looked like a WASP Harvard Business School grad with about twenty years tacked on top. The shelves behind him were lined with videocassettes. By the titles, Geoff could see mainstream movies ranked alphabetically with hardcore porn interspersed throughout. The top shelf was smaller, with a dozen or more videos facing outward, on display. Cheap, hardcore porn with distinctly violent covers. Rapes, bondage. Several other cassettes were untitled but placed alongside. Geoff could only imagine what those held.

Raul saw him looking and smiled faintly.

"Yours?" Geoff asked.

"Mine. Having a creative outlet passes the time."

"We brought something," Jammer said, gesturing to the backpack. "First payment on that thing we talked about."

Raul sighed and pulled the bag over to peer in. He closed it, puffed on his cigar, and said, "I've been looking at bags of cash all my life, and that's not the amount."

"No, not the full amount. It's the first *payment.*"

"That's not what I told you, Jammer."

The pimp licked his lips. "Well, I got this new partner and he wanted to meet you. We'll get the rest of it in a few days, a week outside. We got something going to pull the rest of the cash in."

"How much is this?"

"Fifty."

Raul let his shoulders slump. "Fifty thousand," he murmured. "I say come to me when you've got two hundred thousand dollars together, and you show up with a partner uninvited and a quarter of the money."

"I told him you wouldn't be smiling on that," Strike said.

Raul sighed. "I'm a busy man." He turned his attention to Geoff. "So, you wanted to meet me." He spread his hands wide. "Here I am. You probably expected with a name like Raul to find some little spic, didn't you?"

"I didn't know what to expect."

"Maybe you thought I was some easy, friendly guy? You could trip in here with this piddling amount of money and we'd negotiate some better contract?"

"That must be what he thought." Strike stood behind Raul, grinning as he warmed up.

"You tell him about my degree from Cornell?"

"Uh-uh. Didn't tell him nothing."

"You tell him about me being a bastard kid?"

"Not me," Strike said.

Geoff watched the two of them carefully. All this had a singsong quality, a routine they had done before.

"Maybe that's it," Raul said. "Maybe Jammer found out somehow, told his new 'partner' that my venerable old papa nailed the maid down on a vacation in Puerto Rico and I'm the product. He was a good, responsible sort, though, so he made sure I went to the best schools, long as I stayed away from his family." He gestured to his video on display behind him. "I send an autographed copy of each one I do. I hear it sends him into a flying rage every time. One day, I figure his heart will give out. Is that the sort of thing you wanted to know, new partner?"

"No," Geoff said. "Interesting, though. What I had in mind was speeding up the process a little. We'll be coming through with the cash, but I simply wanted to meet you and be clear on the deal. Jammer and I are new partners, and I wanted to see myself where my money would be going."

"It's going right here," Raul said, touching his chest. He leaned forward, speaking softly. "What you should know when it comes to my business dealings is that it's very important to me that people do what I tell them. Now understand this. I'm going to show you the absolute limit of my patience by letting you walk out of here on both legs. Because maybe this time, I'll believe that *you* didn't know any better."

He turned to the pimp. "But for you, Jammer, you know me. And you disregarded me. You think I've gotten soft? I've been traveling for weeks now. If you think I was just letting go of what happened, you are sadly mistaken."

"What happened?" Jammer looked confused. "What?"

"Oh, shut up." Raul took on a plaintive tone that Geoff didn't believe. Geoff wondered how the man had ever survived in such a position. His whole manner had a theatrical quality, as if he were acting the way a drug lord was supposed to act. "What use to me is a man who can't follow instructions?"

"No use, man, no use." Strike winked at Jammer.

Raul looked over his shoulder at Strike and slapped him lightly in the belly with the back of his hand. "Stop clowning around behind me. Tell me, what good is a man who can't follow instructions?"

"God damned if I know." Strike shook his head, mock-solemn.

Jammer kept his mouth shut while Raul stared at him.

Finally, Raul said, "I let Strike wink and grin because he's a good boy and he does what he's told. I'm a reasonable man and I understand different people have different talents. Now maybe you'll understand whores if you can't understand the drug business. Whores are your business. I'm talking about the caliber of the woman I'm getting these days."

Jammer gestured toward the stern. "I didn't send those two!"

"I *know* you didn't." Raul exploded suddenly and cracked Jammer across the face and backhanded Geoff. Jammer sat back, rigid with fear.

Geoff could have stopped the blow, but he had decided to wait. The man's ring had cut his cheek, and he let the blood trickle down to his collar. *That's two,* Geoff thought. *First Carly, now me.*

Raul continued to rage. "The *stupidity* I have to deal with every day! If you had sent those two, I would have had you drowned right now!"

"Do it, man!" Strike laughed and Lee chuckled along.

"Limp bags of flesh, not a bit of life in them. They cower and shiver like dogs in the rain. I'm telling you that I'm not a happy customer, and if you want to come crawling in with your little bag of money, if you want that territory, then you have one skill and you better make me happy with that one little thing you can get right. Are you listening?"

"I'm listening." Jammer's voice shook.

Raul looked at Geoff briefly.

"You've got my full attention," Geoff said, mildly.

Raul tossed the backpack to Strike. "Put this away."

Strike pulled a big aluminum suitcase from a side locker and opened it. It was filled with cash, mostly hundreds. Strike began stacking the contents of the backpack.

"See that?" Raul said. "There's over eight hundred thousand in there. That's walking-around money for me. That's my equal to your little jar of pennies you keep at home." He gestured to Lee, and the big man hit Jammer in the ear with the back of his hand. "Coming here so far short with this 'partner' means you must not respect me. It means you think you've got something on me."

He gestured again, and this time Lee came around in front of Jammer, set his considerable weight, and threw a hook deep into the pimp's belly.

The blow lifted Jammer out of the chair. He fell against Geoff, gasping for breath. Geoff pushed him back into his chair. While the pimp was doubled over, Raul said to Geoff, "I hope you're paying attention. Maybe you can learn from his mistakes."

"I'm learning." And he was. He now understood how Raul had earned his position. His manner wasn't just a posture; the man was a genuine sadist. His eyes practically sparkled.

"Notice how your partner can't breathe, how he's turning bright red?" Raul said conversationally to Geoff. "A good blow to the stomach will do that. It's awful. You must have had the breath knocked out of you before? You feel like you're dying, but you're alive to watch it. See how he's getting his breath in now, he just sipped a little in? Lee, do it again, same way."

Lee followed through, swinging his big fist into Jammer's stomach like a sledgehammer.

"All right, you think I've got his attention?" Raul asked.

"You know it," Strike said.

Raul rested his elbows on his knees and said into Jammer's ear, "I've had one woman in the past who has given me a fight, the potential for the type of action my viewers expect. A woman who will put a little enjoyment in my day filled with small, scared men like you. That Carly of yours. Maybe you thought I had turned soft. Maybe you thought I was forgetting." He began rolling up his sleeve, putting his arm right under Jammer's eyes. He revealed an ugly scar the length of his forearm. "Maybe you thought, 'If Carly can get away with this, use that straight razor of hers, then maybe I can pay Raul fifty instead of two hundred thousand.' "

Jammer began shaking his head. A trail of saliva fell from his lips. He got his voice. "I don't know. I didn't know."

Raul continued. "But it was far simpler than that. I've simply been traveling for the past few weeks. And while I surely could have sent Strike and Lee to kill her, you, and everyone you know, I thought I'd rather feature her in one of my special shows. So I'm going to buy her from you and give her an excellent role."

"You should have told me," Jammer croaked.

Raul patted his head in a friendly way. "Not to worry. I'm convinced now that you didn't know. I'll be leaving for L.A. tomorrow and I'll be back by the end of the week, so you have her here by Saturday, midnight. You give her to me, and the remaining balance, and I will forgive this intrusion on my time and you will have your territory and be behind the scale with your partner." His lips curled on the last word. "Naturally, if she's not here, I will have you both brought here and I will go to work on you. I'm not as interested, personally, but there's a market for shows with boys. Do you understand?"

"Yeah, sure." Jammer wiped his mouth as he looked over at Geoff. "She's with him now."

Raul turned to Geoff. "In that case, do you understand?" he asked, softly.

"She'll be here," Geoff lied. He looked Raul in the eye and even managed to look scared. All part of his boardroom repertoire.

But perhaps Raul was a sharper judge of such things than Geoff's former competitors. Raul looked at him skeptically, then snapped his fingers. "Lee, I need to make an impression on this man."

Geoff lunged off toward the galley, reaching for the knife he had seen earlier on the cutting board. He heard the big man behind him. Geoff grasped the knife and swung back with it, pivoting on the ball of his foot.

"Shit, shit," Jammer was screaming.

Lee blocked the knife just in time and held on to Geoff's hand.

Geoff didn't try to overpower the big man. Instead, he let himself be pulled forward and then kneed Lee in the balls. That still didn't put him down.

Strike appeared at Geoff's shoulder and jammed a little gun right under his chin. "I'm gonna spread your brains."

Geoff stopped.

"Not in the boat," Raul said, casually. "Sit him down."

Lee used his fist on Geoff like he had on Jammer, then slung him into a chair. "Motherfucker," Lee said and hit him in the face. Strike kept the gun on Geoff and said, "Don't do him yet, Lee, the man still wants to talk to him, hear?"

"I hear." Lee stepped back around the chair to wrap a massive arm around Geoff's neck.

Jammer was babbling apologies. "I didn't know, I didn't know he was going to do this shit, Raul, you've got to believe me."

"You should've known." Raul's voice was silky. He stood over Geoff and drew on his cigar, making the tip glow. He blew smoke into Geoff's face. "You'll have her here, Saturday, by midnight. Or else I go to work on you. This is to let you know that I'm sincere."

He pressed the burning embers against Geoff's temple.

CHAPTER 22

Steve could scarcely breathe when the phone rang. It was around noontime and he had been waiting at the boat all morning.

He picked up the receiver and said hello.

"You and Lisa must not be as close as I thought," Geoff said. "The money isn't in the accounts."

"I've got it," Steve said. "With me, in cash."

Silence.

Geoff's voice was flat when he finally spoke. "That's not what I told you."

"The only way I can count on getting Lisa back safely is to make an even swap with you."

"You can't even count on that."

"Let me speak to her."

"I'm in a phone booth. She's not with me."

"How do I know she's still alive?"

"You don't."

Geoff hung up.

Steve sat down heavily in front of the nav station. He saw the picture of Buddy, dead all these years. He told himself that, at the very least, Geoff's ego would allow nothing less than making Steve sweat it out a little while for changing the rules.

But that logic didn't stop Steve's hands from shaking. For a moment, he was swept with nausea, knowing Geoff could just as easily go back and take his revenge out upon Lisa directly.

Steve forced himself to calm down, once again telling himself that his guilt was something neither he nor Lisa could afford until she was back safe.

He checked the time. Alex was due. Steve went up into the cockpit and swept the parking lot with his binoculars. Alex's truck rolled in, right on time. Steve released a sigh of relief when Alex flashed his lights.

Steve met Alex at his truck and told him about the phone call.

"Jesus," Alex said, rubbing his face. He was still sitting behind the wheel, a revolver lying on the seat beside him. "I'll do whatever you say. But it seems to me, the best we can do is move ahead. I've got to believe he wouldn't kill her until he has the money—and there it is."

Alex gestured to a small suitcase on the floor, a little bigger than a briefcase. "Got it all in hundreds. The folks at the bank spent a little time trying to talk me out of taking cash, but it's all here." Alex handed him the bag. "Here, you do the heavy lifting." Alex took out a long ski bag, which presumably carried the rifle. He slipped the revolver into his belt holster and pulled out his shirt so it was covered. "I'd hate to be robbed on the way to your boat."

In *The Sea Tern,* Steve set aside ten thousand dollars from the

forty thousand of cash that he had been able to liquidate from selling their remaining stocks and savings account. He added the remaining thirty thousand to the case. "There. Come and get it,
Geoff."

Meanwhile, Alex laid out the contents of the ski bag: the rifle
and scope, ammunition, a pair of walkie-talkies, night binoculars. Steve threw a coil of climbing rope onto the table.

"What's that for?"

"I'll get to that," Steve said. "Let's figure this out fast and get
into position. Ideally, he brings her and we give him the money,
and that's the end of it. I'll find a way to pay back the company
and let the police chase Geoff."

"You got to figure he's going to try to kill you, though. He's
showed his face all along."

Steve nodded. "The question is, will he come here at all? It
seems to me, there's at least three options: The first one, he brings
her here. The second, he runs me all over town to pay phones
until we get to some spot where we can exchange her."

Alex grunted. "So I still need to follow you. Because he might
just run you around and kill you."

"The third option is that he just shows up here by himself.
Tries to take the money and tells me Lisa will be released later."

"And you don't think a bullet in his leg would make him talk?"

Steve shook his head. "He's convinced me."

They went into the cockpit. "I've rented a car in case we need
to follow him back to his place. You should plan on taking your
truck, so we can switch off." Steve spread out a Boston street
map. "We're in a spot where he could come and go from about
five directions: north on the expressway, or drive into
Charlestown, or he could cross over the bridge and go into the
North End. He could go into Boston proper, or just continue on
and pick up the entrance ramp to go south on the expressway.

When he drove away last time, I saw him go over the bridge in an old van. So you should move your truck over the bridge."

"Over the bridge? How will I get to it in time?"

Steve smiled faintly. "You haven't acquired a fear of heights any time recently, have you?"

CHAPTER 23

Jammer checked his watch. He was sitting in the kitchen of the little house, watching Geoff make his preparations. Carly was in the bedroom scrubbing the place down. It was almost midnight.

Jammer couldn't remember when his judgment had been so bad. He should have let Geoff beat him into the pavement sooner than take him in to meet Raul.

The guy just didn't know what was what.

Geoff didn't know his *limitations*. Jammer liked the way that sounded, something he'd heard on a television talk show once.

And what truly amazed Jammer was that he suspected Geoff was foxed by *Carly*. That some of the attitude Geoff was showing Raul was because Raul had smacked her around a little. To Jammer, risking your life for a woman was like risking your life for a favorite flavor of ice cream.

Geoff had held out for so long while Raul branded a big scar on the side of his head, sweat streaming down his face, jaw clenched. Wouldn't beg. Jesus. Strike and Lee had dumped them off in Quincy. Strike put a piece of paper with a phone number in Geoff's pocket and told him to call before bringing the chick back. And to be on time.

Now, Jammer fit a cigarette through the mouth of the mask and watched the tip glow. He thought about how hot that tip was. He knew if he himself had suffered that kind of burn, he would still be in bed with an ice pack and screaming at his whores to get out and score some more painkillers. But Geoff had been up and out all day long, and had just come back with all sorts of shit to hook up a water pump for the chick in the freezer.

Nuts. Fucking nuts.

Geoff began to run water in the bathtub and put in the hose attached to the electric pump. He ran the other end to the freezer and shoved a metal tube into one of the airholes. The girl began to scream at him when he did, knowing what was coming. Geoff drilled a little bracket onto the tube and the side of the freezer so she couldn't push the tube out.

Whistling tunelessly, he walked over and threw the switch. "Running water, honey, just like I promised."

The girl lost it, practically rocking the heavy freezer, so hard did she fight in the metal box. Jammer grinned uneasily behind his mask. Why Geoff had to get so fancy killing her was beyond Jammer. And why now? Didn't it make more sense to be sure they had the money before killing her?

Although, there was something exciting knowing she had to die. But Jammer's sense of commerce recognized how pretty she was and killing her seemed like a waste. If it had been *his* job to do her, he would make it quick. None of this slow drowning bullshit, that was too much like those James Bond movies. He said, "Uh, shouldn't we do this after we get the money?"

Geoff made a shocked face, hammed it up big time to show Jammer he had just stated the obvious. "God damn! Why didn't I think of that?"

Geoff switched off the water pump and unlocked the freezer. The girl came out, shaking. She looked like she might tear into Geoff herself. But she lowered her head, and Jammer had to give Geoff some points there—he was teaching her who was boss.

Problem was, it seemed like Geoff figured the same shit would work on Jammer. And Jammer was his own man.

"Read this," Geoff said to Lisa, handing her a newspaper. He clicked on the small tape recorder.

She read the morning headlines and date.

"Now this."

Obediently, she read, " 'Steve. My kidnapper tells me that you have changed plans on him. He has punished me by turning on the water pump. The box I am in is now one third full of warm water. It is already beginning to grow cool and will be cold within an hour. If you follow your remaining instructions, he will give you directions to where I am. If you fail to follow your instructions or if you detain him in any way, then the water pump will start on a timer.' "

Then she tried to add a message of her own, telling her husband that she loved him.

Geoff snapped off the tape midway through her statement. "That's enough. You can do all the hugs and kisses when he comes to pick you up."

Whether Geoff was lying to her or not, Jammer didn't know. The guy had balls and he *acted* like he knew what he was doing. Like the way he had them all wearing rubber gloves and getting the place cleaned up so the police wouldn't be able to trace them later.

The guy was good on the details . . . but then he would pull a stunt like being a wiseass to Raul . . . from where Jammer sat, it looked like Geoff had screwed up everything. Besides, Jammer had never wanted a partner for keeps and he sure didn't trust Geoff to deliver to Raul the money and girl as promised. Jammer figured *he* would go to the marina and collect the money. He would take care of Geoff and Lisa afterward, once he was sure he had the cash. Then he would bring Carly to Raul.

He took the gun out from behind his back and pointed it at Geoff. "I'll take that tape."

————————————————

Inside the box, Lisa heard the metallic click, but didn't recognize it at first as a gun being cocked. She did recognize the warning in the man's tone and that there was a confrontation.

She pressed her ear against one of the air holes.

"You wouldn't know what to do," Geoff said.

"If you scared him as good as you said, he should be waiting there with the cash."

Steve. *Were they talking about Steve?*

"And you're just going to go down and take it?"

There was a pause. "No."

"Then what?"

"I'll have him drive around. You know, to different phone booths."

"What numbers?"

"Huh?"

"Which phone booths?" Geoff's voice sounded as if he were trying to come across as reasonable. But even inside the box, Lisa could hear his contempt. "Where?"

"Around! Look, you've fucked up everything so far."

"What's going on?" the girl said, coming into the room.

"Both of you, over here," the other man said. "Tie him up with this."

"No," the girl said.

"Fine with me. I'll just take this hammer here and hit both of you hard enough so you stay down. Your choice."

"That's not necessary," Geoff said, quietly.

Lisa could hear a faint rustling as the girl apparently tied Geoff up. After that, it sounded as if the other man bound her as well.

"I'll be back," the man said.

"You do that," said Geoff. "And you be sure to kill him."

Lisa moaned, holding back her scream.

During the past two days, she had cried and begged whenever they brought her up to the bathroom. They thought she was completely broken. Sometimes she thought she was too.

From her waistband she took the shard of glass she had managed to break off of the juice bottle on the two bolts the night before last. It was about five inches long and very sharp. She made a simple handle now by wrapping her kerchief around the wide end.

She figured it was good for one cut before it snapped.

———————————————————————

Geoff shook his head in disgust. He had expected something like this from Jammer—he had been watching him carefully as soon as he realized the man had taken the revolver from Geoff's bag. He pulled at the ropes binding his hands to his chair and said, "Honey, back over here. I've got a knife in my back right pocket. You should be able to reach it."

She could. It took them fifteen or so minutes all told, and a few nicks on Geoff's hands. But he was free. He quickly let her go.

"What are we going to do?"

"If the guy wants to go in point, I'll let him. But I'm going to make sure he doesn't screw it up."

"What about her?" Carly gestured to the freezer.

Geoff bent down and flipped on the timer for the water pump.

"You don't have to do a thing." He kicked the side of the freezer and said, "Listen up in there. We're going to find out if Steve will come through for you. He's got two hours."

"Please," Lisa said. Her voice was so clear, so controlled. Like her old self, not what he had been hearing for the past couple of days. It surprised him. "Geoff, don't do this. Open this thing and look at me if you're going to kill me."

He was interested for a moment, but shook it off. To Carly, he said, "Show me how you've cleaned." He walked around the small house with her and saw that she had scrubbed virtually every inch of the place. All their belongings were packed into two suitcases. He brushed her hair back and kissed her lightly on the lips before saying, "You be ready when I get back. I want you wearing the dress and the wig."

"What about her?"

"She's not your responsibility anymore. Mine either."

"Is she going to live?" Carly looked troubled, but he could see she wanted to believe him. She didn't want to think of herself as a murderer. She didn't want to think of him that way either. He had promised never to turn her over to Raul, and so she had good reason to pray that his word was true.

So he told her the truth, "I have no idea if she's going to make it or not. That's entirely up to her husband."

CHAPTER 24

Lisa heard the door slam. She peered through an air hole, and saw the girl standing alone in the kitchen.

Lisa didn't have to fake the shivery sound in her voice when she said, "This water is getting cold already. Please, if you can't let me out, at least give me a blanket."

The girl turned her way, but didn't answer.

Lisa put the piece of glass between her knees and carefully began to run the rope up and down the sharp edge.

"*Please,*" she repeated.

"Just shut up and leave me alone," the girl said.

———————————

Geoff walked a quarter mile to the side street where he had left the Plymouth he had stolen earlier that day. He slid behind the wheel and touched the two bare wires together, sparks flying. It was a big old car, equipped with a huge V-8. Just a tap on the accelerator slammed him back into the seat.

He headed out onto the expressway north, toward Steve's marina.

As a teenager, Geoff had learned to hot-wire cars one summer from a friend who later landed in reform school. Back then, Geoff had given up joyrides as too small a thrill for the risk of prison time. Yet it was now a source of genuine pleasure, the way he kept finding himself capable of handling each situation that arose. It was as if he had acquired skills all his life that were leading him to this kind of challenge.

Not that he was giving himself such high marks for the situation with Jammer. Geoff had expected trouble, but thought it would come after they had the money in hand. He had to give the pimp some limited credit—after all, Jammer did get the drop on him.

But the joke was still on the Jammer. Geoff knew the pickup would not be straightforward.

That morning, Geoff had called Steve from a phone booth across the river. He had kept the binoculars trained on the marina to see if there was any activity after his call, any sign of police. And so he had seen Steve meet a man in a truck. The two of them carried bags down to the boat.

Geoff had been ready to drive back to the house and drown Lisa right then. But he had seen the sign on the door of the truck, ALEX MARTIN SALVAGE, and the name had seemed familiar. Then he remembered Harrison, a million years back, telling him at the top of the rockface that Steve's only friend locally was some guy who worked in salvage. And the name sounded right.

Geoff had given that some thought and decided he liked it. He had two people to help him out, so if Steve wanted to bring a buddy into the game, that was fair. As long as the buddy wasn't afraid to play hardball.

In the van, Jammer had been watching the boat through his binoculars now for about a half hour—unwittingly doing what Geoff had done most of the day, from virtually the same spot.

Jammer had decided against all of the fancy stuff with the phone booths, sending the guy from place to place. That never worked in the movies, and it seemed like a lot of trouble: figuring out a route, getting all the numbers, timing the whole thing. Besides, Jammer felt he could sniff out cops—and he didn't smell any now. He figured Geoff had scared the guy enough, and "Keep it simple, stupid" was the one thing Geoff knew nothing about. The more Jammer worked it over in his head, the more he felt the best thing to do was put a stocking over his face and walk straight down to the boat.

The fact was, even though Jammer wouldn't be holding on to it for long, he was really looking forward to putting his hands on all that cash.

He told himself it was safe to pick up the money. He told himself that it was one in the morning, that everyone was asleep. Let the guy think there was a chance Jammer would be returning the girl and then take the money, pop him in the head, and drive away before anyone figured out that what they heard was not the sound of a car backfiring.

Jammer started the van and headed over the bridge, ready to do just that.

Braced against the cross-ties just under the bridge, Alex felt the rumble of the passing vehicles overhead as he sighted his scope on *The Sea Tern* once again. From his vantage point, he had a clear view of the parking lot, the whole length of the dock up to Steve's boat, and a clear shot for all of the *Sea Tern*'s foredeck. The restaurant was now closed and the dock had been empty of people for almost a half hour.

Below him, the Blue Water 25 was tied up to a piling. He had a coil of Steve's climbing rope beside him so he could rappel down immediately if Geoff approached by water.

Alex yawned. He wasn't exactly tired, but he remembered the feeling from his tour in Vietnam: It was the effects of balancing fear and boredom in equal measures.

He and Steve had been waiting all day long. Logic dictated that whatever was going to happen would happen soon, under the cover of night. Assuming the bastard hadn't already killed Lisa. Alex couldn't imagine what he would do or say to Steve if the night passed without any hint that she was still alive.

Alex yawned again and rubbed his eyes. He rolled his shoulders and tried to relax. After a moment, he swept the parking lot again with his scope, and realized a van had entered without his noticing. The van pulled into a parking place and a tall man got out.

"See the van?" Alex whispered into his walkie-talkie.

"Got it," Steve answered.

The need to yawn evaporated as Alex saw the man pull something down over his head. "Trouble coming your way," Alex whispered. He sighted carefully, putting his crosshairs on the man as he stepped onto the dock heading to Steve's boat.

CHAPTER 25

The man had no face.

That's how it appeared to Steve when the man stepped under the dock lights. Instead of features, there was just blankness under the baseball cap. Then Steve realized the guy was wearing a stocking. And that it wasn't Geoff; this man was a good couple of inches taller.

Geoff had never suggested he had partners, and Steve's mind raced with the implications. Did this mean Lisa wasn't being held against a timer? That Geoff was out of it somehow? Or simply that he sent someone in his place—he didn't trust Steve not to bring in the police?

Steve was crouched on the narrow finger dock for the boat across from *The Sea Tern*. The revolver was heavy in his hand.

The guy had an athletic bag hanging over his shoulder. His

hand was inside the bag. When he reached the stern of Steve's boat, he leaned in and said in a hoarse whisper, "Hey, in there. Got something you're going to want to hear." He held up the small tape recorder. It hissed loudly and Lisa's voice came on, sounding shaky and scared: " 'Steve. My kidnapper tells me that you have changed plans on him. He has punished me by turning on the water pump.' "

Steve stepped forward quietly and put the gun on the man's back. "Turn it off."

Startled, the guy began to resist.

Steve shoved him forward, knocking him against the stern of the boat. The recorder snapped off, but Steve had heard enough. He ground the gun barrel into the guy's spine. "Convince me I shouldn't break your back."

The guy went still. "Take it easy, man. We've still got the girl."

Steve reached into the athletic bag and found a revolver. He put it into his belt and said, slowly and clearly, "It's this simple: You take me to her and you can walk away with the money. You don't, and I will shoot off little pieces of you until you do."

Steve draped the backpack with the cash over the man's shoulder. "There's the hundred and fifty thousand."

The guy seemed to regain himself. "You can't fuck with me. She'll drown in that box. My partner will do her if I don't come back."

"You're coming back. I'm going with you."

"Can't do it, man. But you've got my word we'll let her go."

"I already told Geoff that's not good enough."

The guy drew breath in sharply and twisted his head around. "You know his name?"

"Of course."

"You recognized his voice?"

Steve was puzzled. "I recognized him. He came right down to my boat."

"Without a mask?"

"Is that what he told you?"

"Shit!"

"He's made no attempt to keep his identity from me." Steve knocked the man's hat off and drew the stocking up. "And what's yours?"

The guy whirled suddenly, knocking Steve's gun hand aside while reaching for the revolver in his belt. Steve twisted away, clasping the kidnapper's gun to his waist. The guy shoved him back abruptly and took off down the dock, running.

Grabbing the walkie-talkie, Steve whispered urgently, "Don't shoot him, Alex. Follow him."

The kidnapper sprinted.

Steve jogged after him and was in the rental car by the time Alex's voice came over the walkie-talkie again. "I'm behind him. He just crossed the bridge, heading toward Ninety-three south."

Across the river, Geoff shook his head. He was disgusted with Jammer. He had just raced over the bridge and run a red light.

Panicked.

Geoff watched the guy under the bridge climb up, apparently using a rope ladder. He took off after Jammer in his pickup truck. Minutes later, a Chevy crossed over the bridge as well. Geoff recognized Steve's profile.

"Wagon train," Geoff said, aloud. He swung the Plymouth behind.

The guy is all over the road," Alex said over Steve's walkie-talkie. "He's scared."

"Are you ready for me to come up?"

"No. I'm going to switch on my plow lights now and turn off the headlights. That should look different enough in his mirror for now."

"I want to stop him before he goes into a house or building. He's got the money, it wouldn't take him but a minute to go in and kill her."

"I know, buddy. I know."

A big car swept up beside Steve and his stomach clenched. He took a quick look over. It was impossible to see through the darkened windows. He exchanged the walkie-talkie for the gun quickly. But when the car continued on, doing about eighty, he picked it up again and said, "A big Plymouth just blew by. Watch out for that."

Alex saw the car in his mirror and he laid the rifle across his legs so that the barrel rested just on the edge of the open window. Not the best arrangement, but the best he could do.

The car slipped by him as well and raced on past the two cars Alex had kept between him and the van. A moment later, the car passed the van, too.

Alex found he had been holding his breath.

Just another speeder, late at night.

Alex's hands were slippery on the wheel, and he fought the urge to simply pull over and stop this insanity—he was too old and too smart to be playing with guns.

Equally strong was the urge to chase that van down right then and try to force that bastard to tell him where Lisa was being held.

Alex made himself take a deep breath and exhale. He told himself that Lisa's life depended upon how he and Steve handled themselves.

A few minutes later, the van took the exit for North Quincy.

Lisa finally heard the break in the girl's voice. "Listen, it won't be that much longer. Your guy will come through with the money, so just hold out awhile longer."

Lisa wondered if the girl believed that. She said, "It's just that I'm so cold."

"I can't."

"You *can*. It was bad enough before, but now he's put this water in here and I'm freezing. You've got a key. *Please* get me a blanket."

The girl swore.

Lisa bit her tongue, letting the silence grow.

A few moments later, she heard the angry click of the girl's heels on the linoleum and a zipper being opened.

Lisa massaged her right arm vigorously, hoping that neither her cramped muscles nor any squeamishness would keep her from doing what had to be done.

Jammer was in a fever. He tromped on the gas once off the highway and took a hard right, looped around, and then headed off along the river's edge. He had screwed up, no doubt about it. The scared corporate type Geoff had described didn't fit with the Steve Dern that Jammer had run into. And Dern knew Geoff's name, and Geoff knew Jammer's.

It'd been a mistake trusting Geoff for even a second.

But, the way Jammer was looking at it, he could still come out of it just fine. He had managed to get away with the hundred and fifty thousand. Not bad, seeing as Dern was holding the gun on him.

Now all Jammer had to do was close things out with Geoff and turn Carly over to Raul. As for Lisa, even though she hadn't seen his face, he figured the safest thing was to put her down, too.

"You can do it," he said into the empty van.

He figured there was a good chance Geoff had broken free of his ropes. Since Jammer no longer had the revolver, he would have to be ready when he went into the house. But as pumped up as Jammer was, he felt he could take on Geoff in a hand-to-hand fight, now that he knew what to expect. Especially if he took along a little advantage.

~And that he had.

Steve hit the exit ramp and found the hard right and marina sign that Alex had mentioned. He floored the Chevy, making the tires scream. Moonlight glinted on the water up ahead. There were marshlands just before it, scrubby lots to the right. A warehouse to his left, an occasional house.

Up ahead, he saw Alex's truck just turn the corner. The walkie-talkie crackled and Alex said, "Okay, he's pulling in behind a gray house. There's a mailbox, Eighty Shore Road."

As Jammer swung the car into the driveway behind the house, he noticed that the kitchen light was still on; all of the others were dark. Just the way he had left the place.

Jammer ran his hand down his chest and left arm, feeling the muscle, the coiled strength. He rested his hand on his belt.

The belt buckle specifically. Junior. He'd had it custom made. A larger-than-fashionable buckle, smoothly contoured with rounded edges. It fit nicely in his palm—and when he pulled the buckle away a four-inch blade gleamed. The blade was curved into a shallow hook, razor sharp on both edges. The way the buckle fit in his palm, the blade stuck out between his fore and index fingers.

So when he punched, he stabbed. And he could slash open a guy's throat without having to change grip.

He grinned, more confident with the steel in his hand. He slid it back into his belt, figured that if Geoff had managed to get himself free from the chair, a little distraction might be called for. Show him the money with his left hand; then do him with his right.

"I'm good with this, Mr. Mann," he whispered. "I'm good enough tonight."

He went into the house, ready to prove it.

Alex heard a woman scream.

He froze.

A quick look in the rearview mirror showed Steve's car about a half mile back, and closing fast.

The woman screamed again.

Alex cast another look in the mirror before grabbing the rifle. He threw the door open and ran up the driveway. He felt stiff and awkward. He knew he had waited too long. That time sitting in the car waiting for Steve might have been only a few seconds, but that's all it would take for the man to kill her.

Alex pounded up the stairs of the old house and kicked the door.

It held.

He kicked it again and this time the wood splintered around the lock as the lights of Steve's car washed over him.

The woman screamed again, her voice loud now that he was in the house. "Lisa!" Alex called.

"Help me!" he heard.

He ran through a dark hallway to the outline of light around a doorway. He kicked the door open and in the sudden harsh light, he saw the red, he saw the blood. It took him a half beat to realize it was one woman stabbing the other. "Hold it!" he cried, bringing the gun up to his shoulder.

And he almost killed her. Almost killed Lisa. He had the gun trained right on her head; he didn't recognize her until she turned his way. He almost killed her because she was the one attacking the other woman.

She screamed, "Alex, behind you, behind you!"

Too late, he turned. Too late, he saw that the man had a blade, a little thing that seemed to grow out of his hand. The man shoved it into Alex's side.

Lisa screamed with him.

Alex stumbled, felt suddenly weak. "Steve."

The man yanked the knife away and punched him in the rib cage with it. He pulled his arm back to do it again and Alex hit him in the face with the gun butt.

That straightened the guy out, made him reel for a second. Alex tasted the blood in the back of his throat. He was badly hurt. Jesus, he knew that. A lung, maybe.

Alex's knees were wobbly, but he brought his strength to bear again and jabbed the guy in the chest, trying to bring the barrel around.

But the guy slapped the gun barrel away and stepped in close.

Alex called out for Steve once more. The effort made him cough blood. He was desperately short of breath.

The guy punched him hard on the shoulder and twice more in his rib cage. While the blows didn't hurt so much as the first time, Alex knew he had taken three more stab wounds. He fell to the floor. He tried to raise the gun, but his arms just weren't working right anymore. The rifle seemed enormously heavy, and he couldn't get a grip with his blood-slick hands. He fumbled with the gun and then dropped it altogether.

"Alex!" Lisa cried, and she came up behind the man. She took him by the hair, that long ponytail of his. She pulled him back and cut at his neck. He howled, and shoved her away. He screamed to the other woman, "Hold her, Carly, hold her!"

Alex saw the other woman do just that. She threw Lisa up against the wall. The guy put his hand to his neck and then looked at the blood on his hand, wonderingly. "That fucking bitch," he said. "I'm going to cut her to pieces."

Alex focused himself. He drew a hideously painful breath and carefully put his hands on the gun and slipped his forefinger inside the trigger guard—and then he lifted that dead weight off the floor.

The big-caliber bullet took off most of his assailant's head.

Alex tried to swing the gun onto the girl, but someone reached over him suddenly and yanked it away.

"Hell of a job," the man said, kneeling beside Alex as he lay dying. "You did one hell of a job."

CHAPTER 26

Steve came to. He was cold and wet, lying on the floor. He groaned, pushed himself up, and realized that he was lying in water.

There was a whining noise, a mechanical sound.

He swayed on his hands and knees. His head ached terribly and he was confused as to where he was and why.

Then he remembered running into the house after Alex, the dark shape that had come just behind him—and the sudden, crashing blow.

And the screams.

The gunshot.

"Lisa!" Steve steadied himself against the wall as he stood. The water flowed down the hallway. He hurried into the lit room, the kitchen. His gun was gone.

"Lisa!"

Blood was splattered on the ceiling and wall. The man Steve had fought down by the boat was lying on the floor, his head a bloody ruin. Steve wouldn't have been able to recognize him, if not for his clothes.

The water.

The water was pouring from a big floor-mounted freezer. An electric pump was rigged up to it and a big padlock was snapped to the hasp. The water was brimming from the top lid. Corks had been plugged into the two holes on the side.

Steve lost it momentarily. A sound came from deep in his chest as he fell to his knees and ripped the pump away. Water pulsed across the floor. He called her name repeatedly, expecting no answer and getting none.

The lock wouldn't give way against his hands. But then he saw a crowbar on the counter. Even in that state, as he ripped the hasp away, he knew Geoff had left the tool so he could find her.

Steve threw the lid open. Water splashed onto his legs, red-tinged water.

He backed away from the horror inside.

It wasn't Lisa.

Alex was crammed into the tiny space. His body shifted as the lid opened. His head broke the surface of the water.

"That's the bad news," Geoff said, behind him. "The good news is Lisa still wants to talk to you even though you showed up late to the party."

Steve whirled, the crowbar raised.

Geoff raised the revolver so that it was at eye level. "It'd be suicide."

Steve hesitated.

"I thought so. You are definitely CEO material. Always thinking. Unlike your poor schmuck of a friend who blew in here and almost saved the day. Alex was his name, right?"

"That's right." Steve's voice was hoarse.

"I was impressed. I told him so, too. Just before he died."

"You knocked me out." Steve was still swaying on his feet. He felt stupid and slow.

Geoff slapped his forehead, mockingly. "I *forgot* to tell him that. He called for you a couple of times. Guess he died thinking you had let him down. My mistake."

Steve tried to shut Geoff's words off. He closed his eyes, briefly, then said, "Where is she?"

Geoff nodded toward the window. "Take a look." He flipped a light switch by the door and a floodlight revealed Lisa and another woman in the backyard. The other woman was aiming a rifle—Alex's gun—at Lisa. The woman's neck and shirt were bloody.

"The junior varsity did real well," Geoff said. "Seems Lisa had a piece of broken glass and managed to cut Carly. Even took on Jammer."

Steve opened the window.

"Keep your voice down," Geoff warned.

Steve ignored him. To Lisa, he called, "Are you hurt?"

The way her face broke, the sudden relief he saw there made tears well in Steve's eyes. He didn't deserve her.

"I thought he'd killed you," Lisa said. She started toward the window.

"Get back!" The girl jabbed Lisa with the rifle; hit her hard in the chest. "Give me a reason, you bitch!"

"Carly was soft on Lisa," Geoff said. "Seems Lisa has been conning us for days. Made us think she was weak. Carly tried to help her out, and Lisa cut her for it. Ugly scar from her ear down. If it had been a little deeper, maybe Lisa would have gotten away."

He looked Steve in the eye. "Now my biggest challenge is to make sure Carly doesn't kill her unless I give the word."

"You want a challenge, put the gun down."

Geoff shook his head. "You're not ready. You were out cold just a few minutes ago."

"Let me worry about that." Steve put the crowbar on the counter.

Geoff kicked Steve in the face. It was a high, fast kick that surprised Steve completely and knocked him off his feet. Geoff got in close and pressed the gun barrel right under his chin. "Listen. Maybe you *do* deserve the big desk at the big company. But in the game of life and death, you just don't seem to be cutting it."

He stood up. "You lost round one. So I'll be taking Lisa with me tonight. Don't give up though—as long as you do what you're told, you're going to get another chance."

Steve was able to cut himself loose within half an hour, which was about how long Geoff had said it would take.

Steve set about cleaning the kitchen.

He washed the blood and brain matter off the walls, having to stop twice to run into the bathroom and vomit.

He moved the rental car half a mile away and walked back. Then he rolled Alex and the other man into the sections of old linoleum that Geoff had told him he would find in the cellar. From there, Steve drove back to Charlestown in Alex's truck and loaded the dive boat onto the trailer. He came back to the house, put both bodies onboard, and found a boat ramp in Hull.

A part of him wanted the police to find him. A part of him desperately wanted to explain why he was covering up a murder— weighting the bodies and dumping them at sea. As the dark waves closed over them, Steve said a brief prayer.

As he closed his eyes just before dawn, lying in his bunk in *The Sea Tern,* he told himself that the part of him that wanted to talk to the police—and to God—would just have to be silent for the time being.

Because Geoff still wanted to play.

CHAPTER 27

You still looking for a hobby?" Bannerman said, as he sat down across from Lazar at the coffee shop on the corner of Columbus and Berkeley. "Something to take your mind off not getting laid?"

Bannerman had taken to doing that lately, attributing Lazar's gloom to a lack of sex. That was fine with Lazar. Maybe there was some truth to it, too. His loneliness was so real it felt like a physical thing, a weight on his chest that sucked the breath and life out of him. Lazar wondered how long it had actually been . . . but then his brain switched like a train track to wondering about Charlotte's sex life.

Eleven months since she had moved out on him. Eleven months since she had become someone he didn't know. Someone who said she wanted different things from life. She wanted to leave social work and go back to school. She couldn't give any more at the woman's shelter; she couldn't worry along with other cop wives; she couldn't worry alone at home another night. She had said she couldn't—and didn't—love him the way she once did.

She had moved in with a girlfriend, saying she needed her space. At least for a trial period: a week or two. "Maybe, I'll be back," she had said, her voice tired. She hadn't looked at him when she said it, but still he hoped.

He had walked around like a zombie for five or six days until he finally gave in to a nasty little suspicion that had been growing in his head like a tumor. That night, he had waited outside her girlfriend's place and then followed Charlotte as she drove into Boston. She had parked just off Columbus Avenue in the South End. It was an area that was undergoing gentrification: meaning poor blacks were being shoved out so the buildings could be gutted and rebuilt for rich whites.

He had never cared one way or the other about being black. He knew he was supposed to, but it wasn't something he really thought about much. But that night he was all wrapped up in a rage that swelled him, made him feel twice his size. And that night he cared as he watched her through the binoculars go up the stairs to this place with an overnight bag. He suddenly knew with absolute certainty that she had been screwing around on him, and he knew the type of guy it would be: some rich white guy who had bought up a string of these places and was turning them over for a fortune.

That's what all this shit is about, Lazar had told himself. Charlotte couldn't stay with him because she had found someone better. Some white guy just trying out a black chick for a change.

He could see how good she still looked, the bounce in her step as she went up the stairs, free from him and going to meet her new man. Lazar saw the button she pushed, and he knew he could find the apartment from there.

He left his service revolver under the car seat and went in after her.

He told himself he was going to talk it out with her. Confront her with words. Make her explain herself and say the things he needed to say. But as he strode up the stairs, he felt the rage about to burst, and knew he was going to be on the wrong side of a domestic for the first time in his life. Lazar had a black belt in karate, and when he kicked in the apartment door the crime scene flashguns were already bursting in his head, displaying the bodies like big broken dolls on the floor.

But instead of finding Charlotte with her man, he found her with two little kids and their mama. They were obviously poor, the woman was probably part of the shelter. Lazar saw that Charlotte's overnight bag held children's clothes and books.

After a moment of incredulous silence, Charlotte simply said, "You followed me? You followed me?"

That had sealed her decision to move out to a new apartment. He had been too disgusted and ashamed of himself to put up an argument, and had stayed away when her brother helped her make the move. And then Lazar kept away. To give her credit, she had never once thrown the incident back at him directly. Listening to her these days, it sounded as if their marriage was just something they had once done together for a short time. She said they really needed to move forward on the divorce. Last week, she had called and told him she was starting to date again. Her tone had been just the slightest bit defensive, letting him know she was being honest and didn't expect to find him pounding down any doors.

"Congratulations," he had said and hung up.

He felt the jealousy surge through him again, starting from his heart out to his arms, his stomach. He could feel it right down through his legs to the soles of his feet; it even flowed from his fingertips and lips onto the coffee mug. He wondered if they had enough soap back in the kitchen to clean it off. He was a goddamn health hazard. Customer after customer coming in and being infected by the jealousy in him, a middle-aged, black cop. Mooning over his wife behind a face as impassive as that of a statue.

"What are you glowering about?" Bannerman said.

Lazar realized he had been drifting. "My effect on people," he said.

"Huh. Well maybe this will take your mind off Charlotte." Bannerman held out a manila folder.

"Screw you," Lazar said without any heat. "What is that?"

Bannerman pulled the folder back against his chest. "You're not going to waste our time, right? I'm only giving you this because you'd pound me if you found out I knew and didn't tell you."

"Give."

Bannerman handed the file over.

Lazar read it and shrugged. "Ball's van parked over at that garage near the Wang Center. Back window gone, bullet in the dashboard. Big deal."

"That's what I say." Bannerman called for a cup of coffee. "Waste of time."

"Not a line on Geoff Mann when I ran his name. Or on the chick, Carly Duncan. That was a surprise—there weren't any busts for soliciting."

"Yeah." Bannerman looked mildly curious, then turned back to his menu. "She was a knockout, though. Maybe Jammer just has her out on calls."

Lazar swallowed the rest of his coffee and snapped his fingers at the waitress. "Ginny, make Bannerman's coffee to go."

Bannerman protested. "Hey! I was planning on pancakes."

Lazar had to grin, amazed at how a little distraction could change his mood. Maybe he would find some woman for himself, get on with *his* life too. "Bannerman, you're looking a little fat these days. So come on, before their shift changes. I want to see if the attendants can place Jammer at the garage that night."

"Yeah, sure. That's going to happen. About a thousand people have been in and out since then."

"Damn right. Leave the pancakes before another thousand go through today." Lazar breathed in the warm smells of the diner as they walked up to the counter, glad to be back with himself, if only for a while.

Bannerman had called it.

The three attendants had looked at Lazar as if he were an idiot. Didn't he know how many people flowed through there every day?

"What now?" Bannerman asked, as they left the garage.

"Okay, so we lie to Jammer. Tell him he's been identified getting out of the van that night," Lazar said. "See what he says to that."

Darlene opened the door. "Haven't seen him."

"How about the other girl, your roommate," Lazar said. "Carly, isn't it?"

Over Darlene's shoulder, the apartment looked a mess: pizza boxes and Chinese food takeout cartons in the kitchen area. A porno movie was playing on the television and a man with a big white belly wearing just his underwear came up behind her and said, "Just who the fuck are you? She's on my dime."

Lazar showed his badge. "Think there's some time for us on that dime?"

The man mumbled, "No problem," and hurried away.

"He's just a friend," Darlene said.

Bannerman made a face and shuddered. "Ugly friends, Darlene."

Darlene smiled slightly. "You know."

"So where's Jammer?"

"Haven't seen him, honest to God. Or Carly. Couple, three days, anyhow. Maybe they took a trip. Try another time, okay?" She started to ease the door shut.

Lazar put his foot in the door. "Who's the blond asshole? What is he to Jammer and Carly?"

"Huh?" She looked back over her shoulder.

"Not the pus gut," Bannerman said, disgustedly. *"His* hair is greasy black. We're talking about Geoff Mann."

She shook her head. "I never had the pleasure, honest."

Lazar stared at her and saw only emptiness in her eyes. The little trace of humor he had seen in her before had vanished. He took his foot from the door. On the way down the stairs, Bannerman mimicked her, " 'Honest.' How many times a day do we hear that?"

"Let's go ask Mann himself. Let's see if he says it the same way."

"Why do you care? You've got two days coming to us, why do you want to screw around with this shit now?"

Because I don't want to go home to my empty house was what Lazar thought. What he said was "This is a rich kid. If we find out he's involved in murdering Ball, think how the papers will snatch that up."

"I'm thinking instead how Mann made you look stupid, pulling those bananas out of the bag. I'm thinking maybe you just hate having a wiseass get away with something."

"Could be. But think of it this way: a sexy photo of that Carly, a headline about a handsome rich guy getting involved in murder, hookers. Would have gotten away with it if two smart cops didn't track him down . . . it's good stuff."

Bannerman grinned, knowing Lazar was playing with him.

"Maybe you've got something there. The stuff promotions are made of."

I don't keep tabs," the super at Geoff's building said. He had a thin face and a shock of gray hair even though he looked to be only in his early forties. They were standing on the front steps of the red brick building.

"What can you tell us about him?"

"Nothing." He held his thumb in a book and was obviously impatient. "These are nice apartments. Privacy is one of the things you get with the rent."

Lazar and Bannerman's eyes were now intent upon the man. "He thinks we're wasting his time," Bannerman said. "Don't you hate that, you sit down with a good book and some schmuck shows up at your door trying to sell you something?"

"I hate that," Lazar said.

"I wasn't saying—"

"The thing is, we're not schmucks selling something," Bannerman said. "We're cops asking questions."

"Look, I don't *care*—"

"He doesn't care," Lazar said. "He doesn't care if we waste *our* time, Bannerman. Our time screwing around with him doesn't count."

"I didn't say that."

"Hey, I'm just a dumb cop," Lazar said. "But my hearing is good."

"No, no."

Bannerman said, "I think you're misunderstanding Mr. Calhoun here, Lazar."

"Oh, you got to explain this to me because I'm *black,* is that it, Bannerman? Is that it, Mr. Calhoun?"

"No, of course not." Calhoun looked nervously between the two cops. He edged closer to Bannerman.

"Well, what's so hard here?" Lazar demanded.

Bannerman widened his eyes slightly. "How about it, Mr. Calhoun?"

Calhoun took his finger out of his book and held his palm up. "Okay, let's start over. I know you're busy. It's just that I have a lot to do and I don't know why I have to waste my time on these things if Mr. Mann isn't here to deal with them."

Lazar let his indignant expression fade away. Quietly, he asked, "What are 'these things'?"

"Well, I have no way of knowing if anything was stolen. And maybe it was a friend who took the car, but I don't think so."

"Maybe *who* was a friend?"

"Mann's got a parking space out back and he's got a BMW. Or he had one."

"And somebody picked it up?"

"Yeah. Guy showed up, bold as brass. He had a key, got right in, and took off."

"And Mr. Mann wasn't around to complain?"

"Well, that was just this morning. Mann *could have* been back since the break-in. I left a note and just put a padlock on the door . . . but no, he hasn't been by to ask for the key. So I suppose he hasn't been around."

"The break-in?" Lazar repeated.

Calhoun told them about the man who had run by with the sledgehammer and mask.

"Did you report this?"

The super shrugged and didn't meet their eyes. "Stuff happens. I have no way of knowing if anything was stolen. I called in to his apartment, nothing looked that messed up."

They pressed him for details, but he couldn't come up with much other than he thought the thief was probably white, fairly big.

"And you haven't heard from Mann in how long?" Bannerman asked.

The super looked at the calendar on his watch. "Two days ago."

Lazar said, "Mr. Calhoun, did you go through Mann's apartment, go through all the rooms?"

Calhoun looked indignant. "Of course not. I called out and he didn't come to the door. I simply put on a padlock. He's got to pay for a new lock himself, a real one, and I want him to select the kind before I go to the expense and trouble myself."

Bannerman and Lazar exchanged glances. "Would you have a key to that padlock, Mr. Calhoun?"

Calhoun brought them up to the third-floor apartment reluctantly.

"I mean it," Bannerman said. "We can go away. We've got nothing definite saying the guy is in trouble. But really, you should have looked in the bedroom. What if the guy bashed in Mann's head with that sledgehammer?"

"Oh, I doubt that."

"Uh-huh. But look, if you smell anything really bad, you know, like when a mouse or squirrel gets stuck in the walls? Well, maybe you could just look in then, and give us a call."

"Yeah, yeah," Calhoun said. He unsnapped the padlock and stepped back. "Just stick your head in and if he's not there, you've got to leave unless you get a warrant, right?"

"Right," Lazar said.

Bannerman made a face. "Holy shit. Smell that, willya?"

Calhoun backed further off, looking a little green.

The two cops hurried into the apartment. "Jesus, is it in here?" Lazar said.

"I don't smell anything," Calhoun said from the doorway.

Lazar and Bannerman took in the place fast. It was nice, with high ceilings, light wood furniture in the foyer, a clean, well-laid-out kitchen.

Bannerman whistled, looking into the living room.

"Christ," Lazar said, opening the bedroom door.

Photos of the man were all over the place. Sports scenes, enlargements of Geoff Mann caught at the height of action: skiing off the edge of a rocky cliff, fifty feet in the air; doing a high jump; boxing; motorcycle racing; running for a touchdown; pole vaulting, the pole bent way back; hang gliding; windsurfing; sailing; parachuting . . . the detectives laughed out loud, playing the game of finding the suspect in every photo.

And the sports equipment: skis, fencing gear, a compound bow and hunting arrows, a punching bag, boxing gloves, two bicycles, tennis rackets, a weight set, rock climbing rope . . .

"Look at this," Lazar said. A kayak hung from the ceiling in the bedroom.

Bannerman waved him back to the living room. "Check this out."

An ice axe was imbedded in the wall. Plaster was strewn about the floor. "Temper, temper," Lazar said.

"Maybe the guy with the sledgehammer," Bannerman said.

A huge television sat in the middle of the living room, and there were at least a hundred videocassettes in the rack.

"Stroke stuff?" Lazar asked.

Bannerman looked at the titles. "No. Action flicks: *Eiger Sanction, Treasure of the Sierra Madre, Raiders of the Lost Ark, Pulp Fiction.*"

Calhoun stepped into the room. "There's no smell here. What are you two talking about?"

"Hope you got a damage deposit," Lazar said, jerking his thumb at the ice axe, as he and Bannerman brushed by the super on the way to the bedroom.

Bannerman opened the closet. "Hey, Lazar, check this out." He held up a white karate uniform, a gi. Around the coat hook hung a black belt. He reached in and pulled out a nunchaku, two pieces of hard wood attached by a thin chain. He threw it over to Lazar.

"That's Mr. Man's property," Calhoun snapped.

Lazar whipped the nunchaku over his shoulder. The handle slapped into his palm, and then he made it whistle through a fast backhand; snapped it around his back and caught it behind his ear before tossing it back to Bannerman.

"Yeah, you've still got it," Bannerman said. He gestured to the room, the equipment, the black belt. "But this boy is in some kind of shape."

Over the phone, Lazar was bounced through the personnel office at Jansten Enterprises until finally a Ms. Barry told them that "Geoff Mann is no longer employed by the company." She told him Mann's starting and ending employment dates and said that it was company policy to reveal no more.

"He left last week," Lazar said to Bannerman. "Don't know if he was fired or quit."

"Getting more interesting," Bannerman said.

So they went to Jansten Enterprises themselves and showed the receptionist their badges. Bannerman said, "We would like to speak to the president."

"Are you sure you don't want Security?"

"We're sure," Lazar said, cheerfully. "Tell him it's in regard to a former employee, Geoff Mann."

Her eyes widened slightly. "The acting president is Mr. Dern. I'll call to see if he is in."

She said into the phone. "Monica, the police are here to see Mr. Dern about Geoff Mann."

After a few minutes, a cool-looking woman wearing white linen came out and walked them back to the executive offices. "Mr. Dern isn't in," the secretary said. "However, I talked with Mr. Jansten, and he agreed to meet with you." She was quiet and professional, with short blond hair. They walked past a glassed-in conference room with a huge boardroom table, big enough for thirty people. Lazar found himself straightening his tie, and when he looked over at Bannerman, his partner winked. But he looked nervous, too.

Jansten's secretary was a tougher sort and looked at both cops critically as she spoke into the intercom. "They're here," she said.

As they walked into Jansten's office, Lazar heard her speak crisply to the other secretary. "Monica, Mr. Jansten is only in a few hours a day now, and we've *got* to nail down some of these dates."

"I know, but Steve's been busy, and hasn't returned my calls—"

"Well, where *is* he?" the older woman asked.

Then Jansten waved them to the chairs. He was a powerful-looking old man with ruddy skin. "What's Mann done now?" he boomed.

But as Lazar got closer, he noticed the weariness around Jansten's eyes. The old man sat down heavily after shaking hands with both detectives.

Lazar began. "Mr. Jansten, would you know if Mr. Mann's car was leased?"

"It was," Jansten said. "In fact, I had them make a BMW available to him as sort of a 'welcome to Boston' gift."

"Would you know if it has been repossessed?"

"I don't. But it should have been by now if people are doing their jobs right. If Mann has a problem with that, he can talk with our attorneys. Did he send you concerning *that?*"

"No, he didn't send us. Just a routine question."

"Ah. The famous 'routine question.' What's he done?"

"He may be a witness to something we're investigating," Lazar said, smiling. "The TV shows have made the routine question phrase a problem, but we really do have them sometimes."

"All too often," Bannerman said, ruefully. "Anyhow, we haven't been able to get in touch with him."

"Have you been to his apartment?"

"Yeah. He's not there."

"Then how can I help you?"

"Do you know how we can get in touch with his family?"

"Maybe it's in his personnel file. Give me your card, I'll have it couriered over to you this afternoon." A smile touched Jansten's lips. "It would be pretty interesting to know what kind of family he had. Met one of his girlfriends once, beautiful young girl out in San Francisco. Spent some fund-raiser dinner whispering in my ear, ingratiating herself for his benefit. Kelly. Don't know her last name. She said his parents died when he was young. Grew up with his grandparents. I would have figured wolves myself."

"An aggressive guy?"

"Certainly. I encourage that around here."

"So did he quit or did you let him go?"

Jansten hesitated the barest instant, his eyes momentarily blank. Lazar read the look: He saw it every day. Jansten wanted to tell his story, but he wanted to come out clean himself.

He told them about the rock climb, about Harrison's fall, and how Dern's wife had slapped Geoff. "I thought he was going to attack her."

"Jesus," Bannerman said. "Sounds violent at the upper echelons of American business."

Jansten laughed. "You've got no idea, young man."

"Is that why you fired Mann?" Lazar asked.

"Partially. That he would try such a stunt proved he wasn't ready for the role. You probably know that he's a sports nut. Could've been a pro athlete, the sport of his choosing. That's a fine background for a salesman, but top executives need to demonstrate a little more balance. He's made some money for us, though, no doubt about that."

"But you let him go anyhow."

"Sure. It was him or Dern. And Dern has the brains, the balls, and the maturity to make this company thrive. Mann's got the first two attributes, but when it's all said and done, he's a nut."

"You think Mann saw it that way? Him or Dern?"

Jansten smiled, tiredly. "If Geoff knows anything, he knows who he has to beat."

"Could we speak to Mr. Dern?"

"Talk to his secretary, have her set something up. When you see him tell him that I'm looking for him myself."

CHAPTER 28

Just after three, Steve walked into a striptease bar in the Combat Zone.

He watched a surprisingly pretty young woman take her clothes off onstage before a hooker came up behind him and pressed herself against his back. "Like what you see?" she said into his ear. She put her arms around his waist as if they were old friends.

He nodded.

"Hard not to, isn't it?" She looked up at the other woman and slid her hand along his leg. She hesitated, perhaps seeing some resistance in his face. She drew away. "Are you a cop?"

"Just a guy looking to get laid," he said.

God help me, he thought.

She laughed. "Guess that's clear. Sure, let's go."

He followed her onto the street and turned up toward Chinatown. Steve was aware of the way it looked, following this woman with jet black hair and a tight pink miniskirt down the street. On one level it embarrassed him. But mostly he was impatient with the wasted time.

She said, "You got some cash, honey, for the man? We get there, he's going to want thirty for the room." She said, with studied casualness, "I'm going to want double that, unless you want something special. Just say it if you do."

Once in the apartment building, a tough wiry-looking man wearing jeans and black T-shirt drifted out of the lower-floor unit and looked Steve over carefully. He snapped his fingers. "Rent's due."

Steve paid, and followed the hooker up the stairs. She was even more overtly provocative, swinging her hips and looking back at him, saying, "This is gonna be so good."

He couldn't help but wonder if anyone ever really believed her.

The room was musty smelling, with cracked plaster walls. It was dominated by a huge platform bed. She slid the window open, smiled blankly at him, then started to pull the tube top off. He put his hand on hers and said, "Wait. Let me tell you what I want."

She nodded, warily.

"I want to buy a handgun."

Her eyebrows rose. "Yeah?"

Steve gave her a hundred dollars. "That's for the sex we didn't have, plus a bonus. I'll give you another hundred when you hook me up with whoever has one to sell. I'm looking for a revolver, a thirty-eight or three-fifty-seven."

She sighed. "How about we just keep it simple and fuck? You look like a nice guy, what do you need a gun for?"

"Indulge me."

She took a piece of chewing gum from her purse and looked at him appraisingly as she peeled the wrapper. "I thought you were a little different from the average guy I see around here. You sure you're not a cop?"

"Positive."

"Lift your shirt." She felt along his chest and back, apparently looking for a wire. She then asked him to stand, and she checked him out thoroughly and perfunctorily. All her flirtatious behavior was gone. "All right. I know a guy. I don't want Tommy downstairs to know I'm doing this, okay?" So wait here with me a few more minutes, which is about all it takes usually, then walk down past him with a guilty look on your face and go back to the bar. I'll call this guy, see if he can meet you."

She put the hundred in her purse. "Got to admit, this is easier."

An hour, and three dancers later, she slid up beside Steve at the bar. She ran her hands over him again, checking him out. She kissed him loudly on the cheek and whispered, "Got something for me?"

She held his hand as she walked him to one of the tables in the back, where the lights were even lower. A middle-aged man with a fringe of gray hair sat looking at the girl onstage. He ignored Steve and said to the hooker, "You know the chick on the runway, Jenny?"

"Sure. You like Chastity?"

He laughed. "That her name?"

"Yeah. Hey, I'll introduce you to her." The woman grinned and held both of Steve's hands in hers as he palmed her the hundred. "It's my new sideline. You two should talk."

"I should, huh? How well you know this guy?"

"Well enough. Twice now, I checked, and he's clean as a

whistle." She bumped her hip against Steve, making a joke of it.

"Huh." The guy pointed to the chair beside him, his eyes still intent on the dancer. "We'll talk once I can concentrate."

Steve sat down and Jenny sauntered away. The gun dealer looked like an aging hippie: His gray hair was long on the sides and he wore wire-rim glasses and a Grateful Dead T-shirt. Steve ordered himself another beer and sipped it until the dancer left the stage wearing only a cowboy hat.

The man turned to him. "Okay, this is how it works. We rent a room, which you pay for, and I'll show you the stuff. You want it, I'm gonna want to see cash right then. You're gonna need five hundred, minimum. I've got some absolutely top-rate pieces here. Don't waste my time if you haven't got that on you now."

"I've got money."

The dealer nodded. "Let's do it."

On the street, the man stopped at a Cadillac convertible and took a big black case from the trunk. They continued on to a hotel that smelled of roach powder. The registration clerk was protected by Plexiglas.

The dealer rapped on the window. "One of your finest."

"You got it, Ed."

Upstairs, he spread the weapons out on the bed. "Okay, you got your automatics. Nice Beretta there, that's a nine-millimeter, fifteen-shot magazine. This Glock's got a seventeen-shot. Or that Colt, that's a thirty-eight with a seven-shot." His glasses winked as he looked at Steve. "Don't know what sort of application you have in mind."

Steve didn't answer and Ed continued. "An auto's fast, but you've got those shells ejecting. You're gonna want to pick them up later. That might be a drag. I got a silencer for the Colt if you want. This Uzi I modified myself so it's fully automatic. Pull the trigger, it'll squirt enough lead to take all your troubles away. Again, you're gonna have a ton of shells strewn about."

He threw a few revolvers on the bed. "If that's a problem, these will solve it, but you can't use a silencer. This Colt King Cobra's got a nice short barrel. It's a three-fifty-seven, six-shot. Or if you're not worried about concealment, this Smith and Wesson forty-five with the long barrel will take care of big game." He took out a small gun that fit in his palm. "Two-shot American Derringer twenty-two, good for close work." He swept his hand across the bed with obvious pride. The room smelled of gun oil. "What's your pleasure?"

Steve hefted the guns and chose the Colt revolver and the der-ringer. He paid for them and two boxes of ammunition for each.

"How do I get in touch with you if I want something else?"

The dealer raised his eyebrows. "Just what are you into?" He went on, clearly not expecting an answer. "You want me, just call the front desk here and leave a number for Ed from . . . Mr. Grim. That's what I'll call you. I can get you rifles, military weapons. You need plastic explosives, I can get C-4. I can get you detona-tors, dynamite, hand grenades. If it's in the armament business, I can get it. I've got access to military, police, and a bunch of wacko private parties you wouldn't believe." He put Steve's guns into a heavy paper bag and handed them over. "Buddy, you just made an excellent purchase." He fanned the cash Steve had given him. "And I'm going to get to know that Chastity better. Life is good."

There was a heavyset black man sitting in the cockpit of Steve's boat when he returned. His stomach tightened and he thought, *Geoff's got a new partner.*

The Colt was loaded and Steve shifted the paper bag to his left hip so he could draw the .357 with his right hand if the guy started anything.

Steve said, "What are you doing on my boat?"

The man stood up. "Mr. Dern?"

"That's right."

"I'm Detective Lazar." He showed a badge. "I've been waiting for you. I'd like to ask you some questions about Geoff Mann."

CHAPTER 29

What a long day, Geoff thought. It was just after six in the evening. He had been driving around for so long, it felt as if a drill bit were spinning between his shoulder blades. Just driving up and down the state highways, killing time. The van stank of coffee, take-out food, and sweat.

He had the van jammed way back behind a hedge. The house and driveway were visible through the brush. The place was secluded, private. Something he had noticed the first time he was there. Back then, it had been a mere detail.

A bedroom for him alone would be nice, he thought. But he knew he would have to watch Carly. Make sure she didn't hurt Lisa. Geoff knew Carly wanted him to tell her it was all right, that he didn't care about the scar.

But he did.

He winced whenever he looked at her.

Although he was proud of the way she had fought, the way she held on to Lisa, he found himself thinking more and more about how Lisa had fooled them. The way she had fought Carly and Jammer.

Damned impressive.

He looked back. Lisa was staring at him, murder in her eyes. He couldn't blame her. Tape over her mouth, hands bound. She was back in the shit again.

"Hey, a shower for both of you," he said.

"For her?" Carly asked.

Geoff smiled to himself. She was such a kid. For *her too, daddy?*

Jansten's car turned into the driveway. The old man was alone.

"For everybody." Geoff put on a baseball cap and pulled the brim low. "Right after he turns off his alarm system."

When Jansten opened the front door, his face was already cast in an expression of impatience. "What?" he said, before recognizing Geoff.

Geoff raised the gun.

Jansten reacted fast for an old man. He tried to shove the door closed, but Geoff pushed his way into the foyer.

"What the hell are you doing!"

Geoff put the gun to Jansten's forehead.

Jansten blanched, but his voice was strong and contemptuous. "Get the hell out of my house."

"No boardroom here, Jansten. Just me and my gun."

"Get out!"

Geoff punched him once just under the rib cage. The blow knocked the breath out of Jansten. Geoff waited, saying nothing, as Jansten's face turned bright red and he gasped for breath. Geoff thought of Raul, peering at Jammer. Geoff felt something close to puzzlement. Was this what he had become?

Finally the old man said, "I don't know what you've done—I didn't tell them anything."

"Tell who?"

"I had nothing to tell them."

"Who?" Geoff prodded him with the gun.

"The police."

"What police?"

Jansten looked confused and frightened, although he was trying to hide it. He shook his head.

Geoff cuffed him with an open palm. "Who? What did they want?"

"Two detectives."

"A black guy and a white guy?"

Jansten nodded as he covered the side of his face with his hand. "They came to the office this morning, wouldn't tell me why. They just said it was routine. I just told them you didn't work for us anymore."

Geoff's mouth was dry. Those two cops.

He returned to Jansten. The man was looking at him with bright, shrewd eyes. Trying to figure out just how much trouble he was in.

Jansten said, slowly, "I don't know what you've gotten yourself into, and I don't want to know. If you need cash, I can probably scare up a thousand or so dollars here and then you should just go. I won't pursue this because I'll know that you could always come back. I won't tell a soul."

Geoff said, "Are you expecting company tonight or tomorrow? A cleaning lady?"

Geoff saw the old man thinking so he shoved him hard against the wall. "Who?" he shouted. "Right now, who?"

Jansten shook his head, apparently too frightened to lie. "No one."

Geoff shoved Jansten to the phone. "You're going to leave a message with the service that your secretary is to cancel all your appointments for the next two days and to have no one disturb you with phone calls. That you're not feeling well and you need the rest."

Jansten tapped out the number with a shaking hand. Geoff listened in, his ear next to the receiver. Jansten's voice had a quavery sound and the woman taking the message said, comfortingly, "You sure don't sound good, Mr. Jansten. You should go right to bed and take it easy."

"Good idea," Geoff said, after hanging up the phone. "Let's go upstairs."

Geoff left Jansten's body beside the bed.

In the hallway, Geoff caught sight of himself in the mirror and it pulled him up short. His hair was dank with sweat, and blood trickled from his temple where Jansten had gouged him.

Geoff felt tired all of the sudden.

Killing the old man had been so different from stabbing Jammer's cousin. Not that the old man hadn't given him a good run.

He had.

The old man had looked at him close and said, "Don't take what little I've got left."

Geoff had glanced away, feeling something like sympathy, at least for the moment.

And hope had sprung into Jansten's eyes and he had turned away fast, saying, "Let me get you that cash. I'll get you the cash and you can go and that's it."

"Stay here," Geoff had said, but the old guy had already made it around the corner into his bedroom, talking fast about how he kept close to a thousand bucks in the house for emergencies and if this wasn't one, he damn well didn't know what qualified. His voice was still quavering, but he was trying to hold it together, still talking even when Geoff strode in after him saying, "I don't need your goddamn money."

The old man opened his dresser drawer and came out with a gun.

He was bringing it to bear when Geoff nailed him. Two shots, one under his arm, one in the throat. The old guy dropped his gun, but still kept coming. Managed to claw Geoff in the temple before Geoff clubbed him to the floor.

Now Geoff felt ill.

He peered closely in the mirror. Was he crazy?

As much as he tried to justify killing Jansten, he couldn't find a good enough explanation. He told himself Jansten had pushed him into it, but he knew that wasn't true. He told himself he needed the use of the house. He told himself he owed Jansten some payback for humiliating him in front of the others.

But none of it stacked up. Whereas killing Ball had exhilarated him, Jansten had only his brains and guile to pit against Geoff. Physically, he had been no match.

Black despair seeped through Geoff, feeling very much like shame. Jansten had been so frail in comparison. This wasn't the way Geoff wanted to see himself.

And now the police were involved. They would be after him in earnest once Jansten disappeared. Geoff had not been overly worried before when the two detectives had taken his name up in Jammer's apartment because they would have no way to tie him in to Ball's death once Jammer was dead. And Geoff had intended to leave Jansen's house so it would look as if Jansten had surprised a burglar. Geoff had figured the Sea Crest police and Boston police wouldn't connect a robbery and murder with a mugging death in Roxbury.

But now that the Boston police had already interviewed

Jansten, his murder would definitely send them back to the subject of the interview, Geoff Mann.

Geoff considered leaving the state right then. He wasn't afraid exactly, certainly not of getting hurt or killed. And capital punishment held no terrors. But prison, that did scare him. Years in a little cell, the drab, mundane existence . . .

The thought of a cell squeezed his heart.

Having *nothing to do.* Three steps across the room to the bars, then back again to the cement walls.

The boredom would suck him dry.

Geoff hugged himself now, the wave of despair giving way to the soft gray of depression. With unsettling clarity, he saw himself as nothing more than a brutal killer. A kidnapper and killer.

Lisa.

He felt a flicker of hope. He hadn't killed her yet. Maybe he wouldn't.

He had to admire her. She had managed to keep her head. Conned them day after day. It made him respect her and feel a shade weaker himself.

But more than anything, the thought of her made him relax a little. Like waking from a bad dream and realizing he was still in control. Maybe he would give her that chance she had been asking for. Not a good chance, but a chance.

That made him feel better.

For a few seconds, he even envisioned Lisa as his new partner. Now that he had seen her strength, he found himself making the comparisons between her and Carly. Lisa was not only closer to him in age, she was clearly more sophisticated, more appropriate for a man like him. And a beauty in her own right . . .

Abruptly, he pushed away those thoughts. He *was* crazy if he thought she would ever love him after what he had done. And Carly would do just fine.

Better than fine. She seemed to love him no matter what . . . he could put it down to her youth, her naïveté. She wasn't stupid; there was too much intelligence shimmering behind her eyes for him to think that. More than anything, she seemed to read something in him that she chose to see as his love for her. He didn't know if that was true or not, but he felt a sudden rush of sentimental affection that made him laugh aloud, sweeping the blues away.

———————————

Lisa didn't know whose house it was until she saw a picture over the mantelpiece of Jansten with a young woman. As Carly took her from one room to the next, a tear slipped down Lisa's cheek. She had heard the gunshots.

She wiped her face with her bound hands and stood straighter. The least she could do was let them know how she hated them.

"Honey?" the girl called.

"Right here." Geoff came in from the hallway, the gun in his belt. His eyes looked bright but Lisa noticed he avoided her eyes. He smoothed the girl's hair, making her smile uncertainly.

"Where's the guy?" Carly asked.

Geoff didn't answer her. Instead, he took the tape off Lisa's mouth, looking at her now, challenging her to say something. "Listen. The house is off by itself. Your screams wouldn't be heard, but they would be very irritating to me and Carly."

"What a shame." Lisa's voice was hoarse with her contempt.

"I'll show you a shame, girl," Carly said, her hand slipping into her purse.

Geoff snatched away her purse and took out the straight razor. She tried to get it back, but he held her away with his forearm. "I'll tell you when and if we need to do that. I've still got plans for Lisa. Now take her upstairs and shower her off. She stinks."

He cut the line binding Lisa's hands as if it were ribbon. "I'll be right outside the door. Don't give Carly any trouble." He slipped the razor into his back pocket.

Carly took Lisa up to the bathroom. A moment later, Geoff threw in some clothes, a pair of jeans and a striped, button-down shirt. Jansten's presumably. "Put her in these afterward."

Once the door was closed, Carly gestured toward Lisa's clothes. "Get them off. He's treating you like the frigging queen." She turned the shower on and the bathroom quickly filled with steam.

Lisa hesitated, then stripped off her filthy clothes. She looked at herself in the mirror: Her hair was filthy and there were dark shadows under her eyes. She smelled bad to herself.

Carly looked in the mirror at her scar and then she turned her attention to Lisa. For a moment their eyes locked, and Lisa saw such fury there that she braced herself, ready to go at it again.

But then Carly said, "Just get in the frigging shower, okay?"

Once Lisa was inside, she let the water rush through her hair and she lost herself in the heat. When she finally stepped away to soap herself off, she saw that the girl was still standing right outside, looking in at her. The girl stepped closer, and Lisa couldn't help but notice how young she was. Not much more than twenty, if that.

"It's just that I tried to help you," the girl said. "I opened that box because you said you were cold. And you cut me for it."

Lisa resisted the urge to slap the girl's face. She resisted the urge to remind the girl that she had kidnapped Lisa, helped store her in a box, and had helped kill Alex. That very likely Jansten's body was lying somewhere in the house. Instead, Lisa leaned forward and said, "After Geoff jerks me and Steve around some more, he'll probably kill us. What do you think is going to happen to you after that?"

Carly watched Geoff tie Lisa to one the beds. He was surprisingly gentle, touching only her hands and arms. Lisa was fully dressed in the clothes he had given her. "We'll bring you some food," he said.

In the hallway, Carly said, "Why don't you just fuck her and get it over with?" She brushed past him and went into the bathroom. She pulled her hair back from her neck to look at the scar. "I see how you're looking at this. It's over with us now, isn't it? I'm useless because I'm ugly."

Geoff came in behind her and looked over her shoulder into the mirror. He reached past her and opened the medicine cabinet and found some disinfectant. "We'll shower first, and then I'll put some of this on." He kissed her above the ear and held her close. "Is that what she said to you? I heard you whispering in here."

"Are you going to leave me behind?"

"It's not going to happen that way."

"What way is it going to happen?"

He unbuttoned her blouse and slowly pulled it off her shoulders, looking at her in the mirror the whole time. "See how beautiful you still are," he whispered. He touched the edge of her scar gently. "We'll fix that. When we leave here, we're going to Miami. They have more plastic surgeons than palm trees down there. Both of us will need new faces to start our new lives."

"Our new lives?"

"Ours. Just you and me."

Her eyes welled up. "When?"

"Ssssh. You'll see."

He took her into the shower. As they made love, with the steam billowing up against the old man's walls, she wondered if Geoff was lying. And, if so, was it just to her? Or to himself as well?

CHAPTER 30

The guy show up?" Bannerman said over the phone.

"Finally. Not that it was so bad waiting." Lazar was at the phone booth at the edge of the marina parking lot. "Nice life out here."

"Learn much?"

"Nah. Dern's not as old or the kind of stiff you'd think would be president of a big company like that. But he wasn't volunteering anything. In fact, he was pumping me. Why I was investigating Mann? Who had filed charges? That kind of thing."

"Nosy bastard."

"Probably." Lazar looked back at Dern's boat. The guy was belowdecks now. Lazar couldn't shake the feeling that the man wanted to talk more, but he had deftly shut off Lazar's attempt to probe further.

Lazar continued, "Did the courier deliver Mann's personnel files like Jansten promised?"

"No. I got his secretary on the phone just a few minutes ago. She was on her way out. Ice water, that chick. Said Jansten hasn't authorized it, hasn't said a word about it."

"Shit. Must've forgot."

"Yeah. Anyhow, she said he had left a message with the service saying he was going to be home for a couple of days. She said to get back to her then."

"Fuck that. You explain that we're officers of the law?"

"Sure I did. Made it sound like I'd have her ass in jail later tonight. She explained she worked for Jansten, and if he wanted his privacy at home in Sea Crest, he had the right."

"She told you that, did she? Told you he lived in Sea Crest?"

"Good executive secretaries have to be politicians too, you know."

"If you say so."

"So the Sea Crest police came through. Got his number and address. But this can wait until we're back."

"Give it to me anyhow."

Bannerman read him the information, his voice caught somewhere between amusement and exasperation. "You've got to get laid, man. We don't have that much on Mann, and you're ready to roust this captain of industry at home. What exactly has Mann done? As far as I can see, he likes a girl who *might* be a hooker, he's been away from his apartment for a while, and he's got an ego so big he needs to plaster his walls with pictures of himself. This isn't the kind of evidence we arrest people on in this country. I say we're due our two days off and we should take them."

"Ball was killed with a sword and then Mann and Jammer disappear at the same time. Doesn't that interest you?"

"Not even a little bit. Just because your life is boring and lonely, mine isn't."

Lazar laughed. "Thanks for clarifying. See you Saturday, dick-head."

"Saturday."

Lazar got onto the Southeast Expressway, heading for home in Norwell. He sighed heavily the first time the traffic backed up, and realized abruptly he had been doing that a lot. Sighing.

He dreaded his days off.

Partly it was the house. Memories of her in every goddamn nook and cranny. Maybe he should just sell the damn place, end up in a cockroach-infested Brighton apartment like a normal divorced guy.

He wished he could talk to her. He wished he could get a clear answer about why it had all changed. Why what was once a good thing—what was once their *life*—was now worthless.

Lazar rubbed his forehead, trying to shove the whining, hurt-puppy voice out of his head. He abruptly thought of Mann's apartment.

All of those photos, but none of them showed the guy with a woman or anything that suggested family or friends. Jansten said something about grandparents, a girl in San Francisco. The personnel file would have a next-of-kin phone number. Hell, maybe Lazar would call it and Mann would answer. Got himself fired and scurried back to grandma and grandpa for free food and clean laundry.

Lazar glanced at his watch. Just before seven. Maybe he would stop by Jansten's instead of calling. Standing at the man's door, he'd be much more likely to get Jansten to move things along. With Lazar standing right there, Jansten might even be willing to send somebody back into the office over the weekend, find Mann's file.

Get this fat cop off my porch.

Lazar grinned as he took the exit for Sea Crest.

———————————

Carly brought a bowl of soup and a sandwich to Lisa. The revolver was on the tray. Carly put the food aside and undid the
ropes on Lisa's feet and one of her hands so she could sit up.
"There. Feed yourself."

Lisa noticed that there was less menace in the girl's voice than
before and her hair was drying as if she too had just showered.

"You were wrong," the girl said simply.

Lisa was famished. She ate the chicken sandwich and tomato
soup without saying a word. This was the most complete meal she
had eaten since they had kidnapped her and she wasn't going to
risk offending the girl.

When she finished, the girl said it again.

"How do you know?" Lisa said quietly.

The girl flushed. "Because he loves me."

"Did he say that?"

The girl's expression grew stony. "You think that's a joke? A
girl like me?"

"No."

"I know what he feels. He doesn't have to say it—I can make
a man feel things a tightass bitch like you never could."

Lisa was silent.

That seemed to make the girl angrier. "What makes you think
you're so different? What makes you think you're better? It's just
clothes and . . . this rich-bitch attitude!"

"Does my having money justify what you've done to me? Does
that make it all right to put me in that box? To kill Alex and
Jansten?" Lisa looked closely at the girl.

Carly looked away. "You don't know anything about me. I was
just a kid when Jammer turned me out."

"I see . . . so what he did to you makes it all right?"

Carly's face flushed. "It makes that fucker dead! It means that
it's my turn to get what I want. I'm young enough, I can wash

those years away, and nobody's going to know. And if no one knows, it's like it didn't happen."

"So you're just going to pretend I didn't exist when Geoff kills me?"

The girl shrugged, but again she looked away from Lisa's eyes. "I don't want to talk about that. It might not happen anyway. Geoff can be real sweet when he wants. And if you want to stay on my good side, don't kiss up to him." She walked over to the mirror and looked at her scar. "He says we're going to get this fixed. Maybe if we both make enough of a change, he'll let you go. I mean, you wouldn't be able to identify us any longer."

"Do you actually believe that?"

The girl was silent and then she came and sat beside Lisa. "Look, I know what you've been going through, and I'm not saying I like it. Me and Darlene—she's one of Jammer's other girls—sometimes we would look up and see the disgusting shit we're doing day in, day out . . . and we say like, 'How did I end up here?' And I know that's different from what you're in, you know, this situation. But I know you've got to be thinking the same thing."

"You know that, and yet you're keeping me." Lisa looked at Carly and said quietly, "Please help me out of this."

Carly shook her head. "I can't go against Geoff. He's the only guy who's ever taken care of me." She blushed. "Maybe that sounds stupid, coming from a whore. But I've got feelings too."

"You think I don't?" Lisa couldn't keep the desperation from her voice. Her lower lip trembled. "You're willing to do this because you're waiting for him to say some *words* to you? What do you think is going to happen the first time you cross him? He's doing this to me because Steve beat him out of a job. And I embarrassed him, maybe. I slapped him."

"Why?" Carly looked at her closely.

"Because he was risking lives. For his stupid damn *job,* he was

risking lives. Proving something that no one else needed proving.
For what?"

"Huh. You're too rich to know what it's like to be poor. He was
rich, now he's lost it. This will get it back."

"Rich? Maybe someday we would be. But for now, I don't
know how Steve raised the money he did. Believe me, I know our
finances. There isn't any more."

The girl smiled. "You think you know everything. Geoff says
that money he got from your husband was just flash money. He's
going to do some payback on a guy who hurt me and he's going
to make us rich. Geoff is going to take me all over the world."

"How nice," Lisa said, feeling the hysteria she had been holding back push to the surface. "How nice to know you've got a
good reason for killing me."

Lisa willed herself to look away from the gun.

The whole time she had been talking, she had been conscious
of it on the tray. So when the doorbell rang downstairs and Carly
automatically reached for the gun, Lisa didn't hesitate.

It was as if she had been poised for this moment all her life.

Geoff sat up abruptly on the sofa. He had been asleep and it took
him a second to realize where he was. The doorbell rang again. He
got to his feet and hurried to the window.

It was the black cop. Lazar.

Geoff's blood began pounding and he looked for other cops.
He quietly moved the back windows and peered out. No one that
he could see. That didn't mean anything, though.

He went back to look at the cop. No gun in his hands. His car
pulled right up in the driveway. Ringing the doorbell.

Maybe the guy just wanted to talk to Jansten again.

Geoff let his breath out. Maybe, just maybe, if they were quiet,
the man would go away. Geoff felt disoriented, not ready for this.

That's when he heard the sound of a struggle upstairs. The

scrape of wood on wood that he figured must be the two of them struggling on the bed.

"Shit," he said under his breath and ran for the stairs.

He was halfway up when one of them screamed and the gun went off, filling the house with a hollow boom.

Geoff checked himself on the stairs and turned back as he heard the front doorknob rattle. The cop kicked the door, and Geoff saw the doorjamb splinter around the lock.

Both of Geoff's guns were upstairs.

He threw himself over the banister and landed just a few feet away from the cop as he kicked his way into the foyer.

CHAPTER 31

Police!" Lazar yelled.

Giving that warning almost cost the cop his life right there because it gave Geoff the split second to grasp Lazar's revolver with his left hand and jam his index finger between the trigger and trigger guard. The cop tried to yank the gun away, and Geoff rammed him in the face with his elbow.

Lazar twisted his head and the blow broke his cheekbone. The cop shoved Geoff hard and let go of the gun. That surprised Geoff and he fell back, off balance. Before he could transfer the revolver to his right hand, Lazar pivoted on one foot, kicked the gun away, and then did a fast spin and snapped off a kick at Geoff's stomach. Geoff was able to block the blow with his forearms, but the force of it knocked him down and he slid across the marble floor. The big cop glided forward, and Geoff lashed out at his knee. Lazar turned just in time and took the hard kick against his thigh.

It slowed him down long enough so that Geoff could roll to his feet. The two of them circled in the foyer, the cop's breath rasping. Geoff's own breathing was coming pretty fast too. This cop was as skilled as anyone Geoff had ever taken on in competition. And he was surprisingly quick for his size. Lazar's eyes flickered to the floor, and Geoff risked taking his eyes off the cop for a split second to see the gun lying in the corner.

Lazar jabbed his fingers at Geoff's Adam's apple.

Geoff blocked him just in time. "Good try," he said.

That widened Lazar's eyes, but he didn't say anything. He kept circling for an opening. He snapped off another kick which Geoff sidestepped neatly.

Then Geoff went to work. He feinted with a groin kick, and followed up fast, hitting Lazar's collarbone with the knife edge of both hands. Lazar bunched his heavy shoulder muscles just in time, but from the way his breath gusted out, Geoff could tell the blows had done some damage. When he connected another solid punch to Lazar's cheekbone, he started laughing; he felt so good.

The cop was winded and hurting.

Geoff went for his eyes, his fore and index fingers rigid, his whole body exultant.

Maybe it was Geoff's overconfidence. Maybe it was just Lazar's skill. But the cop parried the jab away, grasped Geoff's wrist, and twisted his arm behind his back before the younger man even realized how much trouble he was in.

Geoff tried to throw himself forward so that he could roll onto his back and yank the arm away. But Lazar wrapped his left arm around Geoff's throat and kicked his legs out from under him. The two of them fell to the floor, Lazar on top. Geoff roared in pain— the man was going to break his right arm, he could feel the elbow joint giving way. Amazingly, he couldn't see any options: Lazar's gun was out of reach. Even if he could have reached it, Geoff needed his left arm to reach behind his back and try to counter the awful strength of the cop by holding his right wrist.

Geoff saw Carly's legs coming down the stairs in front of him.

Suddenly the cop let go of Geoff and went for the revolver himself.

From above Geoff's head another gun spoke, impossibly loud in the foyer. Carly had his revolver, the one he had taken off Steve.

The wall behind the cop splattered with blood and the cop dropped his gun, his right arm now useless. He fell to his knees, fumbling for the gun with his left hand.

Geoff said, "Hold it, Carly."

He shoved the cop away and picked up the revolver himself. Geoff coughed and massaged his throat. As soon as he could breathe freely, he kissed Carly and gave her a hard squeeze around the shoulders. She was bone white and shaking. "Good girl."

He went back to stand over the cop, and then, abruptly, kicked him hard on the shoulder, right over the gunshot wound. That got a reaction from the cop, a strangled kind of scream. Geoff said, "Lazar, you let a woman beat you. How's that appeal to that sense of humor of yours?"

Is she dead?" Geoff asked.

"I wish." Carly slapped Lisa in the face. "She fought me for the gun, but I got it back and cracked her a good one. That's the second time she tried to kill me."

Lisa moaned and raised her head slightly, then let it fall back down. There was a lump on her forehead.

"I've had it trying to help her." Carly's voice was cold and flat. "I think you should get rid of her."

"You do, huh?" He spoke up cheerfully. "Wake up, Lisa. We brought you some company." Geoff went back into the hallway and grabbed Lazar. They had tied his hands and hobbled his legs with a short length of rope so he could walk but not use any of those kicks. Not that he looked like he was in any condition for that anymore. His face was swelling around his broken cheekbone and his arm trembled visibly as the blood poured down his sleeve, covering his hand. He looked at Lisa blankly at first, and then Geoff could see a stirring of interest. Lazar licked his lips and said, "Who's she?"

Geoff smiled. "This guy's a tough one, Lisa. Kind of fat-looking, but he's got an exit wound as big as my fist out the back of his shoulder, and he still wants to meet the ladies. Lisa Dern, please meet Detective Lazar of the Boston Police."

"Geoff, let him lie down," Lisa said. "Please."

"Please fuck yourself," Carly snapped at her.

Geoff put his arm around Carly and kissed her again. "You were ready for her. Saved me, too."

In spite of everything—of Lisa and the wounded cop staring at them mutely, of the fact of Jansten lying dead just a few rooms away—Carly smiled delightedly. Loving Geoff's attention.

Geoff smoothed her hair. "Honey, do me a favor and get me a couple of those white towels and facecloths, some disinfectant, and maybe you can give this guy a couple of those codeine pills we found."

She looked confused.

"I've got plans for these two, honey. Now just do as I ask."

Carly did, and came back moments later with what he had requested.

Geoff took her razor from his back pocket and cut Lisa's arm free from the bed. He made a hobble for her like Lazar's.

To the girl, he said casually, "Honey, put the gun on Lazar and kill him if he moves." Without further preamble, he took Lisa by the hair and shook her head hard. He held the razor up to her face. "You clean this cop up and keep him alive, at least until I'm ready to talk to him. And if you ever—ever—touch Carly again,

Steve won't be able to tell you and Lazar apart by the time I finish spreading you both around this room."

———————————

Geoff left Carly with the gun, and then came back about five minutes later and nailed a sliding bolt lock to the outside of the door. The two of them left, without a word, and Lisa heard the bolt slide home.

Lisa rubbed her face quickly, her hands still shaking. She took a deep breath and turned to Lazar. "Let's see if I can help slow down that bleeding."

He gritted his teeth as she helped him pull off his sport jacket and shirt. She spread disinfectant on a folded towel and taped it against the big wound on his back and did the same with a small washcloth over the puckered wound just under his collarbone. The towel in back was soaking red already. She gave him codeine and water and had him lie down on his side, keeping the shoulder wound high. She put pillows under his legs, figuring he might be going into shock. His color was tinged gray under the brown of his skin. "I wish I knew what I was doing," she said.

He grunted. "Me too." His eyes flickered open and he reached over to squeeze her arm. "Wished I knew what I was doing, I mean." He grimaced. "I was on my own, no one knows I'm here."

Tears filled Lisa's eyes. She didn't realize until then how much she had been counting on him being the first of the cavalry.

"Tell me what's been going on," he said.

Lisa quickly sketched what had happened, from the rock climbing incident onward.

"Jesus," Lazar groaned. "A fucking nut. Why the hell didn't your husband come to us? I just left him, for Christ's sake."

"Steve's all right?" she said, eagerly. "I just saw him that second at the house and Geoff was still up there."

"Oh, yeah. Your husband was on your boat."

Lisa felt a momentary panic, a brief flash of rage. She closed her eyes and forced herself to think. "No," she said, firmly. "No, he couldn't go to the police." She told Lazar again about the way Geoff had locked her in the freezer, of the tapes she had recorded for Steve. "I'm sure he had Steve convinced that he would kill me if he brought in the police—and he would've, too."

Lazar grunted. "Maybe. So Geoff's got the money now . . . why do you think you're still alive?"

She told him about Carly's comment that Geoff wanted to get back at another man, that the money he had raised from Steve was just flash money.

"You don't know who that would be?"

"No."

"Doesn't give us any idea why he still needs us."

"I've had lots of time to think about that. From me, he wants an audience. He alternates between treating me terribly and then being considerate. It's as if he respects you inordinately if you stand up to him, but he's got to beat you down immediately to show you he's stronger. He sees himself in competition with Steve. It's not just revenge, it's like he's trying to prove something through us."

Lazar nodded. "The guy actually complimented me when we were fighting. Like I'd sunk a good hook shot playing basketball."

The two of them were silent for a moment. As Lazar rested, his eyes closed. Lisa touched her forehead gingerly. Her head still ached abominably.

"You think your husband will make it to you again?" Lazar asked.

"He'll try." That Lisa knew. Whether or not she would ever see him again, she didn't know. This policeman struck her as very hard, very tough. And he hadn't succeeded. She said, "Steve is very resourceful."

Lazar's eyelids were growing heavy. "He better make it sooner rather than later. My guess is Geoff let us have this little talk to loosen me up so I'll tell the truth as to when I can expect some backup. I wouldn't tell him before."

"So what are you going to say?"

Lazar sighed. "The truth, I guess. We've got at least two days before anyone will notice I'm gone. Better Mann knows that than to think they will be here tonight. Then he'd just kill me and move you. He's going to want to keep you alive until he gets whatever he wants from your husband. Proves whatever he has to prove. Me, hell, my ass might be fried already. But I won't beg him, I won't give him that. From what you said about him, as soon as I do, he'll kill me." Lazar held Lisa's hand and she squeezed it back, hard. "The longer we stay in his face, the more chances I'll have to kick his teeth in. The more chances you'll have to settle back on that nice boat with your husband."

CHAPTER 32

Steve had been awake for hours when the phone rang just after seven in the morning. "You're in for a treat," a woman's voice said. "Go to the Dunkin' Donuts on Boylston Street. There's a phone out front. Be there in twenty minutes."

He was there in fifteen. When the phone rang, the woman said, "The corner of West Newton and Columbus. The liquor store. Ten minutes."

There was a van following him a few cars back, but it took off up Columbus when he reached the liquor store and he never saw the driver. From there, the woman sent him on to two other locations, to a phone booth in front of the *Boston Herald* building, and then back across town to Newbury Street, in front of the big window of a restaurant. The sidewalk café was doing a brisk business, but everyone disappeared from Steve's view when the phone rang and he said hello.

"It's me," Lisa said.

"Jesus." His knees buckled slightly and then he recovered himself. "Where are you?"

She was gone.

The other woman's voice came on the line. "If Lisa had answered that, I'd have had to kill her," the other woman said. "So she's going to try again to give you a message."

Lisa was put back on. "I'm supposed to make you understand that my life depends upon you telling the truth. That they haven't put me in the box again like before, but they will if you lie." Her voice shook as she said this, and Steve pressed the receiver hard against his ear.

"I will get you out of this, Lisa. You stay alive."

"Love you," she whispered.

He heard the woman say, "Get off the phone." Steve closed his eyes and willed the telephone receiver to give up some clue as to where Lisa was being held. But all he heard was the woman telling Lisa to sit on the floor.

The woman came back on the line. "All right, you heard what she said about the truth. Did you dispose of those two packages and clean up like you were told?"

Steve had the sense that she was reading the question. "Yes."

"Have you talked to the police? At all?"

Steve hesitated, his mind racing. Geoff could have been watching him at any time.

"Answer me!"

"A Detective Lazar came to see me. Wouldn't say what he wanted Geoff for, just said that he had some questions."

"And what did you say?"

"That I haven't seen him since the rock climbing thing."

"Did he seem to buy that?"

"Yes."

"Convince me."

Steve was at a loss. After a moment, he said, "He was just fishing. When he gave me his phone number he said he might be out for the next couple of days . . . whatever he wanted Geoff for, it didn't seem all that urgent."

"Who else?"

"No one."

"Don't lie to me!"

"I'm not."

She paused, and he waited. Then she said, "Final question. Are you ready to do what you're told?"

"Yes."

He could hear her breathing, and he felt that she was trying to make a decision. He couldn't think of anything else to say to convince her—and then she said, abruptly, "Stay there."

She hung up.

Five minutes passed. Steve counted the cars going by, looking for the van. He stood in front of the phone once when a man about his age wanted to use it. The man started to argue, then looked closer at Steve and hurried away.

Steve's knees shook slightly. Had he passed Geoff's little test?

He shivered, even though the day was warm.

Had he failed? Had he just spoken to Lisa for the last time?

A waitress came up to him, smiling cautiously. "Sir? I believe that man is trying to get your attention."

Steve turned. Geoff was inside the restaurant, smiling broadly from a corner table, waving him in. Inviting him to breakfast.

Very good, Steve, the truth shall set Lisa free," Geoff said, cutting into his omelet. "I didn't see the police following, so I sent you on to the *Herald* and came on back here. Just think, if my pimp friend, Jammer, had taken the time to chase you around to a few phones, he and Alex might be alive now."

Geoff was dressed casually in the jeans and an open-neck cotton shirt that he had been wearing the night Alex was killed. But the clothes looked freshly washed, and he was shaved and clear-eyed. There were scabs on his right temple. Burns, maybe. He said, "My friend phoned to say you were forthright about a policeman looking for me. Did this cop say why he wanted me?"

Steve hesitated, then answered. "He just said it was routine."

"Describe him."

Steve did, holding back nothing about Lazar's visit. He spoke slowly and carefully, feeling tightly coiled. Wanting so much to pull the derringer free from his belt and shoot Geoff in the forehead.

Geoff shrugged. "Just a little problem in Roxbury. Has nothing to do with this business of ours."

"And just what is our business?"

"Later. You'll take me out for a boat ride, and I'll give you the specifics." He looked out the window. "Weather seems perfect. What will that boat of yours do? About forty, forty-five?"

"About that. You're having a lot of fun, aren't you, Geoff?"

"Best rush ever. You could have it too, if you loosen up a little. Better than any rockface you ever climbed, believe it." He leaned forward and punched Steve on the shoulder, laughing at the way Steve's face flushed with rage. "Lighten up!"

"Shut up and listen to me, Geoff." Steve's voice was quiet. "You give me the job you want done, and I'll do it for you. Then you owe me one thing—"

"Got it," Geoff said briskly. Putting across a little impatience and sincerity at the same time. "You do what I want, she goes free."

"Bullshit."

That gave Geoff pause. "How's that?"

Steve leaned forward, his voice low. "We both know you're lying. So this is the deal: I do whatever it is you want—and then you owe me a fight. One-on-one. No weapons. Lisa's right there. The winner walks away, the loser dies."

Geoff put his hand out. "What's not to like?"

They towed Alex's dive boat down to Duxtable and left it on the trailer in the town ramp parking lot while Geoff had Steve drive past the gates of Raul's compound. Geoff told Steve he knew the man had money on his boat without telling about Carly or how Raul had burned him.

From there, they went to a marina store and bought a detailed chart of Duxtable Cove. Steve found the approximate location of Raul's mansion on the chart before they put the boat in and powered off in search of Raul's yacht. They found it quickly, the only boat in the mouth of a small cove.

"Take the wheel," Steve said, circling the location on the chart and noting a red nun buoy nearby. He jotted down the coordinates from the GPS navigation system. "Okay, it'll be easy to get back here at night." He took out a pair of binoculars and looked at the yacht. "It's a big Donzi, about fifty feet. *White Angel.*" He put the binoculars down and turned casually to Geoff. "There's a couple of guys in a Mako, looking my way. Just stay where you are and I'll be blocking you from view."

Geoff opened the throttles up and the twin outboards made the boat fly.

"What's your plan?" Steve asked.

"Don't worry about me. All you've got to do is drop me on the boat, get me into the cockpit there. Then give me some covering fire—you'll have your friend's rifle—while I go down for the money. And then you've got to get me off. Simple."

Steve snorted. "Have you ever done something like this?"

Geoff looked at him blandly. "I've been doing all sorts of new things. I'm good on my feet." He sawed the wheel back and forth, making the boat throw up huge sheets of water. "Sucker handles. You do good solid work."

"Yes, I do. And if I learned anything along the way it's that nothing is as simple as it sounds. And that plan of yours doesn't sound simple."

"Me, I always did real well on balls alone." Geoff kept playing with the boat, cracking up the throttles a bit more. Now that they were heading away from shore, the ocean swells gave him an opportunity to launch the boat a little. But still the Blue Water handled well. "Not bad at all," Geoff said. "See, I've come around to Jansten's way of thinking. You and I *could* make a good team."

"You're not listening. What about the guys in the Mako? They probably have automatic weapons, and I bet they're good on their feet, too. And if they come out to meet us while we're on the boat, we've lost the element of surprise. Do you know exactly where the money is being kept? You can't be digging around looking for it while people are shooting at you. What if this Raul has guests on-board? Are you going to massacre all of them?"

"We'll handle it."

Steve shook his head. "Even if these are drug dealers, I'm not killing people for you."

"Lisa's going to take that hard, you ranking a dealer's life over hers."

Steve ignored that. "Besides, you could get killed, blowing in like that."

"Your concern is touching."

Steve ignored that, too. "Let me plan this out."

"Not a problem." Geoff slapped the throttles down so the boat flew over the swells, crashing from one to the next. He grabbed Steve by the arm and drew him close so that he could be heard over the screaming outboards. "Jansten just got it backward: I'm the leader—you're the detail guy. Just make sure I'm the one going in on that boat. I'll want your plan by tomorrow."

CHAPTER 33

Steve went to the Boston Public Library late the next morning. He had already been out to Alex's boat and found some of what he wanted: an underwater propulsion unit and an electric outboard motor that could push his dive boat along quietly at trolling speed.

The book he wanted was in the old part of the library. The place smelled pleasantly of polished wood and old books. The ceilings were barely within a stone's throw. It was altogether an incongruous setting to be checking out a book called *Terror Tools*. The woman behind the counter looked at his card carefully and handed him the book without meeting his eyes.

For the next hour, he brushed up on the art of setting bombs in roads, under car seats, under bridges—down to booby-trapping pens, briefcases, even a police whistle. There was an entire chap-

ter devoted to blowing up boats and ships. And another on what
to look for in a radio-controlled detonator. Some of it he remembered from his days as a navy diver. Some of it was brand new.

Even though he was desperately concerned about Lisa, his concentration was good. It was one of his strengths, one of his ad-
vantages over Geoff. Steve could sweat the details.

After returning the book, he pored through back issues of
Yachting Magazine until he found a foldout ad for the same size
Donzi as *White Angel*. The ad included a schematic of the whole
boat. He ripped it out and put it in his notebook. On the way
downstairs, he stopped at the phones to place a call to Ed from Mr.
Grim.

Okay, here's your C-4." Ed unwrapped two bricks of plastic explosive and several detonators. He proudly pulled out a small
radio-triggering device and showed Steve how to use it. "Flip that,
and ka-boom. What else can I do for you today? I brought along
a few extras." He opened another bag and carefully laid out some
of the guns he had shown before, plus a variety of weapons and
devices, including mace, a blackjack, handcuffs, a Tazer gun, and
gloves with sand lining the knuckles. "Got a shipment of police
equipment," he said. "Back in my L.A. days, a cop with weighted
gloves knocked me on my ass. I only joined the frigging demon-
stration 'cause a girl with nice tits asked me. Lost myself a tooth,
but that chick was crying over me when I came to, and I got myself laid that night. Probably why I'm in this crazy business now."

"Just these." Steve selected two pair of handcuffs. He considered buying the Uzi, too. But he laid it back on the bed, envi-
sioning Geoff spraying bullets into a crowd just for the rush.

Geoff had agreed quickly to the idea of creating a diversion
with an explosion. Said it would do some good just to scare those
bastards straight. He had said it with such vehemence that it made

Steve hungry for the specifics. But so far, Geoff wasn't volunteering any information.

The gun dealer counted the money quickly and said, "Me and that Chastity have quite a thing going. You're helping romance bloom, buddy."

Steve looked at the dealer more carefully. He was wearing a Stones T-shirt and one big hoop earring, like some kind of goofy pirate. His good humor about the hooker seemed genuine. And Steve remembered Geoff saying something at breakfast about Jammer being a pimp. And what had Geoff called the girl the time she was holding a gun on Lisa? Cary? Kelly? Carly. That was it. Carly, like Carly Simon, the singer.

Steve asked the gun dealer if he knew a pimp by the name of Jammer or a prostitute named Carly.

"Do whores give hummers?" The dealer grabbed his crotch.

Steve blinked. "That means yes?"

"Jammer comes through with some sweet chicks. Carly, now she's a stunner. Got an attitude, though. And she's been out of my price range for some time. But I heard Jammer's been kicking her out onto the street for a while, teach her a lesson. I went looking for her a couple of days ago, see if I could help her along. No luck." He fanned the money, smiling slyly. "You've always got the cash, have you screwed her yet?"

Steve shook his head. "Where can I find her?"

"How come you know her name but not where to find her?" Ed was all business now.

Steve held out a twenty. "The address."

The dealer cackled as he added the twenty to his roll. Putting his hand on Steve's shoulder, he brought him over to the window. The man smelled of gun oil, old sweat, marijuana. "Third apartment building from the corner. Fourth floor. That's their window, right there. You might try Darlene if Carly's not there. She's Jammer's other live-in. She's not as fine, but she knows where every-thing goes."

The blond woman opened the door as far as the chain. "Closed for business," she said, dully. "Under repairs."

Her right eye was blackened. Her lip had been split open, and Steve saw the white of an arm cast. She started to shut the door, and he put his foot in the way. "Hold up, please. I know you're hurting, but just give me a minute."

"Mister, I'm really not in the mood." Her eyes seemed out of focus and she looked at a spot over his head. He waited until she slowly turned her attention back to him. "I just took a pill, okay?"

He held a twenty between his fore and index fingers through the door. "Just a few minutes' conversation. About Jammer and Carly."

Now she looked scared. "Haven't seen them." She shoved on the door. "Move your foot, okay? I gotta go."

He left his foot there. "You get beat up about them? Who did it?"

"I didn't say that."

"Then who did it?"

"None of your business. You another cop?"

Steve shook his head. "I'm just looking for a friend." He added another twenty. He saw her considering the money. "It's got to be tough, you can't work when you're hurt like that."

"That's a blessing, man."

"You say the cops have been by?"

She licked her lips, wincing when her tongue reached the cut. "I'll tell you about that." He held back one of the twenties and gave her the other.

She said, "Yeah, twice I saw them. Black and white guys, de-tectives."

"How come?"

"They wanted to talk to Jammer about his cousin, Ball. The guy got himself stabbed. Dead. Over in Roxbury. Anyhow the cops came by, couple of times."

"They find out anything?"

She shrugged. "Dunno. Ask them. Lasser and Bandman or something, I can't remember."

"Jammer have anything to do with it?"

She snorted, didn't bother to answer.

He held out the other twenty. "Did you ever meet a blond guy, about my age and height, named Geoff? He'd know both Carly and Jammer."

She eyed the money in his hand and he gave her the second twenty.

She said, "I told the cops I never met the guy. But I kinda know who he is. He's the guy who helped Carly out on the street when Jammer was gonna beat her. She figures he's her white knight. But she's got some weird ideas, let me tell you."

"Like what?"

"Like this guy's going to come through for her. Like he's not going to let guys like Raul . . . or Jammer grind her up like hamburger."

Steve saw how just saying the drug dealer's name scared the woman. "Raul knows Carly?"

Darlene started to close the door and he shoved back. He said, "How's she know him?"

"How do you think? She's a call girl; he's got a phone." Darlene held up her broken arm. "His guys came by yesterday, beat the shit out of me. I said I hadn't seen them for over a week."

"Jammer and Carly?"

"Yeah. And they wanted to know about the other guy, Geoff. They broke my arm because I didn't know where they were. Wouldn't have told them where Carly was if I did and I guess they figured that out. They said that Raul was back in town early, and he wanted Carly delivered for the screen test last night. Jammer's supposed to deliver Carly to Raul."

"Deliver?"

"Yeah, deliver. She told me what she did. She cut the man, little while ago."

"Jammer?"

"Raul." The frightened look was back in Darlene's eyes.

"It was brave of you to hold out on them."

She stared at him, perhaps trying to see if he meant it. She must have decided he did, because she shrugged and looked faintly embarrassed. "Yeah, well, for the arm and the lip I could take it. Carly really is a sweet girl. Makes me laugh. And Raul's a movie freak. You know the kind I mean? I heard stories. I heard that sometimes he does more than hurt a girl. Most guys out there like seeing a movie of us fucking. But then there's some who want to see us dead. They want to see it *happen*. And Carly cut Raul. I know what he's gonna do if he gets her alone with his camera. And I don't know this Geoff, but if he's like any white knight I've ever known, he's gonna fold soon as Carly turns out to be too much trouble. And believe me, Raul is too much trouble."

CHAPTER 34

"All the food has gone bad," Geoff said. "But there's beer and wine."

They were alone in Geoff's apartment.

"Get this straight," Steve said. "I'm not your friend. I don't want to eat with you, drink with you, or do anything but figure this out so that I can get Lisa back."

Geoff sat on the arm of the couch, sipping a beer. "I suppose you're the one who broke my door in—find anything?"

Steve glanced around at the pictures, the sports equipment, and sighed.

"All right, impress me," Geoff said. "Tell me how I'm going to become rich again tomorrow."

Steve opened up the chart they had bought earlier. He had penciled in a large triangle representing *White Angel* moored inside the little cove, and a smaller triangle representing his own dive boat just outside. "Okay, we anchor the Blue Water just here, out of sight. I go in underwater using the Powersled."

"What's that?"

"It's an underwater propulsion unit. It can haul me along at three miles an hour."

"James Bond. Better be one for me."

Steve didn't answer that. He continued, "I'll set up a charge on the very bow of the *White Angel,* just under the waterline. Then I'll go back and get the Blue Water. Tomorrow night is supposed to be cloudy again, and there won't be much of a moon. With that dark navy blue hull I will be almost invisible. Silent, too, using the electric outboard. Then I'll open up the gas outboards once I'm in close. I expect Raul's guys will want to see what all the noise is about, maybe they'll want to send someone off in their Mako. That's when I set the charge off."

"Just where are you going to get explosives?"

"Alex had everything I needed," Steve lied. "Part of his salvage business. Anyhow, the blast should be just enough to make a small hole in the bow, scare the hell out of everyone, and start the boat sinking. But there should be time."

"You're sounding like a one-man SWAT team. Where do I come in?"

Steve nodded to the picture on the wall of Geoff skiing off a fifty-foot drop. "I know what you're after—that's why I've saved the hot seat for you. Right on the yacht with them. You'll overpower them while they're confused, get the money. You won't have any weapons, since I presume they'll check you out thoroughly. So you'll just have the element of surprise. And your speed. If the money isn't there, if they've moved it off the yacht, then it's a wash. I get you off, then you owe me what we agreed. You think you'll be able to do your part?"

Geoff looked at him closely. "What makes you think they'll let me on board?"

Steve said, mildly, "They want Carly. And you're going to deliver her."

———————————————————

Geoff was stunned. "How did you know her name?"

"You've been screwing up. You mentioned her name, you mentioned Jammer's. You told me he was a pimp. I've asked questions."

Geoff felt the blood rush to his face. He stood up. "You son of a bitch. If you've talked, Lisa's already dead. Count on it."

"Nobody talks more than you," Steve said, irritably. "I just spread some cash around with a few street hookers. Found out that this Carly of yours cut Raul and he wants her back. And that his men are looking for her, you, and Jammer."

"Hookers in the street?"

"Several knew that much about it," Steve lied. "Now tell me what happened with Raul so I can figure the best way to make this work."

Geoff opened his mouth, then shut it. Steve must be lying, he thought. That many people *couldn't* know. . . . Yet Geoff liked what Steve had outlined before. Geoff didn't want to give up on that kind of action. But he didn't like the authoritative tone Steve was taking. Geoff was tempted to hurt him. Find out what sort of double-cross he had in mind. Guaranteed there was one.

And that realization made Geoff relax. .

Because Steve was trying to put him on the defensive. Sitting there looking calm, dropping these little bombs. Well, fuck him.

Geoff smiled. "Sure, I'll tell you what happened."

"Tell me exactly. How you got on the yacht. How many people were with Raul, and how they were armed. Where is the money? What kind of bag or box is it in? Describe it. Describe all of it."

Geoff did.

———————————

Steve listened quietly, taking it all in. When Geoff was finished, Steve remained silent for a few moments, his eyes far away. Then, he said, "You'll need to bring Carly. You won't even get on the boat without her."

Geoff shook his head. "No. I'm not going to risk her."

"We need her."

"Screw you. You're just trying to get her away from Lisa, hope she'd break free, probably."

Steve was mildly shocked. The guy was showing real concern for the hooker. Steve leaned forward, speaking softly. "How do you explain it to yourself? How is it okay to kidnap Lisa, put her in a box—but it's not okay for Carly to be in danger?"

"She's been in danger since she was a kid," Geoff snapped. "Besides, she's mine."

Steve pulled back. "And you want an adventure, don't you?"

"That's about right."

"Well, let me put it to you this way. Adventure doesn't come to people who seek it out."

"Bullshit. In my experience, they *never* happen unless you make them."

Steve gestured at the pictures on the wall. "People like you who take idiotic risks for the sake of the thrill aren't having an adventure, you're playing a game—a sport at best. You've got a choice, and you choose not to risk anything important."

"Nothing but my life," Geoff said, dryly.

Steve spoke slowly, willing Geoff to listen. "You also play Russian roulette like some people play Scrabble. Me, I'm trying to save Lisa. She means more to me than my own life. My adrenaline's pumping right now because if she dies, everything I value is gone. If you really want to challenge me, then play fair. Take a real risk for once in your life."

Steve waited. He saw that Geoff took it in, that he knew it was a challenge, and a transparent one at that. But what Steve had said was true.

"You think having Carly there will stack the cards in your favor?" Geoff asked casually.

"*Our* favor. When you show up without weapons, with her and the money, you'll be doing just what they expect. You show up without her, you won't even get on the boat to see Raul. It's that simple."

Geoff nodded slowly. "You realize that if Carly's with me, I'll have to leave something for Lisa—something on a timer—so if we don't come back, she'll die too."

Steve inhaled. Then he nodded. "I expected that, yes."

Geoff drained the last of his beer and threw the bottle into the trash. "Carly will be there."

CHAPTER 35

Geoff had no trouble renting the equipment, even though the sum of his scuba experience was limited to a one-week certification course during a vacation in the Bahamas. "Give me full gear for two divers: a large man's wetsuit and one for a woman who weighs about one hundred and fifteen pounds. Six tanks, regulators, and an extra set of mask and fins, dive lights."

The clerk whistled. "Six tanks. Busy night ahead, huh?"

"Very."

Geoff whistled on the way out to the van, feeling good as he and the clerk hauled the gear. Damn good. Carly was going to be along to watch him do his stuff.

Back at the house, she tugged at the smaller wetsuit. From the set of her mouth, the quick looks she darted his way, he could tell Carly was afraid of the stark equipment: the lead weight belts, heavy tanks, the gauges, hoses, neoprene, Velcro, and buckles.

"You don't have to worry," he said, teasing her along.

"I don't know how to do this," she said.

"You won't have to," he said. "I'd never ask you to do something you couldn't handle."

Steve finished water-sealing the case he had bought that afternoon. He ran through his checklist: The explosives were ready. The guns were cleaned. Batteries charged for the Powersled and the electric outboard. The boat was fully gassed. He had the sketch of the cove taped up on the bulwark, and from the chronograph beside it he saw he had two hours to go.

Although he had no appetite, he grilled himself a steak. As he chewed the food slowly, he played back the messages on his answering machine: Two from his secretary, desperately trying to reschedule his missed meetings, and one from J.C., his designer down in Charleston. "Steve, I'm just calling to say I'd like to follow up with your guy, Alex Martin, on the Blue Water. Can't raise a call from him." A bluff message from Keiler, head of one of the electronics divisions, kidding him about his "extended vacation" but pressing him for answers, too. There were no calls from Jansten, which was surprising to Steve. He expected there were some pretty ugly rumors circulating by now about the new president. *Unreliable. Jekyll and Hyde personality. Questionable use of funds.*

Steve was faintly troubled by that. But more than anything, he felt distant from that life. That foolish life he had worked so hard to achieve.

What he had before him was all that mattered. He had made his plans, and he was as ready as he could be. Calm under the but-

terfly stomach, calm under the bitter tension that made him wish
the game could start right that minute.

Feeling pretty much the way Geoff wanted him to feel.

———————————————

Carly hated the tears. Hated herself for letting another man twist
her around. "You lied to me!"

That made him mad. She could see it in his face: His under-
standing look vanished, and he turned thin-lipped and cold. "I
need you there."

She pressed herself against him, willing her body to thaw him
again, to give her another chance to show that all she wanted from
him was a chance to run away forever. "Screw the money," she
said. "We've got a hundred and fifty thousand dollars! You don't
need to prove anything else to me."

"It's not the money," he said, as if she hadn't even touched him.

She pulled away. "Like hell, it isn't." Her shoulders began to
heave, and she turned away from him. She knew he hated weakness.

"You've got to know that I can't be pushed. You've got to see
that I'll take care of you no matter what."

"Please, Geoff, please. Let's just get in the van and go."

"You want me to shoot those two down the hall? Just murder
them?"

She bit her lip. "No. I never wanted you to kill anyone, except
maybe Jammer. Just leave them tied up, put some food and water
near them. We can make a call from Florida. Once we've had the
plastic surgery, we can go anywhere, you said it yourself."

Geoff looked at her like she was a little kid. "Lazar is a cop,
and you shot him. We're going to need time to recuperate from
the operations, and we won't make it out of Miami if he can
name us."

"Don't just shoot them. Don't do what you did to that old man."

Geoff smiled at her as if she had just agreed with him. "That's what I mean. These things have to work a certain way. . . . I made a deal with Steve and I'm going to keep it, to a degree."

"A deal! Geoff, you've got his wife—you can't trust any deal."

"I said to a degree. And I know that a hundred and fifty thousand dollars sounds like a lot of money to you, but it's not for the life I have in mind for us."

"*Sounds* like a lot of money? You're damn right it does. I don't care how rich you were before, we can go anywhere in the world—for a while anyhow—on a hundred and fifty thousand."

"I'm not interested in 'a while.' "

She brushed that away. "Geoff, what more do we need?"

"We need to kill Raul and take his money," Geoff said, quietly. "We need to show each other that we're willing to stand together and take down anyone who gets in our way."

"Why?" She laughed uncertainly as she said it, afraid suddenly of what he might answer her. And just as afraid that he wouldn't say it.

He did.

She knew she was supposed to laugh. That this was a real scream. She should be hugging herself it was so funny. She was only eighteen but she had been a hooker for two of those years, and she knew damn well not to believe it when a man said he loved you and that he was going to take you away to be with him forever.

But she didn't laugh.

She didn't cry anymore.

She stood there staring at him while he waited for an answer. Until, at last, she said, softly, "All right."

CHAPTER 36

Y ou can't be serious," Lazar said.

But he saw from the look on Lisa's face, the way she was clamping her jaw tight, that she believed Mann. And given what he had done to her before, putting her in the freezer, he probably was. Lazar felt his knees start to shake, but he kept the bluff tone. "I'm not doing it."

"Up to you," Geoff said. He had them outside, standing on top of the small hill that ran from the top of the house to the ocean. It was just a little before midnight and the floodlights from the back deck provided illumination. The smell of the sea was strong, and Lazar could hear the slap of the waves hitting the private pier. Beside them, the doors and windows of Jansten's Mercedes were wide open. "You probably won't make it if you don't put on the wetsuit, though. Hypothermia."

"We're not going," Lazar said.

Geoff shrugged and pushed his wet hair away from his face. He pointed at Lisa. *"She's* going. Even if I have to toss her in the front seat without a wetsuit, she's going because I made a deal with Steve—he's got a chance to get her back alive." Geoff smiled. "Not a *good* chance, but a chance. As for you, Lazar, I figured, why not? You prefer me to shoot you now, put you in the trunk, that's fine—but Lisa still only gets two tanks of air."

Lazar glanced to the left. Carly was standing about fifteen feet away, aiming the rifle at him. Close enough for her to make a sure hit, but too far for him to get to her. Between the loss of blood and the hobble, he couldn't manage much more than turtle speed. Lazar licked his lips, feeling awfully tired. "I'm still not doing it."

"Shoot him, Carly," Geoff said, indifferently.

"No!" Lisa stepped between Lazar and Carly's gun.

"Oh, give me a reason," the girl said.

Lisa ignored her and grasped Lazar's hands. "Please don't leave me alone."

Geoff hammed it up, acting as if Lazar were refusing to dance with his date. "Come on, Lazar! Put on the wetsuit and get in the car. Her husband has a rendezvous in half an hour with me and Carly. A half hour to do the job, a half hour to get back. If he gives me a good enough reason, you might get another chance."

"And what if he doesn't?" Lazar said, dully.

Geoff nodded to the Mercedes. "Everybody's got to die sometime."

Ten minutes later, he had lashed them to the front seats with clothesline. Lisa was trying to contain her panic. Trying and barely succeeding to remember what she had learned from the three dive lessons Steve had once given her in a pool before she had decided it wasn't the right sport for her. *Too claustrophobic.*

The thought made her laugh now, a hysterical little gasp that made Geoff smile at her oddly as he checked over his work. He had tied two scuba tanks to each of their seats in the back and ran the two regulator hoses over their shoulders using duct tape to fasten them so they wouldn't fall away. He said, "Keep your mouth clamped tight over your mouthpiece as you go off the pier. I'll put masks on you so you can see the pressure gauges, here—you've got three thousand pounds in each tank. That line's got enough slack so you can switch mouthpieces once the first tanks are empty. You'll be in about thirty feet of water. When I dove down tonight, I went through most of that in just under an hour—of course, you might be breathing a little faster than I was."

Geoff began whistling as he wound their legs with a chain and bound them to the seat mounts.

"What difference does it make?" Lazar's voice was shaky; something Lisa hadn't heard from him before. "Dead in forty-five minutes or dead in an hour and a half. We should've made him shoot us both."

"It matters, doesn't it, Geoff?" She talked fast, feeling that if she didn't, she would just sit there and hyperventilate and that was no good. Couldn't get in the habit of running through air if Geoff was going to sink them in that black water. "You're not going to just drown us, you're going to leave us an opening, aren't you, Geoff. You're not just a murderer."

He grimaced as he put a face mask on her. "Technically, I'm afraid I am. So you better make your own opening. There. Test your air." She took a tentative breath out of each regulator mouthpiece. The air rasped through easily enough. She looked over at Lazar and saw that he was doing the same thing.

Geoff took Lazar's wristwatch off and strapped it onto the steering wheel. He taped a dive light to the base of Lazar's headrest and turned it so the beam hit the watch face. It was just min-utes before twelve. "If you're lucky, it'll still be pointing that way once you hit bottom. If you're not—well, you'll know your time is up when your last tank is empty."

He snapped the headlights on, leaned through the driver's door past Lazar and put the car in neutral.

Lazar grabbed him.

The car began rolling down the hill. Geoff snorted. "Give it up, will you?" Lisa could see Lazar's grip was just around Geoff's arm.

The car picked up speed. Carly was left behind, screaming.

Even in that instant, Lisa knew if Geoff wasn't able to meet Steve, then she and Lazar would certainly never get out of the car. But she reached for Geoff anyhow, straining against the rope to get hold of him somehow, to somehow take him down with them. But he pulled away, and stood on the rocker panel, crouching out-side the car. Still Lazar held his arm tight.

They rolled onto the pier and were heading down the center to the dark water at the end. A piling flashed by and as the next came up, Lazar lifted his knee to try to push the steering wheel. She saw he was trying to hit it with the open door and crush Geoff.

But Geoff reached out with his left hand and calmly headed the car down the center. They missed the piling by inches. Then he reached around to his back pocket and something glittered dully in his hand. Lisa saw it was the razor, Carly's razor. "Nice try, guys," he said, as he sliced the back of Lazar's hand.

Lazar cried out into his mouthpiece and let go. Geoff fell in and braced himself momentarily on the center console with the hand holding the razor. Lisa instinctively reached over and grabbed it. The blade bit down to the bone but still she held on—and then it was hers as Geoff let go and shoved away from the car.

The nose of the car dropped abruptly and the headlights lit the surface of the water an instant before they hit.

Metal screeched as the hood buckled. Water roared into the open door and the car canted to the left. Lisa panicked, certain it would roll, certain that they would sink upside down.

Then the weight of the engine pulled the car down and water poured in through her window and rose over their heads. The sound of the air rasping through the regulators changed as they were fully submerged. Silver bubbles burst in front of the dive light beam.

Lisa had a brief glimpse of the muddy bottom below, not too far away, and then the lights winked out.

The dive light shook crazily as Lazar fought in the confined space, trying to free himself from the clothesline. The shockingly cold water found its way into her wetsuit. Her ears hurt, and she swallowed rapidly, clearing them as fast as she could. For a time, the only thing she could hold on to was that she still had air. She was still breathing.

She had no sense of how long it took to reach bottom, whether it was minutes or seconds. She looked to her left and Lazar looked back. It was a surreal scene. His face mask reflected the peripheral glow from the dive light. Air bubbled from his mouthpiece.

Good, she thought. He's still breathing.

She saw his air was just rushing out and she realized hers was, too. Goddamn it, we've got the right, she thought, grinding her jaw against the excruciating pain in her ears. She swallowed and yawned the way Steve had taught her and the air squealed through her ears as the pressure equalized. She looked over and saw Lazar was shaking his head. The pain had to be intense for him, and she wished there was a way she could tell him what to do.

As she forced herself to slow down her breathing, to inhale, one-two-three, exhale, one-two-three, she felt a sharp pain in her hand and remembered that she had cut her hand on the razor.

Remembered she had taken it from Geoff.

She cried out in sudden hope, and, just as quickly, in frustration.

Her hand was empty.

CHAPTER 37

Geoff held Carly's wrist and looked at her watch. "They've been down thirty minutes."

She jerked her hand away. "I'd like to join them, right about now."

Geoff knew she was terrified, sitting there in the van with him outside of Raul's gates. But he liked the way she was trying to tough it out. He drew the four-inch blade from Jammer's belt that he now wore around his waist. "This will give us all we need, once we hear Steve's boat." He thumbnailed what he and Steve had discussed.

She looked more frightened than ever. "You're counting on Steve? How do you know he'll come through? And what if they have guns?"

"We can count on both things: They will have guns, and Steve will come through. As for how we take care of it . . . well, that's where the fun comes in."

"Fun? Jesus Christ, why do you talk that way?"

He put his hand over hers. "Basically, just go along with everything I say. You'll know what to do and when."

Geoff felt good. It was just like before a football game in high school. Everyone else was nervous, either looking like they might puke or yelling at the top of their lungs to prove they weren't scared. He would just sit there feeling good. Knowing that he could move so fast. Knowing with absolute confidence that his body would do the right thing at the right time. That he would do whatever it took to win.

That his luck would hold when the odds were impossible.

Geoff laughed out loud, surprising Carly. She looked over at him, her cheeks wet. "Hey, hey," he said, wiping the tears away with his thumb.

She said, "Don't you know he plans to cut me up in front of his camera? Literally?"

"Sure I do. But he doesn't know what I intend."

"Neither do I."

He kissed her lightly. "You'll see."

Strike counted the money while the Hispanic guy frisked them. The guy took his time with Carly, grinning over at Strike as he touched her. The thing almost got out of hand when she scratched him across the face.

"You bitch!" The man drew back his hand.

Geoff got between them and said to Strike, "Raul likes sloppy seconds?"

Strike's eyes glinted. "The man don't care about that, but he wants them whole when he gets them. How she get cut? She damaged goods, man."

"She did Jammer. He didn't go down easy."

Strike grinned at her appreciatively. "Yeah? Managed to kill your last man, huh?"

Geoff interjected, "Just so we get this straight, she makes this movie, it's ten thousand dollars and all her doctor bills, right? That's the deal."

Strike swallowed his quick grin, and said to her, "That's it, baby. Good deal, considering you cut the man." Strike exchanged a glance with Geoff and the two of them smiled.

Carly thought she might go insane as they tied the Mako to the stern of the big yacht.

How could she have believed Geoff?

She saw that smile between him and Strike. If he could put Lisa down into that car to drown, why should Carly trust his word to her?

Because he loves me, she thought. *Stupid girl.*

She looked at her hands, and then, with a certain reverence touched her arm, feeling the smoothness of her skin, flexing the healthy muscle and bone underneath. She tuned in to her body, appreciating it as hers; appreciating her own beauty.

She felt another flash of rage at Geoff as she touched the scar on her face. How could he bring her face-to-face with Raul? Face-to-face with a man who wanted to hurt her so he could get his rocks off on some goddamn video.

Geoff will ditch me, she thought, abruptly. For a second she was giddy with panic, and she cast about the boat for some way to escape. Strike put the keys to the Mako in his jeans pocket as he knocked on the cabin door. She wished desperately for her razor. She knew beyond any doubt if she had that steel in her hand that nasty punk would be on the floor now with his throat sliced wide open.

Geoff stepped in front of her and winked. She bore down on the panic, forced herself to eat it. She searched his eyes, his body, looking for evidence to assure herself that he would come through. She saw the belt buckle and remembered Junior. She closed her eyes then, and thought about Geoff telling her that he loved her and that he would take her away. She breathed deeply, and she wanted him to kiss her and whisper that everything was all right. But when she opened her eyes, he had moved away.

She checked her watch. They had wasted almost ten minutes getting out to the yacht. It was too dark to see anything, the clouds obscured the moon. She turned and looked out into the darkness, listening for the sound of the motorboat, for Steve.

Maybe Lisa's been stood up, too. The thought gave her no comfort.

"Carly, Carly," Raul's voice said. "I'm so glad you can join me and agreed to be in my little show."

She forced herself to stare at him, show him that she wasn't afraid, even though her insides were curdling. Raul stood there, his arms wide open, making like he was a big movie producer. Laughing at himself. Big soft tub of guts. She knew what he was capable of; knew what he could do to her because of his money and the men surrounding him. But she made herself see them alone in an alley, and she wished again for her razor. Her heart was pounding and her mouth tasted bitter. She couldn't trust her voice to be steady so she didn't answer.

"I'm anxious to get started," he said, and waved her into the cabin.

Geoff jerked his head toward the cabinway, a small smile on his face that she couldn't read. Nevertheless, she walked into the cabin, her legs stiff and numb.

Raul frowned. "What happened to her face?"

Strike said, "Dude here says she killed her man, Jammer. Got himself a cut in before he went down. I say we teach her, right?"

"Did you take away her razor?" Raul asked mildly.

"Checked good, man. She clean."

"I should've cut your throat," Carly said. Her voice sounded better than she thought it would. Clear, unafraid.

Raul chuckled. "Oh, she's terrifying. I'm going to title this one *Pimp's Revenge.*"

Strike grinned, his eyes twinkling with good humor. "Jammer'll like that, man, sitting up in pimp heaven."

Raul snapped on bright lights, and Carly shuddered seeing the video camera on a tripod. The cabin had been rearranged to be dominated by a single bed. The bed and floors were covered loosely with red sheets and she saw a stack of towels on the counter. Beside the bed was an open footlocker filled with leather paraphernalia, gleaming with metal studs.

Carly's breath was rushing in and out.

Raul stepped closer to her. He drew back his sleeve to reveal the ugly scar and then laid it against the scar on her face softly. The intimacy of it made her cry out involuntarily and she backed away. "We're going to get a lot closer than that, Carly," he whispered. "I'll be inside you."

"She thinks she's gonna get ten K and all her doctor bills paid," Strike said.

"That right?" Raul grinned over at Geoff. "I wondered how you got her here without handcuffs."

Geoff put the suitcase of money on the bed. "This is the balance," he said, quietly. "Why don't you just take it and call it quits with Carly."

She looked over at him. *That's it?* She wanted to scream.

Both Raul and Strike laughed.

Raul said, "I've got another idea. Why don't I work on her with a sharp knife for a few hours? Then have the boys drop her in the ocean with lead weights once I get bored. How about that idea? Only question is whether or not you join her."

Carly tried desperately to read Geoff's eyes and face, but all she saw was a sort of pleasant blankness. He didn't even look at her.

The bastards planned to kill her.

And Geoff was doing nothing. In spite of herself, her breath began to rush, and her vision blurred. She wiped away the tears furiously.

Raul stared at Geoff contemptuously, then said to Strike, "Call Lee and have him take this idiot to the house. I'll decide what to do with him after."

"Hey, it only seemed right to make the offer," Geoff said defensively. "Keep that big bastard away from me."

The weakness in his voice was something Carly had never heard before. She still couldn't read him; couldn't tell if he was acting or not. Either way, she figured she was on her own. If only she had *something*. Carly's eyes flickered across the cabin, the galley, the desk. Not even a fork. She remembered Junior and stepped closer to Geoff, but he backed away and said, without looking at her, "Hey, I'm sorry, honey."

She stared at him, not able to stop herself. Trying to read if she had been truly tricked by a man for the final time.

She couldn't tell.

Strike yelled for Lee again, and then pulled a big aluminum case from a side locker and began to put Geoff's money in. Carly saw a huge stack in there, probably as much as Geoff thought there was. She told herself he really wanted it. She told herself he would do something for it, if not for her.

Lee came into the cabin, his massive frame filling the doorway.

"This guy been giving orders for you to stay away, man," Strike said, jerking his head at Geoff. "Called you a big bastard, that's a fact."

Lee walked up to Geoff and shoved him against the wall. "It's the tough guy, huh?" He looked over at Carly and whistled. "You shoulda heard him watching out for your ass, girl, until Raul burned him. Took awhile, but your man give you up like a bad itch."

Outside, the sound of a motor started, close by.

Lee cocked his head to one side, listening. And then it looked like Geoff had punched him, a fast blow to his Adam's apple.

The man went, "Huh!" like he was surprised.

And coughed blood.

Raul turned, his expression irritated, and Strike said, "What?" and then suddenly reached under his shirt.

Lee dropped to the floor, and Geoff yanked the little knife from his throat. Geoff sprang away from the wall toward Strike.

Carly grabbed at Strike's hand as he pulled out a small gun and then Geoff was on him. Geoff punched the little blade into the guy's chest, two, three times, as she held Strike's arm off to the side. The gun cracked twice, bullets flying past her ear.

The kid fell down, clutching himself. There was a click behind them and Geoff whirled as Raul calmly aimed a big revolver.

Carly knew it was over. She saw Raul's finger tighten on the trigger even as she saw that Geoff was already moving. He was going to kick Raul's hand. *He's too late,* she thought sadly.

That's when the boat exploded.

She was thrown back against the galley counter. The front of the boat lifted up and the door toward the bow flew across the cabin and hit Raul.

It knocked him off his feet and the gun fell to the cabin floor. He scrambled for it, but she got to it first.

Immediately afterward, as she climbed into the cockpit, the boat sinking bow first, she couldn't remember if she had actually said it or if she had just thought it.

But then, she must have. Because Geoff had the big case in his hand and he was laughing and kissing her and saying, "I can't believe you!"

So she must have said it. "This one's named *Hooker's Revenge.*"

Right before shooting Raul in the balls.

Geoff had taken the gun from her and put another bullet into Raul's forehead to make him shut up.

The gun flash, the blood, the screaming . . . all of it made her feel dazed and breathless. Geoff was half holding her up.

But she was certain she'd said the words.

Certain.

CHAPTER 38

Geoff thought his heart might burst, he was so proud of Carly. Then he remembered Steve and sobered immediately.

The cockpit lights were still shining, showing the big Blue Water floating alongside. Beyond it, the Mako was floating away, the line free.

Steve wasn't in either boat.

Carly grasped Geoff as the *White Angel*'s bow sank even deeper.

"Where?" she said, and Geoff laid the gun she had used on Raul alongside his leg. He whirled when he heard a noise just to his left.

Nothing.

Then there was the cold touch on the back of Geoff's head and Steve said, "Drop it."

"You know that shit won't work with me," Geoff said.

"Good. Because I don't need you now that I've got her." Geoff heard Steve cock his gun.

Geoff hesitated, but then let the gun and money fall to the cockpit sole. Suddenly, the boat squealed as if in pain, the hull settling as water began to rush over the bow. Geoff reacted instantly and swung his arm back to knock Steve's gun off his head. He then did the opposite of what Steve—or anyone—would have expected.

Geoff threw himself back into the sinking boat.

"Geoff!" Carly screamed.

Steve stood in the cabinway and fired twice. Geoff dove into the chest-deep water and hid behind Strike's floating body. He saw Carly come up behind Steve and try to wrestle the gun away. Steve shoved her away.

"Geoff!" she screamed. "Get out, it's sinking!"

Steve dragged her away.

Geoff waited, listening to her yell for him until it sounded as if they were far away. He remembered the Mako was still within swimming distance. The bow of the yacht sank deeper, and already the water was pouring in from the open portholes as if shot from a firehose. The hull screeched again as the forward bulwark shifted under the press of water.

Geoff rolled Strike onto his back and found the Mako's keys. He thrashed his way up the steep incline to the cabin door—just as the cockpit rail slipped below the surface. A solid wall of black water roared into the cabin, sweeping him in deeper. The last of the lights shorted out and the *White Angel* went down in darkness.

The girl tried to go back down after him. "No!" she screamed, as Steve held her back. She hit him with her elbows and fists, crying, "Geoff, oh my God, Geoff, get out!"

Once the yacht went under, Steve waited until she sagged against the rail, crying, before he let her go.

Steve felt some sympathy, but only a little.

He remembered her holding a rifle on Lisa all too easily. He said, "Tell me where she is."

Carly stared at the black water. "I can't believe it." She turned to Steve, her cheeks wet with tears. "He *did* protect me."

"Where is she?" Steve fought to keep his voice calm.

Carly didn't seem to hear him. She turned back to the water.

Steve spun her around. "What's he got set up, damn it? Did he put her in a box again?"

She seemed to really see Steve for the first time. The hurt, bewildered look on her face turned hard. "You shot at him. You must have hit him."

"Where is she?" Steve shook the girl.

"She's drowning!" the girl spat back. She pointed to the water. "She's under there, just like him."

Steve felt a hand squeeze his heart, but kept his voice calm. "You say she *is*. Meaning she's still alive."

The girl shrugged.

"Is she?"

Steve drew his hand back—and then stopped. He cupped her chin so that she had to look at him. Even in the feeble glow of the instrument lights, he could see the hurt in her eyes. "Look," he said, gently. "You know how you feel about Geoff, how you're missing him? It's been like that in my head for a week now. I'm just about crazy with it. Tell me where she is or I'll hit you and I'll keep hitting you until you do. I'd rather not. I would really rather not. But think how you're feeling, and you know I will."

The girl stared at him and then pulled herself away. She looked at her watch and said, "She's got a little more than a half hour left. Then she runs out of air. He put them in a car and sank them in the water with two scuba tanks for each."

"Each of *them?*"

"Her and that cop, Lazar."

"He found you?" Steve's mind raced, wondering how Lazar had found them.

"Came snooping around," she said. "Snooping cop is going to get it too."

"Where?"

She crossed her arms. "I think I'll just wait."

"How deep?"

"What?"

"How deep was the water?"

She smiled. "I don't know."

He hit her then, hard. "How deep?"

The blow surprised her. "Thirty . . . Geoff said it was about thirty feet deep."

"And how long have they been down?"

"Fifty minutes."

An hour and a half for two tanks at thirty feet sounded about right. Maybe worth a little more. "Where are they?"

"Fuck you."

He raised his hand again and she stared back defiantly. "Go ahead. I've been hit before."

Steve hesitated for a moment, then went to the bow locker and came back with the aluminum case. It looked much like the case that had held Raul's money. He grabbed Carly's wrist and before she could yank it away, he snapped a handcuff bracelet on her. The other end was attached to the case handle. Another set dangled along the case.

"What the hell?"

She tugged at the case and it banged against her leg.

Steve took a key from a Velcro pouch on his wetsuit and turned a lock on the case. Suddenly a red digital readout was visible just under the handle; the number forty-five glowed.

"What's this?" she snapped.

"I'd intended it for you and Geoff. I figured if Geoff had a time limit on the two of you, he would take me to Lisa. You were important to him."

Her chin lifted. "He said that?"

"In so many words," Steve said, realizing it all came down to this. "He might have put you at risk, but he definitely did not intend for you to die." Steve put the key into his pocket. "Now you get to make that decision by yourself."

"Or what?" She stared at the readout. Forty-four minutes.

He waited until she looked up, and then he nodded to where the *White Angel* had been. "Or an explosive charge as big as that removes you from the planet."

CHAPTER 39

The batteries on the dive light were weakening, but Lazar could still read the watch easily enough. He figured the air would last only a few more minutes.

Maybe not even that. They had both been breathing pretty hard.

He thought about what it had been like when the first tank went dry. Thought about how it became hard to draw a breath. How his cheeks had pressed against his side teeth—and then the air stopped altogether. What a blessed relief it had been to put the other mouthpiece in and taste the easy rush of fresh air.

He thought about not having that sweet rush, what the minute or two afterward would be like.

Beside him, Lisa was searching hard, so he tried again, straining his arms at the length of the line so he could run his fingers along the edge of the seat and try to reach down between the gap, between it and the armrest. Lazar bit down hard at the exquisite pain of forcing the torn muscles in his shoulder to work, of forcing his freshly sliced right hand to feel for the very blade that had cut him.

Nothing. The mask gave him tunnel vision and from where he sat, he couldn't see if the razor was inches away or on the other side of the car. Either way, it was beyond his restraining lines. He relaxed, and the cold water overwhelmed him suddenly.

God, he was tired.

When they had first gone down, the saltwater in his wounds had made him scream some of his precious air away. But now he was so exhausted, it almost didn't matter. He thought about Charlotte some more, wondering how long it would take for her to find out what had happened to him.

A week? A month? Maybe never.

He imagined her crying. But, the truth was, he could just as easily imagine her being relieved that she had been separated from him for a year before he was found dead.

Then he caught himself.

Caught himself down there, underwater, minutes away from being a big lump of fish food—and still pissing and moaning about his wife.

He laughed into his mouthpiece.

The sound scattered the little fish that had swum into the open windows of the car, attracted by the light like moths. And that seemed pretty funny too, so he laughed some more. He looked over at Lisa and the light caught her eyes well enough to see that she was begging him to get on the stick, to keep looking for that razor. He liked her, that Lisa.

Lazar closed his eyes and told his wife good-bye. He sucked in a great gust of air and then threw all his remaining strength against the line.

It gave.

Not much, one of the knots just slipped. But he gained an extra two inches of play.

And a painful cut along the tip of his forefinger.

He had found the razor.

———————————————

Carly's eyes were glued to the red digits, down to thirteen minutes now.

They had just charged through town in Alex's truck. Carly had said they weren't too far away by water, but she didn't know how to find the place by boat. Not in the dark, anyhow. Steve had spun the boat around and they had taken more time than he could afford running through the night to get back to the boat launching site. He had run the Blue Water up onto the ramp and thrown two tanks and his dive gear into the back of Alex's truck.

Steve got it when they saw the sign for Sea Crest.

"Jansten," he said. "You're keeping her at Jansten's house. That's how Lazar got to you, he went to question Jansten or something, right?"

She looked at him and then looked back to the numbers.

"Where is he?"

"What?"

Steve shook her. "Where's Jansten?"

She seemed not so much afraid of the descending numbers as mesmerized. "He's in the bedroom. Dead."

Steve raised his hand to her and then pulled it away. He hit his leg softly with a clenched fist. "What the hell was the matter with you two?" he asked, softly.

That startled her. She blinked at him.

Then she sat up suddenly. "Hey, how do I know this is real? Maybe it's just some frigging clock you picked up at the drugstore."

She started to open the case and he snatched her hand away. "Don't. There's a tension release detonator in there."

"Maybe I should do it then. Take you out, too."

He looked at her carefully, but didn't say anything. He turned onto the gravel road leading to Jansten's house.

She stared at him, her hands trembling. She almost did it. Slipped those latches and let it all end right there.

But in the end, she folded her hands in her lap. "I can't go to jail," she said, as they charged past the house.

"Where are they?"

She nodded to the pier. "They went off the end of that."

Steve drove onto the pier and stopped the truck. He hurried out to the back of the truck and pulled on his mask, tank, fins. He grabbed a dive light and quickly tightened a regulator onto the spare tank.

In his head, Buddy's hands beat against slick fiberglass.

Steve pulled the mask down over his face.

"What about me?" Carly said as he stood near the edge of the pier.

He didn't answer her.

"There's only seven minutes left," she cried. "You can't leave me here!"

Steve jumped into the water.

Carly moved herself to the edge of the pier. She watched the light go deeper and deeper. She was silent, until from the corner of her eye, she saw the flicker of change in the digital readout as the seven turned into a six. Before she knew it was going to happen, she burst into tears.

It was dark, and she was cold and wet. As far as she could see, everything from that night Neal had pounded on the door of her mother's trailer had led her here tonight, and she couldn't see how that was fair.

She hiccupped. She looked back up at the house and realized one of the floodlights was still on. That made her tears stop.

She remembered Geoff turning them all off as they left. She *knew* he did.

She stifled a scream.

There was a boat pulled up on the beach, covered with a tarp. It hadn't been there when they had left.

A wave lapped up and moved the tarp near the transom. Even in the poor light, she could see the manufacturer's name.

Mako.

CHAPTER 40

Lisa was almost out of air.

Lazar had been able to slice away the rope binding them within minutes after getting his hands on the razor.

And even though they couldn't pull their legs free of the chain, Lazar had started cutting away the wetsuit around her legs, trying to get enough slack to pull her legs free.

When that first tug on her breath came, Lisa looked at the pressure gauge and saw the needle pegged at zero. She had squeezed Lazar's arm with all her strength and then lain back in her seat, trying to be calm. Trying to conserve the last few breaths until he could strip the material away.

He recognized what was happening and worked furiously.

She knew he couldn't have much air left either. She knew that whatever time and air he spent on her, he couldn't spend on himself. She knew that, and still she couldn't find it in herself to protest.

Hurry, she thought. Her ankle was loose in the chain now, but still she couldn't tug it free. She fought for it, pulling Lazar aside and tugging her leg with everything she had.

Close. But no goddamn cigar.

She exhaled.

Then, slowly, she inhaled. Waiting for rejection.

It came within half a breath. Complete resistance.

The tank was empty.

Still she tried, still she choked and gagged against the mouthpiece trying to find air where there was none. Lazar saw what was happening, and he handed her his mouthpiece and then went back to work on her suit.

She drank carefully from the air. *Bad form to take it all.* Hysteria began to bubble inside her and she clamped down on it tight. *Crazed laughter consumes too much air,* she told herself, solemnly.

The razor bit into her leg and she cried out. She tapped his shoulder, and he came back up to take the mouthpiece.

That's it, she told herself, looking at his pressure gauge. The needle was sitting just above zero.

He gave her back the mouthpiece and went back to work.

She saw a light outside the window.

Lisa rubbed her faceplate, not sure if she was hallucinating.

It was there. A light. She thought maybe this was Death. Or maybe just Geoff coming down to gloat.

That thought gave her a kind of hope. She fumbled for Lazar's hand, looking for the razor. He pushed her hand away and kept working. She yelled into her mouthpiece, determined to live long enough to cut Geoff, cut him any way she could.

And then she recognized who it was and she was certain now that she was hallucinating. She leaned back in her seat as he reached in; she couldn't let herself believe that he was real.

Luckily, that didn't stop her from accepting the bubbling regulator from Steve.

He slid the tank in between them and handed the extra hose and mouthpiece to Lazar. The cop grabbed Lisa's hand and they squeezed each other so hard it hurt. She was laughing inside her mouthpiece and she could hear him do the same. *A little hysteria would be acceptable now,* the solemn voice told her, and she gave in to it for a second or two, and then sobered up fast. She was suddenly very anxious to be out of the car altogether, breathing real air instead of the canned stuff.

She put her facemask against Steve's. She couldn't really see him once the light was blocked out, but, God, she knew he was there.

She drew a deep breath.

It's over. It's over.

She could cry all day if she wanted.

Suddenly, Steve was yanked away from her.

He cried out in pain, a muted underwater sound, but she recognized it for what it was. She reached out for him, terrified, thinking something had him, a shark or a barracuda.

Steve's tank clanged on the roof and Lazar turned the dive light out the front window and she could see Geoff and Steve on the hood, fighting.

And Steve had something sticking out of his back, a big, yellow-handled screwdriver.

Lazar slammed himself to the left and right, but couldn't pull himself free. Lisa tried the same, but as much as she strained, she couldn't quite pull herself free from the chain.

Geoff was trying to yank away Steve's air hose. Steve kept his hand over his own facemask and mouthpiece, like when she had seen him jump off a boat with all his gear. He was trying for the knife he kept on his weight belt, but Geoff's leg covered it as he straddled Steve.

Lisa saw the dull reflection of the razor in Lazar's hand, and saw him reach around the front windshield with it from the driver's side.

But he couldn't get close enough to them.

They were closer to her.

She grabbed Lazar's hand for the razor.

He hesitated, and then she squeezed hard. "Give it to me!" she yelled into the mouthpiece. He handed it to her.

Lisa hit the window with the razor's handle three times.

Lazar turned the dive light so the blade glittered brightly. Steve's head turned their way, and suddenly, he shifted, knocking Geoff back against the front window. Steve had to take his hand away to do that, and Geoff used the opportunity to strip away Steve's mask and regulator.

But Steve kept charging. He kept pushing Geoff back until they slid off the edge of the car. Lazar lunged across Lisa and reached through the window to grab Geoff by his tank.

And Lisa used the razor across the small of his back.

CHAPTER 41

Carly saw Geoff was all wrong as soon as his head broke the surface. He could move his arms, but it was Steve who was keeping him afloat.

A moment later, Lisa and the cop joined them.

"Hurry!" Carly said, as she heard Steve telling Lisa how to disarm the bomb.

Lisa hurried up the ladder with the key in her hand.

"Is it real?" Carly said.

Lisa didn't answer. She slid the key into the lock and switched off the timer.

"Was it?" Carly asked.

"Yes," Lisa said, tiredly. She slumped back against a piling for a moment, then turned to help Lazar. Geoff clung to the bottom of the ladder, his body slack.

Carly called to Geoff, but he didn't answer. "Can't you hear me?" she said.

Steve said, "Lisa, throw me down a rope for him. He's paralyzed from the waist down."

"What about you? You've still got that thing in your back."

"Let Mann drown," Lazar said.

"No!" Carly said.

"Girl, I'd drown you with him, if I had the energy." The cop held himself up against a piling.

"Please," Steve said, his voice weak. "Let's just finish this."

"I'll get the rope." Lisa hurried to the truck and returned with a heavy length of hemp. She tossed an end of the line down to Steve, and then she, Lazar, and Carly pulled Geoff up. Though his arms appeared to still function, he didn't help himself at all.

Carly dragged the aluminum case to the edge of the pier and pulled Geoff's head to her breast. "Oh, baby," she said. "You're hurt bad, aren't you?"

His legs hung over the side, slack, like those of a doll.

He said nothing.

"Steve!" Lisa cried, and turned to Lazar, white-faced. "He's coughing blood."

Lazar staggered over to Geoff and yanked the loop of rope from his shoulders. He said to Lisa, "Go down there with him, and hold on to this. I'll pull you along the pier to the beach."

She jumped into the water. Lazar dropped the line and hurried up the pier.

Carly and Geoff were alone.

"Why did you come back?" she whispered.

He didn't answer.

She cradled his head in her lap. "Does it hurt?"

He opened his eyes. She saw his lower lip start to tremble, and then he clamped his jaw down tight.

"Geoff, talk to me, please."

"I can't feel my legs," he said, finally.

"I thought you were dead. I thought you drowned in that boat."

"Almost did. But I found an air bubble under the cabin roof. I got out before the boat hit bottom. I've always had luck. Always had fantastic luck."

She saw a tear slip down his cheek and wiped it away as if it were just seawater on his face. She said, quietly, "So why did you come back?"

"Crazy."

"Why?"

"Crazy and I'll never walk again for it." His breathing began to rush and he looked left and right, panicking. "Oh, Jesus, oh God, I'm going to be in some prison hospital. Some prison hospital and I'm not going to be able to do anything." He began to shiver, even though the night was warm. "Jesus, Carly, I could last years like this."

"Ssssh." She kissed him on the forehead. "I know. They might never let us out." She looked him in the eyes. "That goes for both of us. So I want the truth. Was it for the money? Did you figure you'd get Steve and make him go back down for the money?"

"The money's gone."

"Is that why, though?"

"No."

"Why, then?"

"You know why. To close it out. To finish with them and to get you."

"You were going to take me?"

She could read it. Read the surprise in his eyes, perhaps with himself. "I told you," he said. "You were going with me. We would have found another way to make some money."

"You love me?"

He nodded. "Seems that I do."

She kissed him on the mouth. "I just wanted to go away with you. I wanted that so bad."

She told him what was in the case, what Steve had said about the detonator. She slid the case on top of them and he put his hands on the latches.

"Take me with you," she said.

He did.

EPILOGUE

They dressed warmly against the October chill and set sail out of Boston Harbor just after midnight. The wind favored them by coming across the beam at a steady fifteen knots. Steve programmed a course into the GPS before coming back to the stern to take the wheel. *The Sea Tern* settled into a fast reach, her wake bubbling white.

Lisa sat beside him. Her hair tickled his cheek and he felt content for the first time in months.

The media had been after every element of the story, characterizing it as the ultimate boardroom clash. Lisa and Steve had seen the picture of themselves inside the ambulance more times than they could count: Lisa, exhausted and bedraggled. Steve, his face shockingly white from loss of blood. Their hands linked.

Luckily, the press liked that. They liked the idea of a wealthy guy fighting for his wife. They liked that Lazar credited them with saving his life, and that they said the same of him. Having a veteran black cop behind them all the way made a huge difference.

As for Geoff, a *Boston Herald* photographer somehow got into his apartment and shot virtually every picture on the wall. The *Globe* ran an editorial titled NARCISSUS LIVES AND DIES IN BOSTON. The story of Geoff's good looks, his embezzled wealth, his shocking level of violence—and most of all, his relationship with Carly—sold a lot of newspapers.

Luckily, every good story needs a hero or two and Lisa and Steve fit the bill.

In truth, without the public sentiment and Lazar's influence with the district attorney, Steve might well have gone to prison for sinking Alex and Jammer's bodies at sea, and for the handgun violations.

As for the assault on Raul's yacht, Lazar told both Lisa and Steve how it had to be before the ambulance ever arrived. He knelt between the two of them on the beach, the flames still flickering on the pier. "You weren't there, you got me? That thing was all Geoff's doing. No one left alive to prove it's not. That gets out, you're gonna have gang shit on top of the cops. One or the other, somebody will get to you."

As it was, they escaped the gangs, the police, and even the press—but not the board of directors of Jansten Enterprises.

"We're looking at a mess, Steve," George McGarrity had said at that morning's board meeting. With Jansten gone, he was the acting chairman. McGarrity didn't meet Steve's eyes. "We don't doubt most of what we heard. We certainly believe Geoff was the instigator here, and while personally many of us admire what you have done . . . the fact of the matter is that you—as well as he— used company funds inappropriately."

Here McGarrity had raised his hand, presumably to catch

Steve's objection, which didn't arrive. "Yes, we realize that your wife was in a terrible spot, and we're sure in such a desperate situation it only seemed expedient to take the money."

Steve looked down at the boardroom table, letting the words wash past him.

So much for wealth and power.

He thought of the speech he could make, how he could castigate them for judging him after the fact. "Just what the hell would you have done?" he could ask. He could talk about the cost of selling his home to immediately pay back the company, even though Raul's aluminum case had been recovered and supposedly the one hundred and fifty thousand would some day be released from evidence. He could talk to them about an executive's ability to make a decision and act. He could even talk to them about Carl Jansten's own robber baron heritage and how he undoubtedly would have taken similar action had he been in the same predicament.

But Steve didn't say any of these things.

McGarrity continued. ". . . and, yes, you have made restitution . . . but with the questions still open about Carl's death and the entangled mess between you and Geoff Mann, I'm afraid this just won't do. Jansten Enterprises has an image to maintain, and that means not only absolute honesty, but the *appearance* of absolute honesty . . ."

Steve walked out.

In the elevator, rushing down to ground level, he did a quick assessment of their finances. The house already belonged to someone else, the contractor had been paid. Steve had never been a believer in golden parachutes and had never negotiated for one. So his salary would dry up within a few weeks.

But the boat was still theirs. After using most of the house equity to pay back what he owed to the corporation, they had enough cash for about four months. Maybe six if they were careful. Most likely he would raise capital for a start-up, produce an even better line of boats with Lisa's help. But he didn't even want to think about that now.

As he and Lisa rose and fell with the motion of the waves, she asked, "Are you going to miss it?"

They looked back on the lights of Boston. He knew if he put the binoculars to his eyes he could have picked out the Jansten building.

He didn't.

Instead, he said simply, "Nothing like I would have missed you."

They sailed on for over an hour at a steady six knots. When the GPS sounded, he turned the boat into the wind and let the sails shiver. They threw the wreath overboard and watched it float on the surface of Alex's grave until it disappeared into the night.

After a time, they let their sails fill and continued on.

Ben looked over at Parker. He thought of the *Newsweek* issue that had just been distributed behind the sandbags that morning. Under the headline, "Collision Course," the cover had depicted high school photos of Johansen with a winning smile, Parker solemn and serious.

"Nervous?" Parker asked Ben.

"Hell, yes."

Both of them started slightly when the telephone on Burnett's belt sounded. He flipped it open. "All right, Mr. Johansen. Give us a second to secure everybody here."

He nodded to Parker, who spoke rapidly into his radio to the SWAT team. "The girl's coming out. Everybody be *god*damn sure you hold fire."

Katy was shoved into the doorway. Around Ben, he could feel everyone relax slightly. This was the first they'd seen of her in the whole stand, and although she seemed terrified, she looked all right otherwise.

"I've got one her age at home," Parker said. He clapped Ben lightly on the arm. "Swap with her."

Ben started across the grass. He lifted his camera slowly to his eye and captured a shot of her standing in the doorway. Her lower lip was trembling. "Hey," he said, as he got closer. "Hey, Katy."

Johansen spoke around the door. "Keep on coming. Once you're in, she goes."

Ben stepped into the gloom of the barn. In an instant, he took it all in: Johansen standing by the concrete wall, the gun on him; the mother and boy, bound and tied to a farm tractor. A shaft of light revealed the mother's face, looking imploringly between Johansen and her daughter. "Please now, can she go?"

"I don't want to," the girl said. "I want to stay with you, Mommy."

"Move it," Johansen snapped.

Ben did a mild double take when he looked at Johansen again. Somehow, the man had shaved and cleaned himself up. Ready for the cameras. "Can I?" Ben said, gesturing to the girl.

Johansen nodded abruptly.

Ben knelt down next to her. "Hey, I've got a girl your age." He pointed to Parker. "So does he." Ben looked back at the phalanx of men with guns and he understood her hesitation. He flapped his hand down to Parker and the agent got his point immediately and knelt down to child level. "Run to him, honey. He knows you're scared."

The girl looked at Ben closely, and then abruptly ran to Parker.

Without thinking, Ben raised the camera and captured two shots of the little girl with dirty blue coveralls and pigtails, running for the kneeling FBI agent.

"Never miss a shot, do you, Ben?" Johansen said. "Now come here, and take off that vest."

Ben hesitated, but Johansen simply raised his gun to Ben's right eye. "You'll miss *that,* in your business."

Ben took off the vest and Johansen had him kneel with his hands on his head while he put the vest onto himself. "Open

your shirt and your pants and show me where the wires are—
and then pull them."

After a moment's hesitation, Ben did.

"All right. You go against that wall and you can keep
shooting. Just save a shot or two for me."

And that's what Ben did. He took shots of the twelve-year-
old boy, looking back at this mother as Heynes and the
cameraman walked toward him. After that, of Parker and
Burnett filling the barn doorway, silhouetted by bright light.
Johansen had all of them pull their wires. "You'll forgive me,
I'm sure," he drawled. "I had a bad experience with these once."

Johansen's diatribe took a surprisingly short time to
complete. "I make no apologies for my actions," he began,
looking into the videocamera. "Although I was saddened that
Thad Greene was pressed so violently into service in the war
against the disintegration of America, I am delighted to hear
the news that he'll recover . . ."

And so on.

A self-serving monologue that placed all of Johansen's acts
of terrorism into "the larger context." This, with a gun jammed
against Mrs. Greene's neck. Most of it had a singsong,
practiced sound. Johansen kept his eyes on the videocamera,
except when he would discuss the "institutions of entropy"
which had "softened and weakened this great country in the
name of equality."

Then he would look at Parker.

When he did that, Johansen's mouth turned ugly and his
voice shook just slightly. Ben almost raised his camera to
capture it, and then decided against it.

Johansen might read it as encouragement.

Finally, he was done.

Johansen bowed his head, and then waved the two
television guys back.

"I've got some questions," Heynes said.

"No," Johansen said. "Just shut up and keep your camera
rolling."

Parker and Burnett stared at the newscaster, and he backed
off, but didn't look too happy about it.

Abruptly, Johansen shoved the woman away. "Thank you, Mrs. Greene. You may leave now. I'm sorry for the trouble." He waved the gun at Burnett. "Walk her out, see that your guys don't kill her."

She seemed stunned, and then her face flushed crimson. She looked as if she were going to say something, but then looked to the gun and the other men, and simply turned away.

"What's going on here?" Burnett asked.

"Do it," Parker growled.

Burnett hesitated.

"Move!" Parker said.

Burnett took the woman away.

"Now how about these guys?" Parker said. "It's time for them to walk."

Johansen shook his head. "The fourth estate stays. If I've learned anything, it's that leadership is all a matter of making the right symbols. Well, I'm going to make one right now."

Faster than Ben could have imagined, Johansen lashed out with the gun butt and cracked Parker on the head. The agent staggered, and Johansen did it again. Blood gushed from a scalp wound. "Get on your knees, nigger."

Ben started forward and Johansen swung the gun to him. "Time for your picture, you whore. Get over here!"

Ben's hands were shaking, but in a glance, he double-checked everything. He had already put the flash on a coil cord so he could hold it off the camera. The power light on the flash was glowing red. He zoomed the lens back to its widest setting.

"You about ready there, Ben?" Johansen smiled slightly as he placed the gun inches from Parker's head.

"Just about." Ben stepped closer.

"You got my flag waving in the background? I looked through a crack in the barn, so I know it's still flying out there."

"I've got it all." Ben's voice was shaking, too.

"Maybe you'll win some more awards here. The niggers have been good for you, haven't they?"

"You're fucking cold, Harris," the cameraman said, letting his videocamera down.

"Keep rolling," Heynes snapped.

The cameraman shrugged and lifted it up, the red light gleaming above the lens.

"Don't do this, Mr. Johansen," Heynes said, his voice conveying just the right sense of urgency and dismay. "I'm asking you—the *world* is asking you—not to do this."

The audio was, of course, rolling too.

Johansen struck a pose and, indeed, a part of Ben knew it was a hell of a shot: the powerful black man staring up at Johansen. Parker was bloodied and confused, but still defiant. Out of focus, the running SWAT team, clearly too late. Johansen held the big gun rigidly in his right arm, his entire body conveying self-righteous judgment.

"Look at me," Ben said, with the assurance of years.

Damned if Johansen didn't comply, the gun moving just slightly as he did so.

Ben reached over with the flash and jammed it mere inches away from Johansen's eyes.

And took the picture.